W9-AAD-943

Kaneland John Stewart Elementary School
817 Prairie Valley St.
Elburn, IL 60119

DEMCO

*To Anna and Thomas, and
to all my family and friends*

GARTH NIX

KEYS TO THE KINGDOM

BOOK TWO
Grim Tuesday

SCHOLASTIC INC.

New York Toronto London Auckland Sydney
Mexico City New Delhi Hong Kong Buenos Aires

If you purchased this book without a cover, you should be aware that this book is stolen property. It was reported as "unsold and destroyed" to the publisher, and neither the author nor the publisher has received any payment for this "stripped book."

No part of this publication may be reproduced in whole or in part, or stored in a retrieval system, or transmitted in any form or by any means, electronic, mechanical, photocopying, recording, or otherwise, without written permission of the publisher. For information regarding permission, write to Permissions Department, Scholastic Inc., 557 Broadway, New York, NY 10012.

ISBN 0-439-43655-9

Copyright © 2004 by Garth Nix. All rights reserved. Published by Scholastic Inc. SCHOLASTIC and associated logos are trademarks and/or registered trademarks of Scholastic Inc.

12 11 10 9 8 7 6   5 6 7 8 9/0

Printed in the U.S.A.   40

First printing, January 2004

KEYS TO THE KINGDOM

Grim Tuesday

Prologue

The blood-red, spike-covered locomotive vented steam in angry blasts as it wound up from the very depths of the Pit. Black smoke billowed through the steam, coal smoke that was laced with deadly particles of Nothing from the deep mines far below.

For over ten thousand years, the Pit had been dug deeper and deeper into the foundations of the House. Grim Tuesday's miners sought workable deposits of Nothing, from which all things could be made. But if they found too much in one place or broke through to the endless abyss of Nothing, it would destroy them and much else besides, before the hole could be plugged and that particular shaft closed off.

There was also the constant danger of attack by Nithlings, the strange creatures that were born from Nothing. Sometimes Nithlings came as multitudes of lesser creatures, sometimes as a single, fearsome monster that would wreak enormous havoc until it was defeated, turned back, or escaped into the Secondary Realms.

Despite the danger, the Pit grew ever deeper, and the shafts and tunnels that preceded it spread wider. The train was a relatively recent addition, a mere three hundred years old as time ran in the House. The train took only four days to travel from the bottom of the Pit up to the Far Reaches. There wasn't much left of the Reaches, since the digging had eaten away much of Grim Tuesday's original domain within the House.

Very few ordinary Denizens ever rode the train. Most had to walk, a journey of at least four months, following the service road next to the railway. The train was only for the Grim himself and his favored servants. Its locomotive and carriages were razor-spiked all over to prevent hitchhikers, and the conductors used steam-guns on anyone who tried to get on. Even an almost-immortal Denizen of the House would think twice about risking a blast of superheated steam. Recovery would take a long time and be extraordinarily painful.

Flying would be far faster than the train, but Grim Tuesday never wore wings himself and had forbidden them to everyone else. Wings attracted Nothing from all over the Pit. Sometimes they caused flying Nithlings to form. Other times, the flapping set off storms of Nothing that the Grim himself had to quell.

The train whistled seven times as it came to a screeching stop alongside the platform. Up Station had been built by Grim Tuesday himself, copied from a very grand station on some world in the Secondary Realms. It had once been a beautiful building of vaulting arches and pale stonework. But the coal smoke from the train and the Grim's many forges and factories had stained the stones black. The pollution from Nothing had also eaten into every wall and arch, riddling the stone with tiny holes, like a worm-eaten wooden ship. The station only stayed up because Grim Tuesday constantly repaired it with the power of his Key.

Grim Tuesday held the Second Key to the Kingdom, the Key that he should have handed to a Rightful Heir ten thousand years ago, but instead chose to keep, in defiance of the Will left by the Architect who had created the House and the Secondary Realms.

Grim Tuesday rarely thought about the Will. It had been broken into seven fragments and those fragments had been hidden away across the vastness of space and the depths of time. He had hidden a fragment himself, the Second Clause of the Will, and had once been sure that no one else would ever reach it.

But now he had learned that the first part of the Will had escaped. It had found itself a Rightful Heir, and that heir had unbelievably managed to vanquish Mister Monday and assume his powers.

That meant Grim Tuesday would be next. As he stepped off the train, he scowled at the open letter he held in his gauntleted hand. The messengers who had brought this unwelcome message to the Far Reaches were waiting now, expecting a reply.

Grim Tuesday read over part of the letter again. The heir was a boy named Arthur Penhaligon, a boy from the world that was one of the most interesting of those in the Secondary Realms. A place called Earth, which had given birth to many of the artists and creators whose work Grim Tuesday copied. *Humans,* they called themselves. They were the most gifted result of all the Architect's aeons-old seedlings, the only creatures anywhere, in the House or out of it, who rivaled Her in their creativity.

The Grim scowled again and crushed the letter. He did not like to be reminded that he could only copy things. Given a good look at anything original, he could make a copy from Nothing. He could even combine existing things in interesting ways. But he could not create anything entirely new himself.

"Lord Tuesday."

The greeting came from the taller of two messengers.

Denizens of the House, but not like the ones in the Far Reaches. They stood head and shoulders above the soot-stained, Nothing-pocked servants of Grim Tuesday who flocked to the train to unload the great bronze-bound barrels of Nothing brought up from below. These barrels of Nothing would be used to make raw materials like bronze, steel, and silver, which would in turn be transformed into finished goods in Grim Tuesday's factories and foundries. Some of the Nothing would be used directly by the Grim to magically fashion the exquisite items he sold to the rest of the House.

The Grim's servants usually wore rags and badly mended leather aprons, and were hunched and slow and beaten-looking. The messengers could not look more different, standing arrogantly in their shining black frock coats over snowy-white shirts, their neckties a somber red, a little lighter than their silken waistcoats. Their top hats were sleek and glossy, reflecting and intensifying the pallid light from the gaslights that lined the platform, so it was hard to see their faces.

Grim Tuesday snorted. He was pleased to see that he was still taller than the messengers, though they were at least seven feet tall. His servants were generally twisted and foreshortened by their exposure to Nothing, but Grim Tuesday was not. He was thin in the fashion of someone who can easily run all day or swim a mighty river. He scorned fancy clothes, preferring leather trousers and a simple leather jerkin that showed the corded muscles in his arms. His hands were hidden, encased in gold-banded gloves of flexible silver metal. Grim Tuesday always wore these gloves, whether he was working or not.

"I have read the letter," grumbled Grim Tuesday. "It matters not to me who rules the Lower House, or any other, for that matter. The Far Reaches are mine and so they shall remain."

"The Will —"

"I've taken care of my part, and far better than that sloth Monday," interrupted Grim Tuesday. "I have no fears on that score."

"The writer of the letter does not think so."

"No?" The Grim frowned again, and the scars where his eyebrows once were met above his nose. "What do you know that I do not?"

"We know of a way that you can strike at the Lower House and this . . . Arthur Penhaligon . . . a loophole in the Agreement."

"Our Agreement?" growled Tuesday. "I trust you are not suggesting anything that would let Wednesday or that fool Friday encroach upon my preserves?"

"No, no. It is a loophole only you can exploit. The

Agreement forbids interference between the Trustees and their properties. But what if you had a lawful claim to the Lower House and the First Key? Then it would be your property, not another's."

Grim Tuesday understood what the messenger was saying. If he could find a way to say this Arthur *owed* him something, then he could take the First Key as the payment. There was only one problem, which the Grim told the messenger — he had no claim against Arthur.

"The former Mister Monday owed you for more than a gross of metal Commissionaires, did he not?" the messenger asked in reply.

"Aye, and many other things, both exquisites and ordinaries," answered Grim Tuesday. His face twisted in anger as he added, "None of it paid for, in coin of the House or in Denizens to work my Pit."

"You know that not having been paid your just debts, you may lay claim to the holdings of the debtor. If you had already served a distraint upon the former Mister Monday, and the Court of Days had decreed that the Mastery and the Key be given up to you, then —"

The messenger's point was clear to Grim Tuesday. If he had asked for payment from Mister Monday *before* Arthur took over, then Arthur would have inherited Mister Monday's debt.

"But I did not serve a distraint," Grim Tuesday pointed out. "And the Court could not in good faith . . ."

The taller Denizen smiled and drew a long roll of parchment from inside his waistcoat. It grew even longer as it came out, till he unrolled a scroll the size of a small carpet. It was covered with glowing gold writing, and several large round seals of gold hung from the bottom, attached with rainbow wax that changed color every few seconds.

"Fortunately the Court was able to hold a special sitting that was deemed to have taken place an instant before Mister Monday was deposed, and I am pleased to say that you have won your case, Grim Tuesday. You may pursue your debt in the Lower House against Monday's successors, and special leave has been granted for you to pursue that debt in the Secondary Realms as well."

"They will appeal," grunted Tuesday, but he reached out and took the parchment.

"They have," said the messenger. He drew a cheroot from a silver case and lit it with a long blue flame that came out of his forefinger. He took a deep draw and blew out a long thread of silver smoke that wove itself through the bands of dark and ugly smoke above. "Or rather, the Steward has. That entity which was formerly Part One of the Will and now calls itself Dame Primus. We doubt that Arthur Penhaligon has any idea about what is going on."

"I like not these legal niceties," grumbled Grim Tuesday. He pulled at his chin with a metal-bound hand, almost talking to himself. "What is done once to the Lower House might be done again to me and my realm. Besides, I see the seals of only three of the Morrow Days upon this document. . . ."

"You need only set your own seal there, and it will be four of seven. A majority, and the Lower House is yours."

Grim Tuesday looked up at the tall messenger. "I would naturally keep the First Key if I am successful in taking over . . . I mean to say, recovering what I am owed?"

"Naturally. All that, and anything you might acquire in the Secondary Realms."

The hint of a smile flickered across Grim Tuesday's face. He could inherit the First Key and everything else that was Arthur's. "And there will be no interference?" he asked. "No matter what I do in the Secondary Realms?"

"As far as our . . . office . . . is concerned, you have

permission to go to this world, this Earth, and do what you need to recover your debt," said the messenger. "It would be best to avoid any . . . shall we say . . . flamboyant looting or destruction, but I think you will be safe from prosecution otherwise."

Grim Tuesday looked down at the parchment. He was clearly tempted, his eyes shining strangely yellow, almost as if they reflected a vision of gold. Finally he pressed one gauntleted thumb against the parchment. There was a flash of harsh yellow light, and a fourth seal materialized, clinking against the others, its rainbow ribbon sending a ripple of light across the parchment.

The two messengers applauded softly, while the mass of servants momentarily stopped unloading the train, till they were beaten on again by the Overseers. Grim Tuesday tucked the parchment into his left gauntlet. The document shrank, till it was no larger than a postage stamp and easily tucked in under his wrist.

"There is one other matter we are charged to raise," said the first messenger. He seemed suddenly more cheerful and less reserved.

"A small matter," said the second messenger with a smile. He had not spoken before and his unexpected speech made some of the servants jump, though his voice was mellow and smooth. "We believe your miners are currently capping a shaft that has broken through into Nothing?"

"It is taken care of," snapped the Grim. "Nothing will not break into my Pit or the Far Reaches! I cannot speak for the other parts of the House, but we have Nothing well in hand here. I understand Nothing as no one else does!"

The messengers glanced at each other. The tiniest scornful glance, too fast for Grim Tuesday to catch, was hidden in the shadows cast by the brims of their shining hats.

"Your prowess with Nothing is well known, sir," said the first messenger. "We simply want something pushed through the sealed passage into Nothing."

"A little something," said the second messenger. He pulled out a small square of cloth. It looked clean and white, but a very close observation with a magnifying glass would show several lines of writing, done in the tiniest letters of dull silver, letters no higher than a single thread.

"It will dissolve, be destroyed," said the Grim, puzzlement on his face. "What is the point of that?"

"A whim of the one we serve."

"A notion. An experiment. A precauti —"

"Enough! What is this cloth?"

"It is a pocket," said the first messenger. "Or was one once. Of a shirt."

"Ripped untimely from a uniform. Shorn from a school chemise —"

"Bah! Riddles and rubbish!" exclaimed Grim Tuesday. He snatched the cloth and tucked it in his right gauntlet. "I will do as you ask, if only to hear no more of your blathering. Take your merriment back to where you belong!"

The two messengers bowed slightly and turned on their heels. The crowd of the Grim's servants parted before them as they strode away towards the banks of elevator doors at the rear of the station. As always, these elevators were guarded by Overseers, the most trusted of Grim Tuesday's servants. Clad in breastplates of dull bronze over black coats of thick leather, their faces hidden by long-snouted helmets, they carried steam-guns and broad-bladed swords called falchions and usually terrified all who beheld them. But the Overseers shuffled away from the two messengers and bowed their heads.

Grim Tuesday watched the two Denizens enter a lift. The doors clanged shut, then a beam of bright light shot up into the air, easily visible through the smog and the decaying roof of the station, till it disappeared into the ceiling of the Far Reaches itself, more than half a mile above.

"Do we move at once, Master?" asked a short, broad-shouldered, and long-bearded Denizen whose leather apron was noticeably finer and cleaner than the other servants. He held a large leather-bound notebook ready and had a quill pen in his hand. Another squat, heavily built servant held an open bottle of ink on his palm. Their faces were almost identical, each with a flattened, broken-looking nose separating deep sunken eyes, one blue and one green. There were five more Denizens with the same basic features, though only three were in evidence at the station.

Together they were called Grim's Grotesques, the seven top executives of Grim Tuesday. He had made them by melding the three Denizens who had once served him as Dawn, Noon, and Dusk into one that was then recast into seven.

"I must return to the works," said Grim Tuesday. "There is still too much Nothing leaking through South-West Down Thirteen and only I can stem it. But someone must go and get this Arthur Penhaligon to sign over his Mastery and the First Key. Not you, Yan. I need you with me. Tan is still below. So it must be you, Tethera."

The servant holding the ink bottle nodded.

"Take Methera. Two of you should be sufficient. Work within the strictures we used before on that world, in their year 1929. Do not call me unless you must, or I shall dock the cost from your pay. Send a telegram, it's cheaper."

Tethera nodded again.

"And if you see an opportunity to quietly expand my collection," added Grim Tuesday with a slow smile, "take it."

"And this scrap of cloth, this pocket?" asked Yan. "Shall you do as the messengers ask? It stinks of upper-floor sorcery."

Grim Tuesday bit the knuckle of his gauntleted hand, then slowly nodded.

"I will. It is no great matter. A Raising of some kind. A Cocigrue or Spirit-eater."

"Forbidden by law and custom," reminded Yan.

"Bah!" snorted Grim Tuesday. "It is not of my making, even should I care for old laws. We lose working time nattering here. Raise steam!"

The last two words were shouted back at the train. Overseers shouted in answer, slapping servants with the flat sides of their falchions to get them to unload the last of the barrels of Nothing faster. Other servants eased themselves between the spikes on the locomotive to disconnect water pipes, while a score of the dirtiest and most malformed Denizens hurried to push the last few wheelbarrows piled with bagged coal up to the locomotive's tender.

Grim Tuesday walked back to the front carriage, followed by Yan. Tethera went the other way, towards the main entrance of the station. This was not only a vast door out into the workshops and industries of the remnant Far Reaches, but, for those who knew the spell, it could also be transformed for a short time into the Front Door of the House, which led out to all the Secondary Realms beyond.

Including the world of Arthur Penhaligon.

Chapter One

Arthur hurried up to his room, the incessant-jangling of the old-style telephone bell getting louder and louder. The rest of his family couldn't hear it no matter how loud it got, but that didn't make him feel any better. He couldn't believe the Will was already calling him. It was less than eight hours since he'd defeated Mister Monday, assumed the Mastery of the Lower House and the powers of the First Key, and then just as quickly handed them (and the Key) over to the Will. The Will in turn had promised to be a good Steward and leave him alone for at least five or six years. Not a few hours!

It was also only fifteen minutes since Arthur had released the Nightsweeper, the cure for the Sleepy Plague that otherwise might have killed thousands, if not millions, of people. He'd saved his world, but was he going to be left alone to get some richly deserved sleep?

Obviously not. Furious, Arthur raced into his room, grabbed the red velvet box the Will had given him, and ripped off the lid. There was an ancient telephone inside, the kind with a separate earpiece. It wasn't obviously connected to anything, but Arthur knew that didn't matter. He grabbed it, unhooked the earpiece, and listened.

"Arthur?"

He knew those gravelly, deep tones at once. The frog-voice that the Will had kept, even when it had transformed itself into a woman. Or something that looked like a woman.

"Yes! Of course it's Arthur. What do you want?"

"I fear that I bear bad news. In the six months since you left —"

"Six months!" Arthur was now confused as well as annoyed. "I've been back for less than a day! It's only just after midnight on Tuesday morning."

"Time runs true in the House, and meanders elsewhere," boomed the Will, its voice clear and loud, almost as if it were in the room. "As I was saying, I bear bad news. Grim Tuesday has found a loophole in the Agreement that forbids interference between the Trustees. With the aid of at least some of the Morrow Days, he has laid claim to the Lower House and the First Key, claiming them as payment for the various goods he delivered to Mister Monday over the last thousand years."

"What?" asked Arthur. "What goods?"

"Oh, metal Commissionaires, elevator parts, teapots, printing presses, all manner of things," replied the Will.

"Normally, payment would not be required till the next millennial settlement, some three hundred years hence. But Grim Tuesday is within his rights to demand payment earlier, as Mister Monday was always behind with his debts."

"So why not pay him?" Arthur asked. "I mean, with . . . with what you normally use for money. So he can't claim anything."

"Normally payment would be made in coin of the House, of which there are seven currencies, each of which has seven denominations. The currency of the Lower House, for example, is the gold roundel, of three hundred and sixty silver pence, the intermediate coins being —"

"I don't need to know the types of coins!" interrupted Arthur. "Why not pay Grim Tuesday in these gold roundels or whatever?"

"We don't have any," replied the Will. "Or very few. The accounts are in a terrible mess, but it appears that Mister Monday never signed any of the invoices that should have billed the other parts of the House for the services supplied by the Lower House. So they haven't paid."

Arthur shut his eyes for a moment. He couldn't believe he was being told about an *accounting problem* in the epicenter of the universe, in the House on which the entirety of creation depended for its continuing existence.

"I've made you my Steward," Arthur said. "You deal with it. I just want to be left alone like you promised. For the next six years!"

"I *am* dealing with it," replied the Will testily. "Appeals have been lodged, loans applied for, and so on. But I can only delay the matter, and our hopes of a legal victory are slim. I called to warn you that Grim Tuesday has also gotten permission to seek repayment of the debt from you personally. And your family. Even your whole country. Maybe your entire world."

"What!" Arthur couldn't believe it. Why couldn't everyone just leave him alone!

"Opinion is divided on exactly who can be claimed against, but the amount due is quite clear. With compound interest over 722 years, the sum is not insignificant. About thirteen million gold roundels, each of which is one drubuch weight of pure gold, or perhaps you would say an ounce, which is 812,500 pounds avoirdupois, or roughly 29,000 quarters, which in turn is approximately 363 tons —"

"How much would that be in dollars?" asked Arthur faintly. *Nearly four hundred tons of gold!*

"That is your money? I do not know. But Grim Tuesday would not accept any currency of the Secondary Realms. He will want gold, or perhaps great works of art that he can copy and sell throughout the House. Do you have any great works of art?"

"Of course I don't!" shouted Arthur. He had felt much better earlier, and had even believed he might never have an asthma attack again. But he could feel the familiar tightening, the catch in his breath. Though it was only on one side.

Calm, he told himself. *I have to stay calm.*

"What can I do?" he asked, making the words come out slowly and not too loud. "Is there any way of stopping Grim Tuesday?"

"There is one way. . . ." mused the Will. "But you have to come back to the House. Once here, you would then need to —"

A loud beep cut off the Will and a new voice spoke, accompanied by a crackling buzz.

"This is the Operator. Please insert two and six to continue your call."

Arthur heard the Will reply, but its voice was very faint.

"I haven't got two roundels! Put it on our bill."

"Your credit has been revoked by order of the Court of Days. Please insert two roundels and six demi-crowns. Ten . . . nine . . . eight . . . seven . . . six . . ."

"Arthur!" called the Will, very distantly. "Come to the House!"

"Two . . . one . . . This call is terminated. Thank you."

Arthur kept holding the earpiece, but it was silent. Even the background buzzing had stopped. All he could hear was the rasping of his own breath, struggling to get in and out of his lungs. Or, rather, struggling inside his right lung. His left side felt fine, which was weird since that was the lung that had been punctured by the Hour Key in his life-or-death battle with Mister Monday.

Three hundred and sixty-three tons of gold.

Arthur lay down while he thought about that. How would Grim Tuesday try to get him to pay? Would he send Fetchers again, or other creatures of Nothing? If he did, would they bring a new plague?

He was so tired he couldn't think of any answers. Only questions. They raced around and around inside his head.

I have to get up and do something, Arthur thought. *I should look in the* Compleat Atlas of the House *or write down some kind of action plan. It's Tuesday already, so there's no time to waste. Grim Tuesday will only be able to do things here in my world on Tuesday, so he won't waste any time. . . . I mustn't waste any time . . . waste any . . .*

Arthur woke up with a start. The sun was streaming in through his window. For a moment he couldn't work out what had happened or where he was. Then the fog of sleep began to clear. He'd flaked out completely and now it was after ten a.m.

On Tuesday morning.

Arthur jumped out of bed. After the fire and the plague of the day before, there was no chance of having to go to school. But that wasn't what worried him. Grim Tuesday could have been doing something for hours while Arthur slept. He had to find out what was going on.

When he got downstairs, everyone else was either out or still asleep. There was the very faint echo of music from the studio, which meant his adoptive father, Bob, was playing with the door open. Arthur checked the screen on the fridge and saw that his mom was still at the hospital lab. His brother Eric was practicing basketball out in back of the house and didn't want to be disturbed by anyone. There was no message from his sister Michaeli, so he figured she was still asleep.

Arthur turned on the television and found the news channel. It was still full of the "miraculous" escape from the Sleepy Plague, with the genetic structure of the virus sequenced overnight and so many sufferers coming out of their comas without going into the final, lethal stage.

The fire at his school got some coverage too. Apparently it had been a very strange blaze, destroying every book in the library — even melting the metal shelves with its intensity — but the building itself had been hardly damaged and the fire had spontaneously extinguished itself. About the same time Arthur had entered the House, he figured.

The quarantine was still in place around the city, but within the city people were allowed to move about during daylight hours if they had "urgent business that could not be delayed." There were checkpoints maintained by police and Federal Biocontrol authorities, who would test anyone passing through. Arthur could still hear the constant dull chatter of quarantine helicopters flying a cordon around the city.

There was no new news, at least none that Arthur could identify as the work of Grim Tuesday. He shut the television off and looked outside. Everything appeared normal. The only people in the street were across the road, putting a SOLD sign in the front yard of the house there.

Which, Arthur thought, was more than a bit weird on the morning after a citywide biohazard emergency.

Arthur looked again. There was an expensive, clean new car, the kind real estate agents always used. There were two men in dark suits, with the usual kind of SOLD sign. But as Arthur looked, his eyes teared up and his vision blurred. When he rubbed his eyes and looked again, the men were much shorter, wider, and misshapen than they had been. In fact, one looked like he had a hunchback as well, and both had arms that reached down almost to their knees.

Arthur kept staring. The two men looked a bit blurry, but as he focused on them, he saw their suits fade. Those clothes were an illusion — the two were actually wearing old-fashioned coats with huge cuffs, odd breeches, wooden clogs, and leather aprons.

Arthur felt a chill run through his whole body. They weren't real estate agents. Or even human. They had to be Denizens of the House, or perhaps creatures summoned from Nothing.

Agents of Grim Tuesday.

Whatever was about to happen had already begun.

Arthur ran back up the stairs, taking three at each jump. Before he got to the top he was wheezing and clutching his side. But he didn't stop. He grabbed *The Compleat Atlas of the House* from his room and went up again, out onto the rooftop balcony.

The two . . . whatever they were . . . had finished hammering in the SOLD sign and had gotten another sign out of their car and were hammering that in as well.

Arthur couldn't quite see what it said till they stepped out of the way. When he read the bold foot-high words it took a second for them to penetrate.

DUE FOR DEMOLITION. THE NEW LEAFY GLADE SHOPPING MALL COMING SOON.

A shopping mall! Across the street!

Arthur put the Atlas on his knees and looked at the two real estate agents. Still staring at them, he placed his hands on the book and willed it open. He'd needed the Key before, but the Will had assured him that at least some pages would be accessible without it.

Who are those people? Are they servants of Grim Tuesday? What does Grim Tuesday oversee in the House? Thoughts tumbled through Arthur's head, though he tried to concentrate on the two "real estate agents."

He felt the book shiver under his hands, then it suddenly exploded open. Arthur almost toppled over backwards. It always shocked him, even when he was expecting it, that the book trebled in size.

It was open at a blank page, but he'd expected that too. A small spot of ink appeared, then stretched into a stroke. Some unseen hand rapidly drew a portrait of the two real estate agents. But not with the illusory dark suits. The Atlas showed them as they had appeared once Arthur rubbed his eyes, wearing large leather aprons that stretched from the neck to the ankle. Only in the illustration they both carried large hammers and had forked beards.

After the illustration was done, the invisible pen started to write. As it had before, it started in some weird alphabet and language, but changed into English as Arthur watched, though the writing was still very old-fashioned.

Immediately following the breaking of the Will, Grim Tuesday embarked upon a course that has wrought great damage to the Far Reaches of the House that were his assigned domain. In the vast room originally known as the Grand Cavern, there was a deep spring that brought a regular and controlled effervescence of Nothing to the surface. The Grim used this elegant provision of Nothing to prepare raw materials for lesser artisans, and to make and mold a miscellany of items himself, copying artifacts created by the Architect, or the work of lesser beings in the Secondary Realms. Yet the more the Grim made such items, the more he wished to make, in order to sell what he wrought to the other Days and even ordinary Denizens of the House.

Limited by the amount of Nothing that rose to the surface of the spring, the Grim decided to sink a shaft to mine the source that supplied the spring. That single shaft has become many tunnels, deeps, and excavations, until almost all the Far Reaches become an enormous Pit, an horrific sore that threatens the very foundation of the House.

To work his ever-expanding mine, Grim Tuesday sought Denizens from the other parts of the House, taking them from the other Days in lieu of payment for the things he sold. These Denizens have become little more than slaves, indentured without hope of release.

As the number of these workers became legion, Grim Tuesday needed more officers to oversee them. Against all laws of the House, and by use of prodigious amounts of Nothing, the Grim melded his Dawn, Noon, and Dusk together and then recast them as seven individuals. In order of precedence they are Yan, Tan, Tethera, Methera, Pits, Sethera, Azer.

Collectively they are known as Grim's Grotesques, for the seven all are misshapen in different ways, since the Grim could only make poor twisted copies of the Architect's great work.

The two Grotesques pictured are Tethera and Methera. Tethera is obsequious to all and speaks honeyed words, but his actions are spiteful and vindictive. Methera is silent and cruel, speaks only to wound, and delights in the afflictions of others.

As with all Grotesques, Tethera and Methera have greater powers than most Denizens, but are lesser beings in all ways than any of the other Days' Dawn, Noon, and Dusk. Beware their breath and the poison spurs within their thumbs.

Despite their fearful mangling and botched remaking at Grim Tuesday's hands, the Grotesques are slavish in their loyalty and love him as dogs love even the cruelest master, their hearts filled with an awful mixture of hate, fear, and infatuation.

Arthur looked across at the two Grotesques. They had hammered the DUE FOR DEMOLITION sign in and were getting another SOLD sign out. Arthur stared at them, a frown deepening on his forehead and tension building in every muscle.

How could they buy the houses so quickly? Are they really planning to build a mall, or are they just trying to freak me out?

The two servants of Grim Tuesday walked over to Arthur's own front lawn. Arthur stared down at them as they started to hammer in the sign. He couldn't believe they were doing it, but he couldn't think of anything he could do to stop them. For a moment he considered throwing something down on their heads, but he dismissed that idea. The Grotesques were superior Denizens of the House and almost certainly couldn't be harmed by any weapon Arthur could lay his hands on.

But he had to do something!

Arthur shut the Atlas and hurriedly stuffed the shrunken book back in his pocket. Then he took off down the stairs at top speed.

They were not going to demolish *his* home and build a shopping mall!

Chapter Two

As Arthur ran down the stairs, he heard the music stop from the studio and then the front door slam. Bob must have seen the Grotesques as well. Arthur tried to shout a warning but didn't have enough breath for more than a wheezy whisper.

"No, Dad! Don't go outside!"

Arthur jumped the last five steps and almost fell. Recovering his balance, he raced across and flung the door open, just in time to see his father striding across the front lawn towards the two Grotesques. He looked angrier than Arthur had ever seen him.

"What do you think you're doing?" shouted Bob.

"Dad! Get back!" cried Arthur, but his father didn't hear him or was too angry to listen.

Tethera and Methera turned to face Bob. Their mouths opened wide, far too wide for mere speech.

"Hah!" breathed the Grotesques. Two dense streams of gray fog stormed out of their open mouths, forming a thick cloud that completely enveloped Bob. When it cleared a few seconds later, Arthur's dad was still standing, but he wasn't shouting anymore. He scratched his head, then turned and wandered back past Arthur, his eyes dull and glazed.

"What did you do to him?" shouted Arthur. He wished he still had the First Key, in its sword form. He would stab both the Grotesques through without thinking about it. But he didn't, and innate caution made him stay near the front door, in case they breathed out the fog again.

Tethera and Methera gave him the slightest of bows, not much more than a one-inch inclination.

"Greetings, Arthur, Lord Monday, Master of the Lower House," said Tethera. His voice was surprisingly melodious and smooth. "You need not fear for your father. That was merely the Gray Breath, the fog of forgetting, and will soon pass. We do not use the Dark Breath, the death-fog . . . unless we must."

"*Unless we must,*" repeated Methera softly.

They both smiled as they spoke, but Arthur recognized the threat.

"Go back to the House," he said, trying to invest as much authority in his voice as he could. It was a bit difficult because he still couldn't draw a full breath and wheezed on the last word. "The Original Law forbids you to be here. Go back!"

Some of the power of the First Key lingered in his voice. The two Grotesques stepped back and the calm on their faces was replaced with snarls as they fought against his words.

"Go back!" repeated Arthur, raising his hands.

The Grotesques retreated again, then rallied and stopped. Clearly Arthur did not have the authority or the remnant power to force them to go, though he had unsettled them. Both wiped their suddenly sweating foreheads with dirty white handkerchiefs plucked out of the air.

"We obey Grim Tuesday," said Tethera. "Only the Grim. He has sent us here to claim what is his. But it need not go badly for you and yours, Arthur. Just sign this paper, and we will be gone."

"Sign and we'll be gone," repeated Methera in his hoarse whisper.

Tethera reached into his jacket and pulled out a long, thin, gleaming white envelope. It drifted across to Arthur, as if carried by an invisible servant. The boy took it carefully. At the same time, Methera held out a quill pen and an ink bottle, and the Grotesques stepped forward.

Arthur stepped back, holding the envelope.

"I need to read this first."

The Grotesques stepped forward again.

"You don't need to bother," wheedled Tethera. "It's very straightforward. A simple deed handing over the Lower House and the First Key. If you sign it, Grim Tuesday will not pursue the debt against your folk. You will be able to live here, in this Secondary Realm, as happily as you did before."

"*As happily as you did before,*" echoed Methera, with a knowing smirk.

"I still need to read it," said Arthur. He stood his ground, though the Grotesques sidled up still closer. They had a very distinct smell, a lot like fresh rain on a hot, tarred road. Not exactly unpleasant, but sharp and a little metallic.

"Best to sign," said Tethera, his voice suddenly full of menace, though he continued to smile.

"*Sign,*" hissed Methera.

"No!" shouted Arthur. He pushed Tethera with his right hand, the one that had most often held the First Key. As his palm touched the Grotesque's chest it was outlined with electric blue light. Tethera stumbled back, grabbing at Methera to keep his balance. Both Grotesques staggered away, almost to the road. There they straightened up and tried to assume poses of dignity. Tethera reached into the front pocket of his apron and drew out a large, egg-shaped watch that chimed as he opened the lid and inspected the face.

"You may have till noon before we commence our full repossession," Tethera shouted. "But we shall not cease our preparations, and delay will not be to your advantage!"

They got into their car, slammed the doors, and drove off, without any engine noise whatsoever. Arthur watched as the car proceeded about twenty yards up the street, then suddenly vanished in a prismatic effect like the sudden, brief rainbow after a sun-shower.

Arthur glanced down at the gleaming white envelope. Despite its crisp look, it felt slightly slimy to his touch. How could he sign away the First Key and the Mastery of the Lower House? They had been so hard to win in the first place. But he also couldn't let his family suffer. . . .

His family. Arthur raced back in to check on Bob. There was no reason for Tethera to lie, but the Grotesques' breath had looked extremely poisonous.

Bob was back in his studio. Arthur could hear him talking to someone, which was a good sign. The padded soundproof door was partly open, so Arthur poked his head around. Bob was sitting at one of his pianos, holding the phone with one hand and agitatedly tapping a single bass note with the other. He looked fine, but as Arthur listened, he quickly realized that while the Gray Breath had worn off, the Grotesques had, as they'd threatened, continued their "preparations."

"How can the band suddenly owe the record company twelve million dollars after twenty years?" Bob was asking the person on the phone. "They've always robbed us to start with. We've sold more than thirty million records, for heaven's sake! It's just not possible —"

Arthur ducked back out. The Grotesques had given him an hour and a half before *full repossession* — whatever that was. But even these beginning attacks were very bad news for the family. They'd be living on the street, forced to get handouts . . .

He had to stop them. If only he had more time to think. . . .

More time to think.

That was the answer, Arthur thought. He could get more time by going into the House. He could spend a week there perhaps, and still come back to his own world only minutes after he left. He could ask the Will and Noon (who used to be Dusk) what to do. And Suzy . . .

His thoughts were interrupted as Michaeli came charging down the stairs, holding the printout of an e-mail, her face stuck in a frown that had to come from more than lack of sleep.

"Problem?" Arthur asked hesitantly.

"They've canceled my course," said Michaeli in a bewildered voice. "I just got an e-mail saying the whole faculty is being closed down and our building is being sold to pay the university's debts! An e-mail! I thought it must be a hoax, but I called my professor and the front office and they both said it's true! They could have written me a letter! Dad!"

She ran into the studio. Arthur looked down at the envelope in his hand, hesitated for a moment, then slit it open along the seam. There was no separate letter inside — the writing was on the inside of the envelope. Arthur folded it out and quickly scanned the flowing copperplate, which was done in a hideous bile-green ink.

As he'd half-expected, the contract was all one way and not in his favor. In a long-winded way, like all documents from the House, it said that he, Arthur, would relinquish the First Key and the Mastery of the Lower House to Grim Tuesday in recognition of the debts owed to Grim Tuesday for the provision of the goods listed in Annex A. There was nothing about leaving Arthur's family alone after that, or anything else.

There didn't seem to be an Annex A either, but when Arthur finished reading what was on the opened-out envelope, it shimmered and a new page formed. Headed *Annex A*, it listed everything that the former Mister Monday or his minions had bought and not paid for, including:

Nine Gross (1,296) Standard Pattern Metal Commissionaires

1 Doz. Bespoke Metal Sentinels, part-payment rec'd, 1/8 still owing plus interest

Six Great Gross (10,368) One-Quart Silver Teapots

2 Plentitudes (497,664) Second-Best Steel Nibs

6 Gross (864) Elevator Door Rollers

Two Great Gross (3,456) Elevator Leaning Bars, Bronze

1 Lac (100,000) Elevator Propellant, Confined Safety Bottle

129 Miles Notional Wire, Telephone Metaconnection

1 Statue, Mister Monday, Gilt Bronze, Exquisite

77 Statues, Mister Monday, Bronze, Ordinary

10 Quintal (1000-weight), Bronze Metal Fish, Fireproof, semi-animate

1 Long Doz. (13) Umbrella Stands, Petrified Apatosaurus Foot

The list kept going on and on, the page re-forming every time Arthur reached the end. Finally he looked away, refolded the envelope, and shoved it in the back pocket of his jeans

Reading the letter hadn't changed anything, except that his determination not to sign it was even stronger. He had to get to the House as fast as possible.

He was about to leave immediately when he remembered the telephone in the red velvet box. It was possible the Will might be able to scrounge up enough money to call him again, so he'd better get that.

Arthur walked up the stairs this time. He didn't think he'd have a full-on asthma attack — he would have already had it if he was going to — but he'd gotten a persistent wheeze instead and couldn't quite get enough breath.

The red velvet box was where he'd left it, but when Arthur went to put the lid back on, he saw that it was empty. The phone had disappeared. Lying on the bottom of the box was a very small piece of thick cardboard. Arthur picked it up. As he touched it, words appeared, scribed in the same sort of invisible hand that wrote in the Atlas.

This telephone has been disconnected. Please call Upper House 23489-8729-13783 for reconnection.

"How?" asked Arthur. He didn't expect an answer,

but the message wrote itself out again on the card. Arthur threw it back in the box and went down the stairs again.

On the way back down, the question came up again in his head. Just one simple word that covered a lot of problems.

How?

How am I going to get into the House? It doesn't exist in my world anymore.

Arthur groaned and pulled at his hair, just as Michaeli came rushing back up the stairs.

"You think you've got problems?!" she snapped as she went past. "It looks like Dad is going to have to go back on tour, like, forever and I'm going to have to get a job. All you have to do is go to school!"

Arthur didn't get a chance to reply before she was gone.

"Yeah, that's all I have to worry about!" he shouted after her. He slowly continued down the stairs, thinking hard. The House had physically manifested itself before, taking over several city blocks. That manifestation had disappeared when Arthur came back after defeating Mister Monday. But maybe the House had returned with the Grotesques?

There was only one way to find out. After a quick

look to check that no one — particularly a Grotesque or two — was watching, Arthur went out the back door and got on his bike.

Provided he wasn't held up at a quarantine checkpoint, it would only take ten minutes to ride over to where the House had been. If it had reappeared, he would try to get in, through Monday's Postern or maybe even the Front Door, if he could find it.

If it wasn't there, he would have to think of something else. Each minute gave the Grotesques more time to do something financially horrible to his family, or his neighbors, or . . .

Arthur pushed off hard and accelerated out the drive, pedaling furiously for a minute, until his wheezing warned him to ease off.

Behind him, the SOLD sign on his front lawn shivered and dug itself a little further in.

Chapter Three

The House *was* gone. At least, its manifestation in Arthur's world had not returned. Instead of a vast edifice of mixed-up architecture, there were only the usual suburban houses, with their lawns and garages and basketball hoops over their garage doors.

Arthur rode his bike around several blocks, hoping some trace of the House remained. If there was just one of its strange outbuildings or even a stretch of the white marble wall that surrounded the House, he felt he could somehow get inside. But there was nothing, no sign at all that the House had ever been there.

He felt strange riding around, looking for something that wasn't there, a feeling made stronger because the streets were deserted. Though the quarantine had been slightly relaxed inside the city, most people were sensibly staying at home with their doors and windows shut. Arthur was passed by only one car on the road, and that was an ambulance. Arthur looked the other way, in case it was the same ambulance he'd escaped from the day before. He was thankful it didn't slow down or stop.

As he finished his circumnavigation of the last block, Arthur began to feel panicky. Time was slipping away. It was already 11:15. He only had forty-five minutes to find some way to enter the House, but he had no idea how he was going to do that.

The sight of several moss-covered garden steps reminded him of the Improbable Stair. That bizarre stairway went from everywhere and everywhen, through the House and the Secondary Realms. But the Stair was dangerous and there was a good chance of ending up somewhere he really didn't want to be. It wasn't worth trying the Stair unless he must. Even then, he probably wouldn't be able to enter it without the Key.

There had to be another way. Perhaps if he could track down the Grotesques' headquarters, he could find their doorway back to the House —

Something moved at the corner of his eye. Arthur twisted his head around, immediately alert. There was something in the movement he didn't like. Something that gave him a slight electric tinge across the back of his neck and up behind his ears.

There it was again — something flitting across the garden of the house opposite. Moving from the letterbox to the tree, from the tree to the car in the driveway.

Arthur put one foot on the pedal, ready to move off,

and watched. Nothing happened for a minute. Everything was quiet, save for the constant drone of the distant helicopters patrolling the perimeter of the city.

It moved again, and this time Arthur saw it dash from behind the car to a fire hydrant. Something about the size and shape of a rabbit, but one made of pale pink jellylike flesh that changed and rippled as it moved.

Arthur got off his bike, laid it down, and got out the Atlas, readying himself for its explosive opening. He didn't like the look of this thing, which he guessed was some sort of Nithling. But at least it was timid, hiding and scuttling.

Arthur could still see a single paw poking out from behind the hydrant. A paw that slowly melted and reformed through several shapes. Paw, claw, even a rudimentary hand. He concentrated his thoughts on that sight, gripping the green cloth binding of the Atlas tight.

What is the thing that hides behind the hydrant?

The Atlas burst open. Even though he was ready, Arthur took a step back and nearly fell over his bike.

This time, the invisible writer wrote quickly and in instant English, ink splattering all over the page.

SCOUCHER! RUN!

Arthur looked up. The Scoucher was leaping towards

him, no longer small and innocuous, but an eight-foot-tall, paper-thin human figure whose arms did not end in hands but split into hundreds of ribbon-thin tentacles that whipped out towards the boy. They sliced the air in front of Arthur's face, though he was at least fifteen feet away.

There was no time to get on his bike. Arthur twisted away from the tentacles and threw himself into a sprint, the Atlas still open under his arm. It closed itself and shrank as he ran, but he didn't try to put it in his pocket. He couldn't pause even for a second or those tentacles would latch on. They might sting, or paralyze, or hold him tight so the Scoucher could do whatever it did —

These thoughts drove him to the end of the street. He hesitated for an instant, uncertain of which way to turn, till the Atlas twitched to his right and he instinctively followed its lead. It twitched again at the next corner and then again a minute later, directing him down a partly hidden laneway — all at high speed. A speed Arthur soon realized he couldn't keep up. Whatever had happened to his lungs in the House had improved them, but he wasn't cured. He was wheezing heavily and the tightness on his right side was spreading to the left. He'd run farther and faster than he'd ever done before, but he couldn't sustain his speed.

Arthur slowed a little as he exited the lane and looked over his shoulder. The Scoucher was nowhere to be seen. He slowed down a bit more, then stopped, panting and wheezing heavily. He looked around. He'd thought he was headed towards home, but in his panic he'd gone in a different direction. Now he wasn't sure where he was, and he couldn't think of any possible refuge.

Something flickered at the corner of his eye. Arthur spun around. The Scoucher was back in its small fluid shape, sneaking again. It was about thirty yards back, zipping from cover to cover, slinking forward whenever he couldn't see it.

Arthur wasn't even sure it was a Nithling. Perhaps it was something else, something made by Grim Tuesday that the Grotesques had set upon him. He needed to know more, but he didn't dare to stop and look at the Atlas while the thing was creeping up on him. He needed somewhere to hide, perhaps a house —

The moment he looked away, the Scoucher stormed out from behind a pile of paving stones next to an unfinished path. One reaching tentacle, even longer than the rest, brushed the back of Arthur's hand as he turned to flee. It wasn't much thicker than a shoelace, and he hardly felt its touch, but when he glanced down, blood was flowing freely. More blood than seemed possible from such a tiny scratch.

Arthur was halfway across a well-mown front lawn when someone called his name from the neighboring house.

"Arthur?!"

He knew that voice. It came from Leaf, the girl who had helped him after his asthma attack, whose brother and family were among the first afflicted by the Sleepy Plague. He'd seen her briefly the day before, while traveling via the Improbable Stair. He had no idea where she actually lived, but here she was on the porch next door, staring at him in surprise. Or staring at the Scoucher —

"Look out!" she cried.

Arthur changed direction, narrowly avoiding a sweep of the Scoucher's tendrils. He jumped over a low brick wall, trampled through Leaf's parents' prize vegetable garden, leaped up the front steps of her house, and charged through the front door. Leaf slammed it shut after him. A second later it was hit by a sound like rain drumming on the roof — the impact of hundreds of tentacles upon the heavy door.

"Your hand's bleeding!" Leaf exclaimed as she slammed home a large bolt. "I'll get a bandage —"

"No time!" gasped Arthur. A lot of blood had come

from the simple scratch, but the flow was already slow-ing.

Arthur opened the Atlas, ignoring its sudden expansion. He added in a low wheeze, "Have to . . . see how . . . fight . . ."

The drumming sound came again. Leaf gasped and jumped back as several tentacles ripped the draft excluder off the bottom of the door and slithered inside. She picked up an umbrella and struck at them, but the tentacles gripped the umbrella and cut it into pieces. More and more tentacles came through under the door. Then they started sawing backwards and forwards.

"It's cutting its way through!" screamed Leaf. She pushed over a plant in a heavy earthenware pot and rolled it against the door. The Scoucher's tentacles struck at the spilled earth for a second, then went back to their sawing. The door had a steel frame, but the tentacles cut through it quite easily.

Arthur concentrated on the Atlas.

What are a Scoucher's weaknesses? How can it be defeated?

An ink spot appeared on the page, but was not blotted up. Words came quickly, and once again were in English and the regular alphabet straightaway. The penmanship was not up to its usual standard.

Scouchers are a particularly unpleasant type of Nithling. They issue from the narrowest cracks and fractures, and are consequently short of substance. Typically they gain a greater and more defined physical presence in the Secondary Realms by consuming the blood or ichor of the local inhabitants. Scouchers in their earlier phases may take a variety of shapes but always have several limbs that end in very fine tentacles, which are lined with tiny but extremely sharp teeth. They use these tentacles to cut their victims, who usually fall unconscious. The Scoucher then laps up the free-flowing blood —

"Arthur! The door —"

"How can I defeat a Scoucher?" Arthur asked furiously.

Silver is anathema to Scouchers, as is ruthenium, rhodium, palladium, osmium, iridium, and platinum. Scoucher hunters typically use silver dust blown through —

"Silver! Have you got anything silver?" Arthur wheezed, clapping the Atlas shut.

At the same time Leaf grabbed his arm and dragged him across the room and into the kitchen. She slammed the kitchen door behind them and threw herself at the refrigerator, trying to slide it across. Arthur shoved the Atlas into his pocket and grabbed one corner of the fridge, rocking it out from the wall as the terrible sound of splintering wood suddenly stopped in the other room.

"It's inside!"

The fridge was barely set down before it rocked forward. Tentacles punched through the flimsy kitchen door and rasped across the steel sides of the fridge.

"Silver! Silver will kill it!" Arthur repeated. He opened the nearest drawer, but all he could see were chopsticks and wooden utensils. "A silver fork will do!"

"We don't have anything metal!" Leaf cried out. "My parents won't eat with metal."

Several tentacles ripped the freezer door off and flung it on the ground. More tentacles swarmed in to grip the edges and the whole refrigerator shifted across the floor with the squeal of metal feet on tiles.

"Jewelry!" exclaimed Arthur as he looked around for something, anything silver. "You must have some silver earrings!"

"No," said Leaf, shaking her head wildly. Her earrings swung too, without any sort of metallic jangle. They were ceramic and wood.

Another squeal alerted Arthur a second before the refrigerator started to topple over. He jumped away an instant before it fell and followed Leaf as she raced through the door at the opposite end of the kitchen.

Arthur slammed the rear kitchen door shut behind him. But this one had no lock, and from the weight of it, could barely stop a determined fist, let alone other-worldly tentacles.

"Come on!" screamed Leaf. She ran down a flight of concrete steps to the back door, Arthur close behind. "I know . . . we *have* got some silver!"

The back door led into a garage that had obviously never housed a car. It was part plant nursery and part storage area, with bags of potting mix stacked up next to boxes identified by contents and date.

"Look for a box marked MEDALS or SKI JUMPING!" instructed Leaf urgently, pushing Arthur on. She turned back herself and locked the door, using a key from the drip tray of a hanging planter. She was just withdrawing the key when several tentacles punched through the door and lashed across her arm. They cut deeply and Leaf staggered back, shocked into silence. She tripped over a tray of seedlings and fell heavily onto a sack of sand.

Arthur took a step towards her, but she waved him back, before pushing her hand hard against the cuts to try and slow the bleeding.

"Silver medals," she coughed out. "In a box. Dad won lots . . . that is, came second . . . silver medals ski jumping. Before he met Mom and became a neohippie. Hurry!"

Arthur glanced at the door. The Scoucher was cutting through it as easily as it had the front door. He would have less than a minute to find the medals, maybe only seconds.

Rapidly he scanned the boxes, dates and contents labels tumbling through his brain. Children's toys from ten years ago, an encyclopedia, Aunt Mango's paintings, tax records, Jumping —

Something splintered behind him and he heard Leaf's sharp intake of breath.

Arthur grabbed the box marked JUMPING, pulling down three others at the same time. They fell on his feet but he ignored the pain, ripping through the cardboard. A shower of small velvet boxes fell out. Arthur caught one, flipped it open, grabbed the medal inside, spun on one foot, and hurled it towards the Scoucher that was coming through the door.

The medal flew true, smacking into the thin figure as it bowed its head to pass through the doorway. The Scoucher took a step back, puzzled, but otherwise seemed unharmed as the medal slid down its chest.

"Gold!" shrieked Leaf.

Arthur was already bending down to get another medal. This time he opened the box and threw the contents in one swift motion. Something silver flashed through the air as the Scoucher charged forward. The medal hit with a satisfying clunk, but did not slide down. It stuck like a fried egg to a pan and started to sizzle like one as well.

The Scoucher let out a pathetic groan and folded in on itself. Within a second, it was rabbit-sized again, but without the shape of a rabbit. Just a blob of pinky flesh with the silver medal still sizzling on top of it. Arthur and Leaf stared as black smoke poured out of the blob — smoke that curled around and around but didn't rise or dissipate. Then the Scoucher disappeared, and the silver medal spun and rattled on the concrete floor.

"How's your arm?" asked Arthur anxiously before the medal came to a stop. He could see the blood coming out between Leaf's fingers. She looked very pale.

"It's okay. There's a first-aid kit in the kitchen, under the sink. Bring me that and the phone. What was that thing?"

"A Scoucher," shouted Arthur over his shoulder as he ran inside. He found the first-aid kit and the phone and ran back, desperately afraid that he'd find Leaf dead on the ground. Strangely, the cut on his hand had completely closed up. Though it had bled profusely for a few minutes, he could hardly see where it was now. Arthur immediately forgot about it as he crashed through the remnants of the door.

Leaf's eyes were shut but she opened them as Arthur knelt by her side.

"A Scoucher? What's that?"

"I'm not really sure," said Arthur. He opened the first-aid kit and prepared a wound dressing and a bandage, suddenly very glad he'd taken the course last year and knew what to do. "Keep the pressure on until I'm ready. . . . Okay . . . let go."

Rapidly he got the dressing onto the deep cuts and bandaged Leaf's arm firmly from the elbow to the wrist. There was a lot of blood, but it wasn't arterial bleeding as he'd feared. Leaf would be all right, though she still needed an ambulance and professional help.

He picked up the phone and dialed 911, but before he could speak, Leaf snatched it away from him. She spoke quickly to the operator, shaking her head when Arthur tried to take the phone back.

"You can't call," she said after hanging up. "I'll tell them some story. You have to go over to . . ."

She closed her eyes, and her mouth and forehead creased in concentration. "Go to the old Yeats Paper Mill on the river. Go under it to come to the House."

It sounded like something Leaf had memorized from someone else.

"What?" asked Arthur. The Atlas had led him to Leaf, but — "How come . . . how . . ."

"The girl with the wings, the one who was with you yesterday," Leaf said slowly. Shock was clearly taking hold. Arthur got a coat out of one of the fallen boxes and draped it over her as she kept talking. "Just then I kind of blacked out and it was like she was sitting next to me. She told me what I just told you. There was more, but you woke me up just when she was getting into it."

"The Yeats Paper Mill?" asked Arthur. "Go under it?"

"That's it," confirmed Leaf. She had shut her eyes again. "It's not the first true dream I've had. My great-grandmother was a witch, remember."

Arthur looked at his watch. 11:32. He had less than half an hour and the paper mill was at least a mile away. He wasn't even sure where his bicycle was. He could never make it into the House before the Grotesques unleashed their full plan.

"I can't make it in time," he said to himself.

"Take Ed's bike," whispered Leaf, pointing to the

black-and-red racing bicycle racked up between three sturdy green mountain bikes. "He won't be back from the hospital for a few days."

Arthur stood up but hesitated. He felt he should wait for the paramedics to arrive.

"Go," said Leaf. She tapped her forehead weakly. "They'll be here in a few minutes. I can tell."

Arthur hesitated until he heard the faint call of a siren. It got a little louder.

Leaf smiled. "Not second sight. Just good hearing."

"Thanks," said Arthur. He ran and wheeled the bike over to the garage door. The lack of an automatic opener puzzled him for a second, till he worked out he had to push the door up himself.

"Hey, Arthur!" Leaf called out as he got on the bike. Her voice was so weak that it came out a little louder than a whisper. "Promise you'll tell me what this is all about."

"I will," replied Arthur. *If I get the chance.*

Chapter Four

Arthur pedaled furiously, coasted till he got his breath back, then pedaled furiously again. He wasn't sure that he actually would get his breath back, as that familiar catch came and his lungs wouldn't take in any air. But each time he felt his chest stop and bind, there was a breakthrough a moment later and in came the breath. His lungs, particularly the right one, felt like they were made of Velcro, resisting his efforts to expand them until they suddenly came unstuck.

He tried not to look at his watch as he cycled. But Arthur couldn't help catching glimpses of its shining face as the minute hand moved so quickly towards the twelve. By the time he got to the high chain-link fence around the old Yeats Paper Mill, it was 11:50. Arthur only had ten minutes, and he didn't know how to get through the fence, let alone get *under the old mill —* whatever that meant.

There were no obvious holes in the fence and the gate was chained and padlocked, so Arthur didn't waste any more time looking. He leaned Ed's bicycle against the fence, stood on the seat, and pulled himself up on one of the posts. Despite being scratched by the top strands of old, rusty barbed wire, he managed to swing himself over and drop to the other side. At the bottom he checked his shirt pocket, to make sure it hadn't been torn off with the Atlas inside. He'd lost it that way before and he was not going to lose it again.

"*Underneath . . . underneath,*" Arthur muttered to himself as he ran across the cracked concrete of the old parking lot towards the massive brick building and its six enormous chimneys. No paper had been made at the Yeats Paper Mill for at least a decade, and the whole place had been set aside for some sort of development that had never happened. *Probably a shopping mall,* Arthur thought sourly.

There had to be underground storage or something here, but how could he find a way down?

Wheezing, Arthur ran to the first door he could see. It was chained and padlocked. He kicked it, but the wood held firm. Arthur ran along the wall to the next door. This one looked like it had been opened recently, and the chain was loose. Arthur pushed it open just wide enough to squeeze himself through.

He hadn't known what to expect inside, but he hadn't thought it would be a huge open space. All the old machinery and huge piles of debris from former internal walls had been pushed to the sides, leaving an area about the size of a football field. Light streamed down in shafts from the huge skylights and many holes in the tin roof.

In the cleared area, a strange machine squatted. Arthur knew instantly it came from the House and was not a relic of past papermaking. It was the size of a bus and looked like a cross between a steam engine and a mechanical spider, with eight forty-foot-long, jointed limbs that sprouted from a bulbous cylindrical body — a boiler — with a thin smokestack at one end.

The limbs were made of a red metal that shone dully even where the sun did not fall, but the boiler was a deep black that sucked up the sunlight and did not reflect it.

There were several huge bottles of the same black metal near the spider-machine. Each one was taller than Arthur and easily three or four feet in diameter.

Arthur sneaked across to a pile of debris and took another look. He couldn't see anyone, so he slinked along to the next pile and then the next. When he was level with the machine, he was surprised to see a very normal-looking office desk next to it. There was a giant plasma screen on the desk, and a PC beneath it. Arthur could see a green activity light flashing on the PC, despite the fact its electric lead was coiled up on the concrete floor, not plugged into anything. He could also see something on the screen. Graphs and rows of figures.

Arthur was just about to creep forward for a better look when a Grotesque walked around from the other side of the boiler. Arthur wasn't sure if it was one of the two he'd seen before. Whoever it was, it was no longer disguised in a modern suit. Its leather apron had what looked like scorch marks all over it, and numerous tools were sticking out of the pockets on the front.

Arthur ducked down behind some fallen bricks and froze. The Grotesque sang to itself as it picked up a huge pair of long-handled tongs from the floor and went over to the dark bottles.

"Double, treble, quadruple bubble, watch the stock market get into trouble. . . ."

Using the tongs with much grunting and shuffling, the Grotesque picked up one of the huge bottles and slowly maneuvered it over to the boiler. It put the bottle down for a moment to open a hatch almost at ground level directly below the smokestack. Then it drew out gloves, a tightly fitting hood, and goggles with smoked quartz lenses from inside its apron. It put these on, picked up the tongs again, and used them to lever the bottle into a position where its neck fitted into the opening in the boiler.

Then it spoke. Three words in a language that Arthur did not know. Words that sent a shiver through the soles of his feet and up his spine. Words that caused the heavy wax seal on the bottle to shatter and release the contents into the boiler.

The contents were Nothing. Arthur saw a dark, oily waft that was both liquid and smoke at the same time. Most of it poured into the boiler, but a few tendrils escaped, winding back towards the Grotesque, who stepped smartly back. It dropped the tongs and drew a glittering blade of crystal that crackled with electric sparks.

The Nothing that had escaped began to eddy and spiral, taking a definite shape. At first it looked like it would become some sort of animal, something tigerlike, with clawed paws and a toothy mouth. Then it changed to become a human shape, but one with bunched tendrils instead of hands.

A Scoucher!

The Grotesque sheathed its crystal blade and eased one of the many rings it wore off its middle finger. As the Scoucher's shape became definite and it lunged forward, the Grotesque flicked its ring. It struck the Scoucher in the face, and once again Arthur heard the sizzling sound. A moment later, the Scoucher was gone, and the ring bounced on the floor with the clear bell-like sound of silver.

The Grotesque laughed and bent to pick it up. Arthur chose that moment to run to the next pile of debris. Instantly, the Grotesque swung around, its crystal blade in its hand once more. Arthur instinctively flinched, but the Grotesque did not rush over to attack. Instead it smiled and flourished its hand at the machine.

"So the Master of the Lower House has come to see my strange device. I presume you require a demonstration? A little foretaste of what is to come at twelve o'clock?"

The Grotesque strode to the side of the machine and turned a large bronze wheel. A shriek came from the boiler, rising in intensity with each turn of the wheel. Smoke suddenly poured out of the smokestack. Weird smoke that was gray and slow and thick, pitted with tiny specks of intense blackness. As the smoke rose and the shrieking grew louder, the arms of the machine rose high in the air and began to jerk and jitter from side to side.

Arthur looked around frantically. Whatever the machine did, it would be bad. He had to find the way into the House!

"Oil up fifteen percent!" shouted the Grotesque and it spoke another word that made Arthur feel suddenly ill. In response, the spider-arms stopped for a moment, then began to dance in a rhythmic, mesmerizing pattern. As they moved, sparks fountained out of the pointed ends of each limb, leaving luminescent aftertrails across Arthur's eyes. Bright trails that were vaguely reminiscent of mathematical formulae and symbols, though not ones that Arthur recognized.

On the plasma screen, the graphs suddenly disappeared, replaced by a spinning BREAKING NEWS logo. It was replaced a moment later by the face of a TV network woman, with the words SUDDEN OIL SHOCK scrolling across the screen. Arthur couldn't hear her over the shrieking machine and the whirr and buzz of its arms, but he could guess what she was saying.

The Grotesque's bizarre machine had somehow sent the price of oil up fifteen percent.

"What stocks does your father own?" jeered the Grotesque. It took a piece of paper out of its apron pocket and looked at it. "Oh, I know. Music Supa-Planet, down fifty percent!"

Again it spoke a strange word that sent a ripple of pain through Arthur's joints. The spider-arms stopped at the word, then began a different dance, tracing out their strange formulae in patterns of light.

Arthur shook his head to try and clear the aftereffect of the bright sparks and the words. On the second shake, he saw something. A little door at the base of one of the huge paper mill chimneys. A metal inspection hatch that was slightly ajar.

The chimneys go below the surface. That has to be a way down.

He ran towards the hatch, with the Grotesque's voice echoing all around, even above the shrieking engine.

"Northern Aquafarms, down twenty-five percent!"

Arthur reached the inspection hatch. As he pulled it open, the shriek of the engine suddenly stopped. He glanced back and saw the Grotesque staring at him malignantly.

"Go where you will, Master of the Lower House. The Machine merely pauses for want of fuel, and I shall soon supply that!"

Arthur shuddered, bent his head, and climbed through the hatch. He was only just inside when the Grotesque shouted something, another word that made

Arthur's teeth and bones ache, and slammed shut the hatch behind him, cutting off all the light.

In the brief moment before the door closed, Arthur saw that the chimney was at least thirty feet in diameter, with well-worn steps that circled around and down. In the total darkness, Arthur descended by feel, careful not to commit his weight to a step until he was sure it was there. Not for the first time, he wished he still had the First Key, for the light it shed and many other reasons.

Finally he reached the bottom. It was slightly flooded, water coming up to Arthur's ankles. The river was close by here. He was probably below its level, Arthur thought uneasily. It didn't help to think of the river suddenly breaking in, not here in the absolute darkness.

But there had to be a way out, a way into the House. Didn't there? Arthur began to think that he had been lured into a trap. Maybe this was just a chimney and he'd been led into it like a complete fool.

Maybe the Grotesque is going to let more water in. Is it already rising?

Arthur began to edge around the walls, feeling with his feet and hands. He was starting to panic, and the cold water was not helping his breathing. He could feel his right lung seizing up, the left laboring hard to make up for its companion's failings.

His hand touched something sticking out from the wall. Something round, about the size of an apple. Something smooth and soft. Wooden, not brick.

A door handle.

Arthur sighed in relief, and turned it.

The door opened inwards. Arthur stumbled in, tripping over the lintel. His stomach somersaulted as he continued to fall.

Straight down!

Just like the last time he'd entered the House, Arthur was falling slowly — as slow as a plastic bag caught on a summer breeze — through darkness.

But this time he didn't have the Key to get him out of this strange in-between place that was neither his own world nor the House. He might fall forever and never arrive anywhere. . . .

Arthur gritted his teeth and tried to think of something positive. He had held the First Key. He was the Master of the Lower House, even if he'd handed his powers over to a Steward. He felt sure there was some remnant magic in his hands, which had once wielded the Key.

There has to be some residual power.

Arthur thrust out his right hand and imagined the Key still in his fist. A shining Key.

"Take me to the Front Door!" he shouted, the words strangely dull and flat. There was no echo in this weird space, no resonance of any kind.

Nothing happened for a few seconds. Then Arthur saw a very pale glow form around his knuckles. It was so dark it took him a little while to work out what it was. The light comforted him, and he tried to concentrate on it, willing it to grow stronger. At the same time, under his breath, he kept repeating his instruction.

"Take me to the Front Door. Take me to the Front Door. . . ."

His wrist clicked as his hand moved away, tugged by an unseen force. He felt the direction of his fall change from straight down into a shallower dive.

"Take me to the Front Door. Take me to the Front Door. Take me to . . ."

Far off, a tiny light caught Arthur's eye. It was too far away to be more than a luminous blob, but Arthur felt sure he was headed towards it, that it would grow and grow until it became a huge rectangular shape of blinding light.

It *had* to be the Front Door of the House.

Chapter Five

To Arthur's considerable relief, the light did grow and it did look exactly like the Front Door. Only this time he was approaching very slowly, so he had enough time to prepare himself for the shock of falling through to the other side — to the green lawn of Doorstop Hill, in the Atrium of the Lower House.

Once he was there, he figured it would be relatively easy to get to Monday's Dayroom. Arthur wondered if it was called *Arthur's Dayroom* now, or *the Will's Dayroom,* or something else completely different. In any case, he would find the Will and Suzy there, and together they would work out what to do about Grim Tuesday and his minions.

Arthur was still thinking about that as he drifted gently towards the Door, when he was unexpectedly thrust forward by a tremendous force. Completely unprepared for what felt like a giant whack in the back, he tumbled end over end and crashed headfirst into the bright rectangle of light.

For an instant Arthur felt like he was being turned

inside out, everything twisted in impossible and painful directions. Then he bounced on his feet on the other side and crashed down onto his hands and knees. Jarring pain in both told him he had not landed on soft grass. It was also completely dark, without even the soft glow of the distant ceiling of the Atrium, and certainly no elevator shafts illuminating the scene. Even worse, there was smoke everywhere — thick, cloying smoke that instantly made Arthur's lungs tighten and constrict.

Before he could begin to feel around or even cough, someone grabbed him by the shoulders and pulled him up and back. Arthur swallowed his cough and instinctively screamed, a scream that was cut off as some kind of fluid enveloped him. He started to choke, thinking that he was in water, but a solid clap on the back stopped that and he realized that whatever the fluid was, it wasn't water and it wasn't getting into his throat and nose. A moment later he was out of it and could feel air again. He had passed through some kind of membrane or fluid barrier.

Wherever he was, everything looked extremely blurry and there was too much color, like he was standing with his nose pressed to a stained-glass window where the colors kept mixing up.

"Relax and blink a lot," instructed whoever was

gripping his shoulders — a calm, deep male voice that sounded vaguely familiar. It only took Arthur a second to remember whose it was.

The Lieutenant Keeper of the Front Door.

Arthur blinked madly and tried to relax. As he blinked, the colors settled down and the blurriness eased, at least when he was looking straight ahead. It was still very blurry to either side.

"Are we inside some sort of multicolored glass ball?" Arthur asked after a moment. They certainly were inside something spherical and there was light shining into it, light that kept shifting around and was diffracted into many different colors.

"We are in a temporary bubble inside the Door itself," explained the Lieutenant Keeper. He let go of Arthur, stepped in front of him, and saluted. As before, he was wearing a blue uniform coat with one gold epaulette. "One that lessens the effect of the Door on mortal minds. Now, we only have a brief respite before you must go through to the Far Reaches —"

"The Far Reaches?" exclaimed Arthur in alarm. "But I wanted to go to the Atrium of the Lower House."

"The Front Door opens on many parts of the House, but the door you entered in the Secondary Realms leads only to the Far Reaches and the Grim's railway station."

"I can't go there!"

"You *must* go there," declared the Lieutenant Keeper. "You have already gone there. I snatched you back, but I cannot keep you inside the Door for any great length of time. You must go where you are going. That is the Law of the Door."

"But . . ." Arthur struggled to think. "Okay, if I have to go to the Far Reaches, can you send a message from me to the Will or Suzy, in the Lower House?"

"That part of the Will is called Dame Primus now," said the Lieutenant Keeper. "I am afraid I am not allowed to send unofficial messages to her or anyone else. I can hold a message for someone, but I cannot pass it on unless they inquire whether I have one."

He unbuttoned part of his coat and reached in to withdraw a watch. It played a haunting melody as he flipped open the case and gravely studied the dial.

"Two minutes, then I must return you to the Far Reaches."

"Can you give me a disguise?" asked Arthur desperately. The Lieutenant Keeper had helped him before with a shirt and cap, so he didn't stand out in the Lower House. Arthur would need a disguise even more in Grim Tuesday's domain.

"That I can do. I hoped you would ask."

The Lieutenant Keeper reached out through the glowing walls of the sphere. When he pulled his hand back he held one end of a clothesline. He reeled it in. As the pegs dropped off, various items of clothing fell into Arthur's lap, including a faded pajama-like top and pants, a strange hooded cape of some rough material the color of mud, and a many-times-patched leather apron.

"Put the work suit on over your clothes," instructed the Lieutenant Keeper. "You will need layers for warmth. Roll up the cape for later."

Arthur put on the pajama-like top and trousers, and then strapped on the apron, which was very heavy leather. As instructed, he rolled up the hooded cape. It was very thick, and difficult to squash down. Arthur didn't recognize the material.

"Stabilized mud," said the Lieutenant Keeper as Arthur looked down on a rolled-up cape that was a quarter as big as he was. "Inexpensive and it offers sufficient protection against the Nothing rain in the Pit. While it lasts."

"Nothing rain?" asked Arthur. He didn't like the way the Lieutenant Keeper said *the Pit* either. He remembered that the Atlas had called it *a huge sore in the foundation of the House.*

"The Pit is so vast that clouds form partway down and there is constant rain," said the Lieutenant Keeper as he reached back out through the barrier and retrieved a pair of wooden clogs stuffed with straw.

"The rain concentrates the Nothing pollution that pervades the Pit and carries it back down. Hence the name."

"But what is the Pit exactly?" asked Arthur. All he knew from the Atlas's earlier reference was that it was some sort of giant mine, and a danger to the House.

"Unfortunately, you will soon see for yourself. I fear you will have difficulty staying out of it. Once in, you should escape as quickly as you can. Now — put on the clogs. Keep your socks. They are not so different as to attract notice."

Arthur slipped off his comfortable, arch-supported, computer-designed sneakers and put on the straw-stuffed wooden clogs. They felt loose and extremely uncomfortable. When he stood up he couldn't take a step without his heels lifting out.

"I can't even walk in these," he protested.

"All the indentured Denizens wear them," said the Lieutenant Keeper. "You cannot risk being given away by your footwear. Now, for the smog. It contains minute particles of Nothing, so it wears down Denizens and will almost certainly slay a mortal. Which hand did you hold the First Key in most?"

"The right," said Arthur.

"Then you must put two fingers from your right hand up your nostrils and your thumb in your mouth while you inhale and recite this small spell: *First Key, grant this boon to me, that the air I breathe be pure and safe, and keep from me all harm and scathe*."

"What?"

The Lieutenant Keeper repeated his instructions and added, "You may need to repeat this spell, as it too will be worn down by the smog, and the residual powers of the Key will fade from your flesh. Do not stay overlong in the Far Reaches, particularly the Pit."

"I won't if I can help it," muttered Arthur. "I guess I can always get out up the Improbable Stair if I really have to."

The Lieutenant Keeper shook his head.

"You mean I can't use the Stair?" asked Arthur. He knew the Stair was risky, but at least it had been an option. Like a parachute or a fire escape. Some faint hope of escape from disaster.

"You would never reach a favorable destination,"

said the Lieutenant Keeper. "Not without a Key, or a well-practiced guide."

"Great," said Arthur dolefully. He carefully put his fingers in his nostrils and his thumb in his mouth. It was difficult to say the spell around his thumb, but possible. He felt a tingling in his nose and throat as he said the words, and at the end of the spell, let out an enormous sneeze that rocked him back on his heels.

"Good!" declared the Lieutenant Keeper as he quickly consulted his watch again. "Now we must return you to your destination. I have done all I can, Arthur Penhaligon, and more than I should. Be brave and take appropriate risks, and you shall prevail."

"But what . . . please tell *someone* where I've gone —"

Before Arthur could say any more, the Lieutenant Keeper snapped a salute, turned on his heel to get behind Arthur, and gave him a very hefty push. Arthur, arms cartwheeling, went straight through the strange liquid barrier and once more fell on his hands and knees on the cold stone floor. His left clog came off and clattered away and his hood fell down over his face.

As Arthur struggled with his hood, a bright light shone on him. Arthur looked up and shielded his eyes from a lantern held high by a short, broad figure. The light was shrouded and blurred by the smoke, so for a second Arthur thought he was looking at some sort of pig-man, then he realized it was the thrusting visor of a helmet. The fellow also wore a bronze breastplate over a long leather coat and had a broad, curved sword thrust naked through his belt. More peculiarly, he had what looked like a miniature steam engine in a harness on his back that was sending a steady flow of smoke up behind his neck, and small bursts of steam from out behind his elbows.

That one small engine couldn't possibly be the cause of the thick smoke behind the looming figure. It was like a fog, so heavy that Arthur could only make out fuzzy lights and occasional blurry shapes moving in its midst. Noise was also muffled. Arthur could hear a distant roar, as if there was a crowd somewhere, but he couldn't see it, and there was also a kind of metallic thumping noise that sounded like machinery.

"There's another loose one!" called the lantern-bearer to some unseen companions back in the smoke. He sounded like he didn't have any teeth or there was something wrong with his tongue. Or perhaps it has to do with the pig-helmet.

"Get up!" ordered the steaming, smoking figure.

"You're in the Grim's service now and must stand in the presence of all Overseers."

"I am?" asked Arthur as he slowly stood up, speaking in a quavering voice that was only partly an act. "I hit my head. . . . You're an Overseer?"

The Overseer swore in a language Arthur didn't know. The Key had enabled him to speak all languages of the House, but without it, he had only kept the power to understand the *lingua domus* that Denizens of the House spoke, not the specialized dialects of each demesne.

"More damaged goods!" the Overseer continued. "Those other Days are always trying it on. Follow me! Obey orders or you'll get steamed."

To demonstrate his warning, the Overseer pulled out a large-bore flintlock pistol — the kind pirates and highwaymen had in films — but this one was connected by a hose to the miniature steam engine on his back. He cocked the flintlock, then pulled the trigger. The lock snapped down, sending a spray of sparks into the air and a whistling blast of steam quite close to Arthur. The boy flinched and jumped aside, to the Overseer's great delight.

"Har! Never seen the like before, have you? Behave and you'll keep some flesh on your scrawny bones."

Arthur jumped again as the Overseer pushed him

deeper into the smog. He only had a moment to glance back over his shoulder, to try and fix his location for a later exit. There was a door there, tall and imposing, easily thirty feet high. But it didn't look like the Front Door. It was made of carved wood and showed scenes of a tall, thin man — presumably Grim Tuesday — making things at a forge and a bench, and being worshipped by hundreds of apron-clad disciples. But the scenes were fixed and unmoving, stained with streaks of grime and pitted as if acid had been sprayed across the surface. Nothing like the constantly shifting, colorful, and vibrant images on the Front Door. Clearly this *could* be the Front Door, because Arthur had come out of it, but it wasn't at the moment. There had to be some secret to its use.

There would be no easy escape through there.

The Overseer pushed Arthur again, shoving him to the right. Arthur saw that he was heading towards the back of a line of sad-looking Denizens that disappeared into the eddying smog. The line was halted, but there was a sudden brief lurch forward as Arthur joined it and a momentary lightening of the smog gave him a brief glimpse of their destination: a long mahogany desk, little more than fifteen yards away, where a Denizen was being presented with a leather apron and a cape that looked even drabber than the one Arthur had.

"Get in line and get yer stuff," said the Overseer with a final push. None of the Denizens looked around as Arthur joined the line. They simply shuffled along, their eyes downcast.

Arthur almost called out that he already had his stuff but he kept his mouth shut. The Overseer might not like his stupidity being publicly announced. Or perhaps there was other *stuff* being given out as well as the leather aprons and capes.

When the Overseer had disappeared back into the deeper smog, Arthur hesitantly tapped the Denizen in front of him on the shoulder. It was a woman, dressed in the sort of strange combination of nineteenth-century clothing that Arthur had seen in the Lower House. This woman had a long, torn dress as the basis of an eccentric outfit that appeared to include at least a dozen scarves wound around her arms and torso.

Arthur's tap on the shoulder didn't have the effect he expected. The Denizen shrank beneath his touch, losing six inches in height without bending her knees. She turned around fearfully, obviously expecting someone much scarier than Arthur.

"Beg pardon, sir," she whispered, tugging at her fringe. "It wasn't my fault, whatever it was."

"Uh, sorry," said Arthur. "I think you've got me confused with someone else. I'm not one of the Overseers or anything. I'm . . . ah . . . one of you."

"An indentured worker? You?" whispered the Denizen in amazement. "Then how?"

She made a gesture with her hand pushing down on her head. She was much shorter than she had been before Arthur tapped her.

"Oh, that wasn't me," said Arthur hastily, almost babbling. "I don't know how that happened. Don't think it was anything to do with me. I hit my head and I can't remember anything. Where are we?"

"The Far Reaches," whispered the Denizen. She was still feeling the top of her head and looking puzzled. "Your contract must have been assigned to Grim Tuesday. You're an indentured worker now."

"Sssshhhh!" warned the next Denizen along. "Keep it down! The last person talking got steamed and so did everyone next to him. *I* don't want to be steamed."

"Where are you from?" whispered Arthur to the woman ahead of him.

"The Upper House. I was a Capital Ornamenter Third Class. I don't understand why I was sent here. I must have done something wrong. Are you one of the Piper's children, or unnaturally shrunk? It does happen here. I didn't think it would happen to me so soon —"

"Quiet!" hissed two Denizens farther up. "Overseer!"

An Overseer lurched out of the smog. He stopped to gaze at the line of Denizens, tapping on his steam-gun with thick, calloused fingers. Arthur saw a ripple of fear pass through the whole line, a kind of slow hunching down that all the Denizens did, while at the same time trying not to show any signs of movement.

The Overseer kept watching for a few seconds, then disappeared back into the smog. As it closed around him, Arthur caught a glimpse of another two or three lines of Denizens, all waiting to be given their basic outfit. There could be even more lines beyond.

No one spoke after the Overseer left. They kept shuffling forward as their turns came. Arthur didn't tap the woman on the shoulder again, fearful of shrinking her even further, and she didn't look around.

When he came to the front of the line, the Denizen behind the desk stopped in mid-action as he was about to hand Arthur a pile of clothing. He was short and shaped rather like a turnip, so stopping made him almost topple over. In order to keep his balance he dropped the clothes and grabbed the table, almost oversetting the name plaque that said SUPPLY CLERK in tarnished gold-leaf letters.

"You've already got yours!" the clerk gasped.

"Got what?" asked Arthur. Pretending to be stupid seemed the best defense.

"Your apron, leather, one of; cape, rain, stabilized mud with hood, one of; and clogs, wood veneer, one pair," replied the Denizen. "So what do I do?"

"I don't know," said Arthur. "Just let me go on?"

Wherever *"on"* was. Arthur had been watching carefully, but hadn't been able to work out what happened to the Denizens in front of him after they got their aprons and capes. They marched around the left side of the table and disappeared into still thicker smog. Arthur also couldn't work out where the aprons and capes and clogs came from. The Denizen handing them out appeared to pull them from the solid mahogany tabletop.

"But I don't know if that's allowed," muttered the supply clerk.

"You could ask," piped up the Denizen who was waiting behind Arthur.

"Ask?" hissed the clerk. He looked around nervously. "You never ask anything round here. That only leads to trouble."

"Well, how about you pretend you never saw me and I just go?" suggested Arthur.

"Next!" said the supply clerk, craning his neck to look to the next person in line. Arthur hesitated for a moment, unsure of where to go. The supply clerk scratched his nose and cupped his hand around his mouth so he could whisper, "Around to the left, down the steps."

Arthur walked around the desk to the left and almost fell down the steps, since he didn't see them until he was almost on them. They were broken in parts, deeply coated with soot, and dangerously greasy. As Arthur cautiously made his way down, he tried to dig up some thoughts out of his brain on how to escape. But no bright ideas flared. All he could think of were the Lieutenant Keeper's words: *Take appropriate risks.*

But what risks were appropriate?

Arthur was still wondering about that when he reached the bottom of the steps. It looked no different from the area above — dark and smoggy, save for a diffused light ahead that could be ten or fifty yards away. Arthur set out for it, his clogs clacking on the stone floor, occasionally waving his arms to dissipate a thick band of nasty-smelling smog. Fortunately, the spell the Lieutenant Keeper had taught him was working and

Arthur was very relieved he'd done it, even though he'd felt stupid sticking his fingers in his nose.

The light came from two lanterns on either end of another wide mahogany desk. This desk was also bare, save for an identical gold-lettered sign that also said SUPPLY CLERK. The particular clerk behind the desk was even shorter and squatter than the one before. He was so shrunken he only came up to Arthur's waist and was barely visible behind the desk.

As Arthur stopped in front of him, he pulled a smoke-grimed lantern with a badly mended handle out of the desktop, his fingers appearing to actually dip into the wood.

"Strom lantern, self-oiling, one."

"*Storm* lantern, you mean," said Arthur.

"Says *strom lantern* in my book," replied the clerk. "Hurry along and join your gang. Just follow the railway tracks behind me. Unless you hear a whistle, in which case, get off the tracks for a while."

"This storm — sorry, *strom* — lantern is broken," Arthur pointed out.

"They're all broken," sighed the clerk, indicating the lanterns at each end of his desk, which were identical. "That's the pattern. I suppose our lord and master has better things to do than fix up the pattern. No use complaining. I complained once and look what happened."

Arthur stared at the clerk in puzzlement.

"Got downsized, didn't I? I was a foot taller and a Maker Fourth Class before I was stupid enough to complain about badly made strom lanterns. At least I didn't get sent down the Pit. Now off you go before I get into more trouble."

"What's your name?" asked Arthur. This clerk might be a useful contact. At least he talked about Grim Tuesday and the Pit.

"Name! Supply Clerk Twelve Fifty-Two. Now get going before an Overseer shows up! Around the desk and follow the rails."

Arthur turned to go, holding his smoking lantern high. But before he disappeared into the smog, the supply clerk coughed. Arthur turned back.

"Mathias. That was my name," muttered the clerk. "I don't know who you are, but something makes me want to tell you. Good luck in the Pit. You'll need it."

Chapter Six

There were railway tracks behind the desk, only ten yards away but unseen until Arthur tripped over the first rail. Inspecting them with the lantern, Arthur saw they were made of some dull metal that looked like bronze, and they were set very wide apart, at least eight feet, which he thought was a wider gauge than any railway back in his world. The rails ran on stone sleepers rather than wood or concrete, and the rubble under and between the sleepers was of some strange material that was the shape and color of wood chips but was very heavy and hard — perhaps another kind of light stone.

The rubble was called ballast, Arthur remembered. Bob's ninety-four-year-old uncle Jarrett — Arthur's great-uncle — had worked on the railways all his life and liked his great-nephews and great-nieces to know the proper terminology for everything from the tracks to the trains. He even had recordings of different types of steam engines they'd had to listen to.

But Great-uncle Jarrett wasn't there to tell Arthur anything about this particular railway, and the boy didn't know which way to go. The tracks ran to the left and right, disappearing into thick smog in both directions. To try to get a better idea of where he was, Arthur crossed the tracks and walked away at a right angle. Having learned that visibility was effectively nil in the smog and general weirdness of the place, he trod carefully, alert for another stairway or a sudden drop.

Crouching down and raising his lantern, Arthur saw the stone floor simply ended as if it had been sheared off clean by an enormous knife. Swirls of smog blew along the edge of the precipice, cloaking how far down the drop might be. Arthur couldn't see the other side at all.

He guessed that he had found the edge of the Pit. Slowly he backed away, not feeling safe until he had returned to the other side of the railway.

Now that he knew he was on the edge of the Pit, Arthur realized that the railway slanted down in one direction. That would be the way he was supposed to go. But if he followed the rails, he would be drawn deeper and deeper into the horrible life of an indentured worker in Grim Tuesday's realm. On the other hand, if he followed the rails up, he'd probably get steamed . . . and unlike a Denizen, would not survive the experience.

I'm in trouble.

It was really sinking in now that he was trapped in a

very unpleasant part of the House. He didn't have the Key, so apart from some faint lingering power in his hands, he had no magic to help him and no weapon. He had no way to get out and no way to communicate with his friends. No one knew he was here except the Lieutenant Keeper — who couldn't tell anyone unless they asked first.

He'd rushed in to try to stop his family from suffering any more financial assaults, but all he'd managed to achieve was to get himself into very serious trouble.

Arthur sat down on the rail, put his head in his hands, and massaged his temples. He felt slow and stupid and utterly defeated. He had to figure out a way to escape. There was no way he could survive going farther down the Pit.

He started rocking back and forth. Somehow that slight motion made him feel better, as if any movement might help him come up with an idea. As he rocked, he felt a slight pain in his chest. Not the internal ache of a stiffening lung, but something poking into him from his pocket.

The Atlas.

Suddenly full of hope, he got the green-cloth-covered book out and rested it in his lap. Then he laid both hands flat on the cover and thought out his question.

How can I get out of the Pit?

The Atlas opened with less than its usual alacrity, and instead of growing to its usual dimensions, only expanded to twice its pocket-sized form. It also kept partially closed, so Arthur had to peer in. Clearly the Atlas didn't like the air in the Pit either.

A single letter was slowly sketched out in ink, then the unseen hand grew faster and wrote a word, then another. As in the first time Arthur had used the Atlas, the words were not in English, and the letters were not any that he knew. But as he looked at them, they changed into a more recognizable form.

There are numerous ways to leave the fearsome Pit of Grim Tuesday. There are the official ways, requiring suitable passes and permits. They include:

> *a. by walking up the service road;*
>
> *b. as a passenger upon Grim Tuesday's train; and*
>
> *c. as one of the Grim's messengers, with a wheel recalibrated for ascent.*

There are the unofficial ways, which are dangerous or self-defeating. These include:

> *a. by flying, with its attendant risks, some specific to the Pit; and*
>
> *b. by destruction at the hands of a Nithling or an eruption of Nothing.*

"No," said Arthur. "I mean specifically how can *I* get out of the Pit now?"

Nothing happened. The page of the Atlas remained still and frozen. No unseen hand wrote, no ink shimmered.

Arthur slowly closed the Atlas and put it in his pocket. For a moment he had thought it would give him some easy way out, some secret way to exit the Pit. It had helped him back in his world, but it either couldn't or wouldn't help him here.

I suppose I could go to an Overseer and ask to see Grim Tuesday, Arthur thought despondently. *And just sign the stupid paper that would give him the First Key and the Lower House . . .*

"Excuse me! I think you're meant to go ahead of me," said a polite voice out of the smog. Arthur looked around and saw the Denizen who'd been behind him in the line.

"They seem quite keen on staying in line here. Name's Japeth, by the way. Former name, I suppose."

"I'm Arthur," said Arthur. He extended his hand. Japeth took it, but before he could close his hand, blue sparks erupted from Arthur's palm and lashed around Japeth's wrist. The Denizen let go with a yelp and withdrew, sucking his fingers.

"You're not an indentured worker!" he exclaimed.

Arthur tensed for the Denizen to call out to the Overseers, who would surely be somewhere near in the smog. Japeth might get a reward, or early release, or something. So he mustn't be allowed the opportunity . . .

"Don't worry!" Japeth added quickly as Arthur bent down and picked up a piece of the weird stone ballast from the train track. "I'm not a snitch, tattletale, dobber, blabberer, squealer, fink, or indeed, easy-mouth. Whoever you are, I shan't say a word, phrase, utterance, syntag —"

"You'd better not," warned Arthur. He tried to sound severe but was very relieved as he dropped the stone. "I'm here . . . on a mission to help all the indentured workers."

Japeth also seemed relieved. He bowed and doffed an imaginary hat. His courtly manners were rather at odds with the extremely ragged velvet pants he wore under his leather apron. His shirt was no longer white, but yellow, and the cuffs were done up with string rather than buttons. Like most Denizens, he was handsome, but his face looked a little squashed, as did his body. As if he'd been pushed down and broadened, an imperfect clay model that had once come from a handsome mold.

"I would be honored to assist," he said. "That is to say, aid, support, succor, abet, reinforce, or give a leg up."

"Thank you," said Arthur. "Um, do you always talk like that?"

"You refer to my constant, even habitual use of a multiplicity of words and terms?"

"Yes."

"Only when I'm nervous," replied Japeth. "I am . . . I used to be a Thesaurus Minimus Grade Two. It is an occupational hazard, danger, or threat that we sometimes become prolix, verbose, long-winded, longiloquent. . . . I fight against it, I assure you. Shall we move on before someone comes looking for us?"

"I suppose we should," agreed Arthur, after a moment's hesitation. He needed more time to think, and they couldn't stay where they were.

"After you," said Japeth, bowing and once again waving his imaginary hat.

"No, after you," replied Arthur, bowing a little himself. He didn't want the Denizen walking close behind him, not with all the ballast stone about. He sounded sincere, but Arthur didn't want to risk being hit on the head and handed over unconscious to the Overseers.

Japeth inclined his head and strode off down the

tracks, his clogs echoing hollowly on the stone sleepers. Arthur followed, still thinking furiously and occasionally tripping over his own clogs. If only he could get a message out to the Lower House. Every idea he came up with had a flaw. He got all excited for a second when he remembered that Monday's Noon had been able to summon a telephone apparently out of nowhere in the House and the Secondary Realms. But even if Arthur could do that, the Lower House's telephone service had either been cut off or required cash payment up front, and he had no money.

But perhaps I could get some, he thought. *Then I could call the Will, or Suzy, or Monday's Noon. . . .*

"What currency do they use in the Pit?" asked Arthur as they continued down the tracks without running into anyone or anything.

"I believe the Far Reaches used to have a very nicely minted gold noble, silver real, and copper bice," replied Japeth. "However, Grim Tuesday has gathered all actual coinage to himself, and everyone else must make do with ledger entries. Like our indentures."

He pulled out a rectangular piece of card that he wore on a string around his neck.

"Do you mind if I have a look?" asked Arthur.

"I can't take it off, remove, or displace it from my person," said Japeth. "But please do take a glance, preliminary examination, indagation, or, indeed, look."

The paper looked like a label, with neat writing in a sickly green ink. It had one column headed EARNINGS and one headed OWING. The EARNINGS column had a single line with *0n 0r 0b*. The OWING column had *4n 6r 18b*. As Arthur watched, the OWING column rippled and changed to *4n 7r 1b*.

"You see why no one ever earns their way free of their indenture. We are not paid until we reach the bottom of the Pit and, even then, only if we find usable amounts of Nothing. But we are charged for every breath of this foul air, and ridiculous amounts for our meager equipment."

"So there is no money, I mean coins or notes, at all in the Pit?"

"So I have been told, informed, clued in," said Japeth. He started to walk along the railway again. "Shouldn't we be getting on, moving along, advancing, progressing?"

Arthur nodded. Japeth was clearly getting more and more nervous, and it was infectious. Arthur hurried after the Denizen, the sound of their clogs clattering faster and faster till they were almost running.

It was just as well they hurried. A hundred yards farther down the track, an Overseer suddenly loomed up out of the smog. He was marching with purpose along the railway, his steam-gun ready. When he saw them, he grunted and waved them past, then followed. Clearly he had started to investigate the delay in new arrivals.

The smog cleared a little in front of Arthur. He saw several groups of Denizens marching away without Overseers. Another group was standing nearby, watched by an Overseer who had his visor up and was polishing his teeth with a cloth and an open tin of white paste. He was shorter than a head by the Denizens he watched, but much broader across the shoulders. His face was really squashed down and two of the teeth in his lower jaw protruded out like small tusks.

"Here you go," shouted the Overseer behind Arthur. "Couple of laggards."

The Overseer rubbed his teeth one last time, slipped the tin under his apron, gave a surprisingly gentle sigh, and clanged down his visor. Immediately a change came over him. He hunched forward, growled, and drew his steam-gun. His backpack steam engine went from a purr to a harsh rattle, pumped out a heavy cloud of black smoke, and vented steam to either side behind his elbows.

"Hurry up!" he shouted. "Get in line."

Arthur and Japeth ran to the group of Denizens, who were milling about, trying to get into a line. But no one wanted to be closest to the Overseer, so whoever ended up there ducked around the back and joined the end of the line. This went on for a minute or so, till the Overseer blasted a jet of steam into the air.

"Stop!" he yelled. "You, stand there! You, stand there! Right, now stand in line."

When everyone was in line, the Overseer marched up to Arthur and Japeth and roared, "Why were you late?"

"I fell on my head," said Arthur. It seemed to be an all-purpose excuse. "Where are we?"

"You are on His Mightiness Grim Tuesday's Pit Railway Service Road!" shouted the Overseer. "You are very lucky!"

"Why?" asked Japeth. "How come? On account of what —"

"Shut up! I ask the questions!"

Japeth shut up. The Overseer growled, then repeated, "I ask the questions! And my first question is . . ."

His voice trailed off as he struggled to get a grimy piece of paper out from the inner pocket of his leather coat. Having gotten the paper out, he had trouble unfolding it. When it was finally unfolded, he held it up to his visor.

The question, when it finally came, was not what Arthur expected.

"You all been branded?" asked the Overseer.

Arthur nodded with the others and kept his head down, hoping to hide the fear that he was sure showed in his face.

"Any swift healers?" asked the Overseer, obviously reading from the paper.

Everyone shook their heads. The Overseer looked across at them, then back at the paper.

"Orright, let's see your soles, then," instructed the Overseer.

Our souls? thought Arthur in surprise. *How can we show our souls?*

He was particularly surprised when everyone stepped out of their right clog, took off their right sock, and started hopping about, each presenting their right foot towards the Overseer.

"Come on, then, no time to waste in the Grim's service," barked the Overseer. "Don't hop about, you idiots! Lie on your backs and hold your soles out."

Arthur, still mystified, sat down with everyone else in a line along the cold stone floor. But as he slipped off his right clog, he looked at Japeth's bare foot and saw what the Overseer was looking for.

The brand was on the sole of the right foot! A brand that ran from the heel to the ball and said in glowing green type: INDENTURED TO GRIM TUESDAY.

Arthur froze for an instant, then pretended his clog was stuck, as he feverishly tried to think about what he could do. The Overseer had a steam-gun, there was the other Overseer somewhere back up along the railway, and certainly many more on the platform above it.

"I knew it!" shouted the Overseer. "There's always one!"

Arthur snapped his head back. For a horrible second he thought the Overseer was talking to him, then he saw the squat figure was standing over one of the Denizens at the other end of the line.

"Swift healer for sure," declared the Overseer. "When were you branded?"

"Yesterday, when I arrived," replied the Denizen dejectedly. "But I don't always heal swiftly, sir. Sometimes it takes days."

"Days! That brand's supposed to last a year. I'll have to ear- or nose-clip you instead. Stand up."

"Oh, sir, please, I'd prefer another branding."

"We don't care wot you want!" roared the Overseer. He rummaged around in his coat pockets and eventually pulled out a shiny metal disc that was several inches in diameter. "Where do you want it?"

"Oh, the nose," grumbled the Denizen. The Overseer grunted and touched the disc to the Denizen's ear. There was a small flash of light, a sizzling sound, and the disc was hanging off the Denizen's earlobe just like an oversized earring.

"I said my —"

Before the Denizen could say any more he was clouted to the ground by the Overseer's large fist.

Sensibly, the downed Denizen lay there, obviously struggling to keep his mouth shut. The Overseer sighed again and rubbed his knuckles.

"Now then, anybody else a swiftie?"

Arthur thought very swiftly indeed and raised his hand. The Overseer lumbered down the line.

"Oh, it's dropped-on-the-head. You sure you know what we're talking about? Show us your sole."

Arthur lay back, slipped off his clog and sock, and showed his bare foot. The Overseer bent down with considerable creaking and grunting and whistled between his front teeth.

"Completely gone! Orright, get up and I'll give you a nose-clip."

"Great, I've always wanted a big round thing in my nose," suggested Arthur as he stood up. He instinctively knew better than to ask for it in his ear straight out. "Or . . . um . . . jangling on my lip."

"Keep yer lip to yerself," snarled the Overseer. He held the disc out and laughed as Arthur flinched. Then he touched the disc to the boy's left ear.

Arthur felt a stab of pain that went right through his ear and into his head, where it bounced around between his eyes. The pain was so intense, he staggered back. He would have fallen if he wasn't caught by Japeth.

"Slow *and* sensitive!" roared the Overseer. "You have to stand on yer own feet here!"

"He's one of the Piper's children," retorted Japeth. "They're different. They were mortals once."

"No special cases here!" shouted the Overseer. He threw a punch at Japeth. Strangely, though Japeth didn't move, the punch missed, as if the Overseer had pulled it on purpose.

Despite his mind being mainly focused on the throbbing pain behind his eye sockets, Arthur still managed to wonder why the Overseer was so loud. The Denizen seemed to have only two modes of communication: loud and deafening.

"No more backchat or I'll steam the lot of you!" roared the Overseer. He consulted his piece of paper.

"Orright! You lot are now called Gang 205117. Remember that! Gang 20 —"

He looked at the paper again.

"Gang 205117. You on the left, you're number one in the gang. You're number two, and you're three, and four, and five, and six, and seven —"

"He counts well, doesn't he?" whispered Japeth, who was still holding Arthur up. But the pain passed quickly, so Arthur managed to stand on his own as the Overseer pointed at him and said, "You're thirteen."

Something about that number made the Overseer stop and scratch his head. He looked at his paper again, but whatever he was looking for wasn't there.

"Ain't supposed to be thirteen," he said to himself after a long silence. "Always twelve in a gang . . ."

"Maybe they throw the Piper's children in extra," said Japeth, as he put out a hand to stop Arthur from swaying into him. "For free. As a bonus, premium, or frill —"

"Shut up!" roared the Overseer. "You, Number Thirteen! You're one of the Piper's children?"

"Y-yes," stuttered Arthur.

"You're not a messenger? Piper's children is always messengers down here."

"No," said Arthur. "I'm not a messenger."

"Thrown in as an extra, then," said the Overseer with satisfaction. His brow cleared at having solved this mighty puzzle and he looked at his paper again and slowly read out the next instruction, pausing every now and then to puzzle over a word or pick off a spot that had obscured the type.

"Gang insert-number-here. You are about to begin your journey to the bottom of the Pit! You will be put on the road and Number One will be given a time candle. You must reach the First Way Station before that time candle burns out. If you do not, you will be hunted down and punished. At the First Way Station you will be given another time candle and you must go on to the Second Way Station before it burns out. This system will continue until you reach Down Station, when you will be put in new gangs to work in the Pit. Praise be to Grim Tuesday!"

Finished, the Overseer folded up his paper and put it back in a pocket. Then he fished around in almost every other pocket before finally dragging out a tall white candle marked with red bands a fingerbreadth apart. As soon as the Denizen who was now Number One took it, the candle burst into flame. The Denizens all stared at it, their faces registering shock, horror, and distaste.

Arthur stared at the candle too. Its lighting had brought home to him, and everyone else, that they really were on their way down to the unknown horrors of the Pit.

"Get going," roared the Overseer.

But as Number One stepped out, the Overseer raised his visor and muttered something. It took Arthur a second to realize that, like the Supply Clerk, what he'd said was, "Good luck."

Arthur was surprised that an Overseer would wish them luck, and worried that they would need it. He almost said something as he went past, but the Overseer had already snapped his visor down and the next lot of downcast Denizens was coming out of the smog from up the line.

Arthur's own gang was heading down, walking in single file next to the railway tracks, with Number One setting a quick walking pace. Arthur hesitated for a moment, but, as before, he had no real choice. He couldn't go back up. There was only the edge of the Pit on the other side of the tracks.

He had to follow the rest of the gang and descend into the smoky darkness.

Chapter Seven

Number One didn't slacken his pace, and for several hours he didn't stop at all. Arthur was hard put to keep up at a walk, and occasionally had to run to catch up. As the wall of the Pit rose up on his left and the service road grew narrower and closer to the railway, Arthur began to get an idea of just how vast the Pit must be. The railway and the road that ran next to it were clearly cut into the side of the Pit, following the edge around in one huge spiral from top to bottom. It was impossible to see with all the smog, but the curve was so gentle that Arthur eventually figured that the Pit must be miles in diameter.

Arthur had no idea how deep it was. He asked Japeth, who also didn't know. Japeth asked Number Eleven in front of him, but that Denizen shook her head and wouldn't answer. None of the other Denizens talked at all. They just followed Number One with their heads bent, eyes fixed on their clogs or the heels of the Denizen in front of them. Occasionally one would look up anxiously and try to get a clear view of the bands remaining on the time candle.

They walked for hours without seeing anything of interest, save for occasional piles of broken train parts piled up next to the line. The Grim's train clearly suffered a lot of broken axles, snapped connecting rods, corroded pistons, chipped wheels, and other damage. Probably because it was affected by Nothing at the bottom of the Pit, Arthur guessed.

He would have liked to look at the various parts, but the gang's first stop only came when Number Six tripped out of her own clogs and fell down, knocking over Number Five, who knocked over Number Four. But they only stopped long enough for the three Denizens to get up and get their clogs back on.

An hour later, Arthur deliberately kicked off a clog himself in order to get a rest, but being right at the back no one noticed except Japeth, and the rest of the gang didn't stop. So Arthur and Japeth had to run to catch up.

That took most of Arthur's remaining energy. He knew he didn't need food and water in the House, but he still felt hungry, thirsty, and depressed. He tried to shake off the depression, telling himself it was only because he was tired. But that was the problem. He wasn't just tired. He was exhausted. He got wearier and wea-rier, and they just kept on walking.

Thoughts of giving in and signing over the Key and the Mastery of the Lower House started to well up as Arthur walked and walked and walked. He simply couldn't think of anything else to do except give up.

He managed to beat those defeatist thoughts back for a while when they left the smog behind and he felt a bit better. He even ran up to look at the time candle, ig-noring the glares of Number One for getting out of line. But the feeling better only lasted for a few minutes. Arthur quickly fell back to his rear position, disturbed to see that the candle had burned down to only the sec-ond band out of twelve. According to his watch, which was going backwards but otherwise seemed to be track-ing time okay, they had been walking for six hours. With ten bands of the candle to go, that was another thirty hours walking.

Even without the smog it was still pitch dark. The only light came from the gang's strom lanterns and the time candle. To make things worse, they soon descended into wet, hanging clouds that were cleaner than the smog but cold and clammy.

Thirty hours of walking to go. I can't do it. But I have to. . . . I have to. . . .

Arthur was already too tired to think about how he could get out of his current predicament, but the thought of having to keep going for another thirty hours made him try harder. He tried to look around more, just in case some opportunity came up.

Perhaps I could hide, and sneak back up later, he thought. *Or somehow ambush an Overseer and take his clothes and disguise myself. Only I haven't seen any Overseers down here so far . . . or there might be a telephone booth and some coins the Grim didn't notice, and I could call up the Will and be rescued. . . .*

The sound of a clog falling off broke into Arthur's daydream. He realized he'd fallen asleep walking and that Japeth wasn't in front of him, but next to him, steering him by his elbow.

It was his own clog that had fallen off. He bent down to put it back on, moving so slowly he felt like he was still in his dream.

"How long . . . asleep?" mumbled Arthur. Everything looked the same. Denizens disappeared into clouds in front of him, led by an indistinct figure carrying a flickering light. There was the railway track to the right. There was another pile of broken wheels and bits and pieces.

"I don't know," said Japeth. "You are brave to be

able to sleep here while walking. I doubt if I will sleep again for weeks."

"I'm just worn out," mumbled Arthur. "Not a Denizen."

"Not a Denizen?" asked Japeth. "But even the Piper's children have become Denizens, of a kind. . . ."

"M' not even that. Mortal. Been in House only once before . . ."

"But you have power! I felt it when we shook hands. You said you were on a mission —"

Arthur shook his head to wake himself up. He was so tired he couldn't even get his mouth and tongue to form words properly. He slapped himself on the face and felt a little spark zap across from his palms. It woke him up . . . a bit.

"It's hard to explain," he told Japeth. "Grim Tuesday is my enemy, and I really do want to help everyone escape from this Pit. But I have to get out myself first."

"There can be no escape from the indenture," said Japeth gloomily, fingering the string around his neck. "Indentured workers are always returned to the Far Reaches, even if you could get into another part of the House. There is no escape, getaway, deliverance, or emergence. We're down here for eternity. Forever, plus the statutory day."

"There must be some way," said Arthur. He felt a little refreshed, either from slapping himself or from his walking sleep. But only a little. A deep weariness lurked in every bone and muscle, waiting to rise up and overwhelm him. "Can't the indenture be cut off or something?"

"Quiet back there!" ordered Number One. He seemed to think he was in charge because he held the candle.

"Stick your nose down your own apron!" retorted Japeth. "We'll talk as much or as little as we like."

Number One grumbled something back, but said no more. However, he *did* increase the pace, with the other Denizens obediently following. It was just fast enough for Arthur to have to run every twenty paces or so, rather than every half hour. Soon, he felt a familiar tightness in his right lung. His throat was also a bit sore and his nose puffy. The spell the Lieutenant Keeper had taught him must be wearing off.

"Even if you could cut off my indenture tag, it wouldn't help," said Japeth as he easily ran next to Arthur. "Grim Tuesday has a master indenture roll, containing every Denizen's contract and listing what we owe and earn. An individual tag will simply re-form if it is damaged or destroyed. The only way out would be if one of the other Days bought out our contracts. And that will never happen. Our Days 'transferred' us to the Grim in the first place, though it would be more accurate or to the point to say we were sold, traded, or bartered."

"There has to be a way," muttered Arthur. At least he wasn't indentured. Not that it mattered when he was heading in precisely the wrong direction for any chance of escape. He was also totally exhausted, with one lung seizing up, the other sore from taking the load, and his nose streaming. It was all he could do to think about putting one foot in front of the other, let alone anything farther ahead.

"By the way," Japeth asked, "where did you get your streaming nose? That would be worth a fortune back in the Middle House."

"I told you I'm a mortal," sniffed Arthur. "I've got a cold."

"Oh," said Japeth. "A cold! Can you transfer it? Then maybe you could bribe an Overseer —"

Arthur shook his head. He had no idea how to transfer his cold, besides maybe sneezing on Japeth, which wasn't something he was about to do. He couldn't understand why the Denizens were so keen to have mortal ailments. Except, of course, that for them they were purely cosmetic, since they didn't feel sick.

Half an hour later the constant wetness of the cloud

began to turn into actual rain, and the gang paused briefly to put on their capes. The rain soon became a steady drizzle, punctuated by the occasional heavy, stinging drop. One fell on Arthur's hand, burning his skin as it slid off with a sizzling noise. But as with the Scoucher's cut, the burn healed within a few minutes, leaving no sign.

Nothing rain, thought Arthur dully. *That's all I need.* The stinging drops kept coming down every few minutes, but most fell on Arthur's hood or cape, leaving pockmarks in the stabilized mud. Arthur was so tired he hardly noticed them. He managed to keep going, but only because Japeth was almost carrying him.

Even with Japeth's help, they were falling farther and farther behind, the candle flame borne by Number One often out of sight, and Number Eleven a dim figure occasionally glimpsed through the rain.

"I can't go any farther," Arthur finally gasped when they lost sight of Number Eleven altogether. "You go. I'll catch up when I've had a rest. I can hide from the Overseers behind all this junk."

Japeth lowered the boy down next to yet another pile of broken train parts. Arthur leaned back against a pair of bogey wheels and his head sank down on his knees. He halfheartedly wiped his nose on his sleeve and thought about casting the breathing spell again. But he was so tired. . . .

After a while, he realized that Japeth was still standing in front of him.

"Go!" said Arthur weakly. "I'll work out some way to catch up. You don't want to get steamed."

"Perhaps a steaming is less to be feared than descending farther into the Pit," said Japeth slowly. "I have seen only despair and fatalism among the Denizens here. But you offer some hope. You are not indentured. You have some latent power. I shall take my chances with you. Rest, and I will watch. Stand guard. Shelter. Shield you. Shepherd. Mind. Watch. Tend. Keep vigil. Watch and ward. Patrol. Do the rounds . . ."

Japeth kept talking, but Arthur felt himself fall far away, the Denizen's voice receding into some distant space. In less than a second, Arthur was asleep.

He woke up to a peculiar whirring sound and the hum of the railway lines. Japeth was shaking him by the shoulder.

"Arthur! Wake up! Something is coming down the line!"

Arthur sat up and immediately started coughing. A racking cough that started deep in his chest and rolled up through his throat. A cough that kept going and going, as if his body was desperate to get something toxic out of his system.

Still coughing, Arthur plunged his fingers into his nose and his thumb into his mouth. Then, in between racking coughs, he managed to sputter out the words of the Lieutenant Keeper's spell. But the coughing continued, his nose kept running, and Arthur was overcome by fear. The spell hadn't worked and he was going to choke to death here in the ghastly Pit. . . .

Suddenly the coughing stopped and Arthur's nose dried up at the same moment. He took a deep breath, luxuriating as it spread through both lungs. He felt fine, though very stiff in the legs. According to his backwards watch, he'd been asleep for three hours.

"We must hide! Conceal ourselves! Take cover!" Japeth warned.

Arthur looked up the track and a large Nothing-laced raindrop hit his cheek, almost splashing his eye. He swore and wiped it off, ignoring the painful stinging sensation, and looked again, careful to keep his hood well forward.

He saw two fuzzy lights coming down the railway line, lights no stronger than his strom lantern, and only about a foot apart. They were too close together and didn't look bright enough to be the lights of a train. The whirring sound was also too quiet, and the rails were only humming very softly, nothing like they would for a full-sized locomotive and its load.

Nevertheless, Arthur hurried around the pile of scrap metal and hunkered down with Japeth behind an upturned bench seat thrown from a carriage, its horsehair stuffing sprayed out like a strange plant. They put their lanterns down the central hole of a huge driving wheel, covered it with a steel damping plate, and sat completely still in the darkness.

Arthur held his breath, fear rising as he stared at the lights and the dark shape behind them.

Chapter Eight

Arthur peered over the upturned bench at the approaching vehicle. Shrouded by the rain and disguised by a nimbus of diffused light, it was extremely hard to make out what it was. Only one thing was for sure — it wasn't a train. In fact, as it closed in, Arthur saw that it was a single wheel about six feet high and two feet wide, running on only the inner rail of the track. Or more exactly, it was two wheels, one inside the other. The inner wheel didn't move. The lights were fixed to the sides of this inner wheel, and there was someone . . . or something . . . sitting inside it. The outer wheel rotated around the inner wheel.

Arthur couldn't see any sign of a steam engine or anything else to make the wheel go. Perhaps it simply ran downhill and could never return to the top. It also seemed an unlikely conveyance for Grim Tuesday, which was a relief. It would be hard for anyone much taller or fatter than Arthur to fit inside the wheel.

Mind you, Arthur thought, *Grim Tuesday might not be like the picture on the station door. . . . He might really be small and slight . . . or not even have a human shape.*

"What is that?" whispered Japeth.

"I don't know," Arthur whispered back. He stared at the approaching wheel. Was it his imagination, or was it slowing down?

"It's stopping! Halting! Arresting! Ceasing to proceed forward!"

"Ssshhh! Don't panic," hissed Arthur. He bent down and picked up a long tube of Nothing-pocked copper, perhaps a former steam-pipe or fire-tube. It was slippery and wet, but felt comfortingly heavy in his hand.

"What if whoever's in it has a steam-gun?" Japeth asked.

"*Ssshhh*," Arthur hissed again. "Maybe it will go past."

But the wheel stopped about ten yards away. The rail stopped humming, allowing Arthur to hear clearly the strange, low sound that still came from the wheel. It took Arthur a moment to recognize it as the constant tick of clockwork. That immediately brought unpleasant memories of the clockwork creatures from the Coal Cellar. . . .

The figure inside the wheel stretched one leg out, then another. The movements seemed normal, not clockwork, but Arthur clutched his metal pipe more tightly. Once again, defeatist thoughts rose up in his mind. Perhaps he should step out and surrender, ask to be taken to Grim Tuesday. . . .

No! Arthur fought back. *I'm not giving in. I'm not surrendering, and I'm not going to sit and wait to be steamed or cut to bits.*

The wheel-rider slipped completely out and stood up behind the left lantern of the wheel. The light, spread and blurred by the rain, made it impossible to gauge the size of the person or what he or she was doing. But Arthur couldn't see any steam wafting out or the shine of an unsheathed blade.

The dim figure raised one hand. Arthur tensed, then as a bright light flashed from the end of the wheel-rider's index finger, he leaped up and rushed forward, swinging the metal tube over his head.

"Haaahh!" he cried, attacking.

"Arthur!" a voice called out.

Arthur slid to a stop and almost fell over. He lowered his copper pipe and squinted at the light, brushing away the rain from his face with the back of his left hand.

"Suzy?" he asked.

"Of course it is, stupid! Who were you expecting?"

Arthur smiled and shook his head as Suzy Turquoise

Blue stepped in front of the lantern. She looked the same as ever, bright-eyed and seriously disheveled. The ubiquitous apron of the Far Reaches was simply thrown over her multiple shirts, and one corner of her mulberry-colored waistcoat poked out from under the apron. Her battered top hat was missing, and in its place she wore an odd little red pillbox with a shiny black strap under her chin. There was also a large cleft stick thrust in her belt, with a piece of parchment stuck in the cleft.

Arthur shook his head again, but his smile got wider. Suzy was not only a great friend and ally, she had a knack for turning up just when Arthur really needed some help. And as far as he could tell, she was never downhearted. Not even here, in Grim Tuesday's Pit.

I wasn't expecting anyone friendly," Arthur said. "But I'm *very* glad to see you."

"'Course you are," said Suzy. "So would I be, down this dismal hole. Who's your mate?"

Arthur looked over his shoulder to where Japeth was standing hesitantly behind the upturned bench.

"Japeth. It's all right, Japeth, she's a friend of mine," Arthur called. "Come out."

He turned back to Suzy and added, "Japeth was in my work gang. He helped me . . . stay alive, I guess. But what are you doing here?"

"Looking for you, of course," said Suzy. "Ow!"

A heavy drop of Nothing-tainted rain had fallen on the back of her hand. She wiped it off with a grimace, ignoring the red welt it left behind. Unlike Arthur and Japeth, she wasn't wearing a stabilized mud cape.

"Got to get my umbrella," she muttered, rummaging inside her shirts. She brought out and opened up a small multicolored paper umbrella of the kind used to ornament cocktails. For a moment it just looked ridiculous, then it exploded into a full-sized umbrella, much as the Atlas did.

The Atlas!

Arthur had a momentary panic as he scrabbled under his cape and apron for his shirt pocket. For an instant he thought he'd dropped the Atlas back on the railway! A second later his hand closed on the rough cloth cover and he sighed in relief.

"Heart attack?" asked Suzy curiously. "Thought you were too young."

"No, just checking the Atlas," said Arthur. He looked at Suzy again and for a moment felt like giving her a hug, he was so relieved to see her. But the moment passed. He offered his hand instead. Suzy took it.

"Delighted, I'm sure," said Suzy formally. "See, I've been learning me manners."

As they shook, the nail on her index finger suddenly shone with a very bright, clear light, almost blinding Arthur. Suzy let go immediately and tugged on the finger till the joints cracked and the light went out.

"Supposed to stop once I found you," she grumbled. "Dame Primus . . . that's her as used to be Part One of the Will . . . fixed it so it would get brighter when you were close."

"But how did you know I was here?" asked Arthur.

"That'd be telling," said Suzy, holding her index finger up to her nose. It lit up once again and she flinched. "Stupid finger spells! That Will was a frog for too long if you ask me."

"But how *did* you know?" Arthur repeated.

"Well, after the telephone was cut off I thought I'd nip over to your world, only Dame Primus wouldn't let me go, cos of the Original Law. I said, 'It's a pretty dumb Law when you can't do anything but everyone else can' and Dame Primus said, 'You'll go to your room, young lady, for the next decade if you're not careful, trouble or no trouble,' and I said, 'Arthur's the Master, he made me Monday's Tierce, you're only the Steward,' and then she sent me to my room. Only I climbed out through the chimney and Sneezer let me use Seven Dials to have a look at what was going on, and I saw the Grotesques had gone through, and then the Scoucher, and I wanted to warn you but your head is too thick or something and won't receive waking dreams, so Sneezer helped me ask the Atlas and it steered you to that girl Leaf who I met when we were on the Improbable Stair, and then I sent a dream to her telling her where the Grotesques had opened their side of the Door in your world, and I . . . Where was I?"

She took a deep breath and rushed on.

"Oh . . . we figured Leaf could tell you and then you could use that door to get back into the House. But then I thought maybe I'd better go and help you out anyway, so I went to see the Lieutenant Keeper and asked him to let me through, but he wouldn't, so then I sneaked back into the Dayroom and looked through Seven Dials again and saw you were going through the Door, so I went down to the Atrium to meet you. But when you didn't show up, I knocked on the Door and talked to the Lieutenant Keeper.

"I sez to him, 'Did Arthur come through the Door?' and he sez, 'Yes,' and then I waited and he didn't say anything so I sez, 'Where did he go?' and he sez, 'The Far Reaches,' and I sez, 'How long ago?' and he sez, 'Two hours by House Time,' and then I sez, 'Let me go through too,' and he sez, 'No,' and I sez, 'Why?' and he sez, 'Even if I could permit it, you can only use that door from the Secondary Realms. Here, you have to go through the House.'

"So I went back to Dame Primus and after a bit of shouting and carrying on she sez, 'Grim Tuesday deserves to have you on his doorstep,' and she fixed me up with all the trimmings to help you out, like this fingernail thing."

"Right," said Arthur weakly. After having hardly spoken for a day it was almost too much to listen to Suzy, who was clearly in a talkative mood. "So how did you get into the Far Reaches and get that . . . that wheel and everything?"

"The Grim uses the Piper's children for messengers," said Suzy, brandishing the cleft stick with the parchment in the end. "Monday's Noon, that used to be Dusk, did a transfer for me to the Middle House, and then a friend of his there sold my contract to Grim Tuesday so I could join his messengers. Then I swapped with Ned to come down the line because my finger glowed when I went near the railway."

Arthur shook his head, his new earring jangling annoyingly against his neck. He was still tired and sore and it was all a bit too much to take in. Then he realized the significance of what Suzy was saying.

"You're indentured!" he said. "That means you're trapped here!"

"Only temporarily," replied Suzy with a shrug. "Once you find Part Two of the Will and take over from Grim Tuesday, then you can release me from my indenture."

"And me," said Japeth. "Sir. Excellency. Eminence. Highness. Majesty. Whoever you actually are."

"He's Monday," said Suzy. "The Master of the Lower House."

Japeth choked on whatever he was going to say and immediately leaned into a very deep bow that put his head almost at Arthur's feet.

"I'm not Monday!" said Arthur. Distress was clear on his face. He *wasn't* Monday. He *wasn't* one of the Days. He was just a boy caught up in great events and as soon as possible he would go back to his normal, uneventful life. "I'm Arthur Penhaligon. I've handed over the Mastery of the Lower House to the . . . to Dame Primus or whatever she calls herself. Please, get up!"

Japeth raised himself a little, but remained hunched over. He retreated several steps, tripped over a broken piece of rail, and fell flat on his back. Arthur hurried over to help him up, making the Denizen even more flustered.

As Japeth straightened himself out, Arthur turned back to Suzy.

"How am I supposed to find Part Two of the Will and take over from Grim Tuesday anyway? I can't even free myself from this Pit! Ow! OW!"

A drop of Nothing-laced rain had fallen on his lip. Arthur frantically wiped it off and hopped around clutching his face till the pain subsided. He didn't know whether it was the Lieutenant Keeper's spell or some residual enchantment from the First Key, but the burns from the Nothing rain healed in a matter of minutes. But he still felt the pain. . . .

"That's why I'm here," said Suzy. "To help you. You might want to look the other way — this is a bit disgusting."

"What is?" asked Arthur, as Suzy reached into her mouth with two fingers.

"This!" said Suzy, ripping out a tooth from the back of her mouth, complete with bleeding roots.

Arthur grimaced and stepped back as Suzy spat blood onto the train tracks.

"Had to smuggle it in as an extra wisdom tooth right at the back," she explained, setting the tooth down on the ground, being careful to shield it with her umbrella. "Got everything we need in it."

Arthur looked down at the tooth.

How could this ugly-looking molar have anything in it? he thought, but he was wise enough in the ways of the House to keep silent for a moment.

As Arthur watched, the color from the bloody roots slowly spread upwards, changing the tooth from white to a deep, even red. Then the tooth began to shimmer and change, its outline becoming blurry and indistinct. An instant later, Arthur was looking down at a fat little wooden doll about an inch high and two inches around, with a smiling face, red cheeks, and a bright red-painted coat with a black line around the stomach to mark where it could be opened. It looked like the smallest doll from a set of Russian dolls, the kind that nested one within another.

"Uh, you sure this is right?" asked Arthur.

"Open it up," said Suzy with a sniff. "See for yourself."

Arthur bent down and unscrewed the doll. When he lifted off the top half his thumb and forefinger were savagely forced apart, nearly spraining them, as a larger doll exploded out.

The second doll was five times the size of the tiny doll he'd just opened. Arthur sighed as Suzy raised an eyebrow.

"Come on," she said. "There's three more dolls inside that one, then the one with the stuff. Don't stick your head too close, mind."

"I'll do it, sir," offered Japeth.

"No, I'll do it," said Arthur. "And don't call me sir!"

"Very good, your sublime serenity."

"Don't call me that either," said Arthur as he gingerly unscrewed the head of the second doll, leaning well back to allow the larger one inside to bound out without doing him permanent damage.

The other dolls quickly followed, and in a few minutes Arthur was unscrewing the head of the fifth and last doll, which was almost as tall as he was, and three times as fat. This time, nothing exploded out.

Arthur warily looked inside the open doll, ready to jump back if there was some delayed reaction or ghastly contents inside. But the doll was empty, save for a canvas satchel at the bottom about the same size as Arthur's school backpack.

"Had to put it inside lots of dolls so the Grim's Sniffers didn't pick it up," explained Suzy. She stuck her umbrella upright in the spoke-hole of a leading wheel, rolled the doll onto its side, and bent in to retrieve the satchel.

Her muffled voice continued from inside. "You

probably missed 'em coming in the back way. Horrid things, those Sniffers. Just the snout of a dog, without the rest of the animal. A nose crawling about on hairy-bristle legs that I reckon the Grim took off a cricket and sized up. Fair made me want to puke."

"One crawled over me when I arrived," said Japeth with a shudder. "A disembodied snout with two tiny eyes and a shrunken mouth, sniffing at my skin . . . I didn't know what it was, or what it was doing."

"They sniff out magic or forbidden powers," said Suzy. "Like wot's in 'ere."

She laid the satchel down under the umbrella and opened it up. It unfolded like a picnic set, revealing two pieces of beautifully crisp, heavy white paper; a stick of crimson sealing wax; four small coiled balls of twine; a box of matches (with a picture of a duck smoking a pipe on it and the words DANGER MATCHES — FIVE TIMES AS FIERY, SUPER EASY TO LIGHT); and two glass jars that were stuffed full of what appeared to be green woolen frog finger-puppets.

"Two sets of Ascension Wings and two sets of stickit fingers," said Suzy. "The wings take us up out of the Pit, all the way to the ceiling of the Far Reaches. Using the stickit fingers, we then clamber across the ceiling to the spire of Grim Tuesday's Treasure Tower. We drop onto the spire, raise the cockerel wind gauge, and climb in as quick as you like, find Part Two of the Will, and set this place to rights. . . . At least, that's what Dame Primus reckons, so it'll go horribly wrong for sure."

"What are Ascension Wings?" asked Arthur. "And why do we have to climb across the ceiling? What's this Treasure —?"

"What's that noise?" asked Japeth. "Begging your pardon."

Arthur heard it too, and looked up into the darkness, pulling his hood forward to shield his eyes. He could hear a really loud hissing that seemed to come from up above. It took him a second to work out that it sounded like a firework fuse being lit, magnified a thousand times, but also very far away.

"Uh-oh," said Suzy. She plucked the folded paper from the end of her cleft stick and handed it to Arthur. "That'll be this. I'm supposed to have warned all the gangs between Up Station and Way Stations One and Two. . . ."

Arthur unfolded the note and quickly read:

DANGER. All overseers, all gangs, all way stations, all workers, and all staff. A sunburst is scheduled for High Noon House Time today, affecting top layers from Up Sta-

tion to Way Station Two. All workers are hereby ordered to stop work or motion at the sound of the thirty-second fuzee, which will be clearly audible. All workers must shield their eyes and must not look up till the all-clear whistle is heard. Should the sunburst reveal Nithlings, then the alarm must be sounded as per Standing Orders 27, par. 4 or by screaming as loudly as possible in unison for three seconds every nine seconds. By Order, Tuesday's Van.

What's a thirty-second fuzee, thought Arthur. *Must mean fuse . . . thirty seconds —*

"Look down!" shouted Arthur as he grabbed his companions and pushed them headfirst down towards the cold, wet stone.

Chapter Nine

Arthur had barely hit the ground, with Suzy and Japeth on either side, when there was a sudden flash of light so intense that he had to shut his eyes even though he was looking at the ground and his hood was pulled over his face.

Strangely, there was no heat or shock wave, though Arthur had flinched in expectation. There was only the initial flash, then a slowly lessening but still brilliant light.

A few seconds later, a faint but piercing whistle echoed down through the Pit, like the cry of a distant bird. The all-clear whistle, Arthur presumed. Scrunching up his left eye and keeping the right completely closed, Arthur risked a look.

What he saw astounded him. A giant glowing ball the size of a hundred hot-air balloons hung in the air about a mile up and eight or nine miles away, like a small, comfortably bright sun. It had banished all the rain clouds, the rain and the smog, and its slowly fading light illuminated the upper reaches of the Pit in all its vastness, a hole so big the far side was just a blurry smudge at least twenty miles distant and so deep that even the sunburst's light could not penetrate its depths.

"So that's a sunburst," said Suzy, with a sniff. "Thought it'd be better than that. More like a big firework, you know, knock the dust out of yer ears with a bang."

"It's bigger than I thought . . . could have thought," whispered Arthur. He'd been to the Grand Canyon and was thinking of the Pit on the same sort of scale. But it was much, much wider than the Grand Canyon and much, much deeper. "The Pit, I mean."

"It's still just a big rotten hole in the ground," said Suzy. "We'd better hurry and get these wings on. Take advantage of the sunburst. Might not be another one for months."

"What is that sunburst thing?" asked Arthur, pointing to the huge glowing ball. It was much less bright than it had been, and the shadows from the Pit were steadily climbing upwards, and faint wisps of rain cloud were re-forming high above. "What does it do?"

"I dunno exactly," replied Suzy. "Ned told me it kind of clears up the Nothing, gets rid of the rain for a while and so on. Grim Tuesday does it to different parts of the Pit every few months. Like clearing out a drain with vitroleum, I 'spect. But it's handy for us. Better to fly in the light. If we ever get around to it."

"Ah, I heard an Overseer say to another something similar to 'need a sunburst soon, for track-checking,'" said Japeth hesitantly. "Which suggests that the track is inspected during the season or interval of this sunburst, and as the sunburst's light falls or descends upon us, we may soon be, ah, inspected. . . ."

Arthur looked back up the railway. He had gone at least thirty miles along the service road, around the edge of the Pit while slowly descending. Up Station had to be roughly a third of the way anti-clockwise back around the side — about ten miles — and about half a mile up. He peered in that direction, narrowing his eyes against the sunburst, which was now only as bright as a highway streetlight. But it had done its work, and, though beginning to darken and cloud over, the air was still clear.

Japeth and Suzy looked too. At first no one could see anything, then everyone spoke at once.

"Smoke —"

"Train —"

"Grim's train!"

They could all see the signs that revealed the presence of the train, though it was too far away to see the train itself. The glitter of the sunburst's light on polished metal, a tall spray of sparks, and a smudged column of black smoke rising straight up. It had to be Grim Tuesday's train, starting down the railway.

"It'll take a few hours to get here," said Arthur rather doubtfully. "Or an hour, at least. Won't it?"

"Right, we have to get the Ascension Wings on," said Suzy. She added, "And they're called that because they only go up. You can lean to change direction, but they only go up. They're a very weak magic, much weaker than regular wings. Easier to smuggle in."

"What about Japeth?" asked Arthur.

"Sorry." Suzy shrugged. "Nothing I can do."

"Perhaps I could take your wheel, Miss Suzy, and catch up with my gang," suggested Japeth. "Then, when you defeat Grim Tuesday, sir, you might take the trouble to release me from my indenture? And perhaps find employment suitable for a former Thesaurus?"

"More like *if* than *when*," muttered Arthur. "And I can't just fly out on you. You didn't run out on me."

"Nor will you run out on me, I'm sure," said Japeth, bowing again. "This is merely a delay, postponement, deferment, or recess. I am sure you will be successful and my release, rescue, deliverance, redemption, saving of my bacon —"

"You said it," said Suzy. "Nice to meet you, Japeth.

Don't worry. Arthur's smarter than he looks. I reckon he'll see you right. Tuesday'll be a pushover compared to Monday."

"Really?" asked Japeth.

"Nah, don't be soft," said Suzy. "I just said that to cheer you up. Shouldn't have asked. Now, Artie, we need to get the wings and stickit fingers on. I'll have to cut some holes in your coat and shirt."

"Don't call me Artie! And why do I need holes in my clothes?"

"Because the wings are stuck on with sealing wax to your shoulders," explained Suzy, indicating the stick of red wax. "With a string through the wax, so when it's time to drop the wings, you pull the string, break the seal, and down you drop, nice as ninepence. Come on."

Still Arthur hesitated. He felt that he was once more being pushed into something that he had no control over. But was there any real choice?

"That train is remarkably fleet, fast, light-footed," said Japeth, who was watching the smoke plume from the Grim's train. "If I am to take the wheel, I perhaps should set forth, depart, leave, or absent myself immediately."

"You're right," said Arthur. He forced a deep breath into his tired lungs and stood up straighter. He owed it to Japeth — and Suzy and everyone else — to do his absolute best and then some more. Giving up was not an option. "I will defeat Grim Tuesday and I will release you and all the other indentured workers. No one should be a slave. Here, or anywhere else."

"That's more like the old Arthur," said Suzy. "There I was thinking this Pit had sucked the guts out of you. In a manner of speaking."

"Thanks a lot," muttered Arthur. He held out his hand to Japeth. "Good luck. I'll do my best to help you."

This time, there were fewer sparks when Japeth shook his hand. But Arthur felt a surge of energy come out of his palm and travel up through his arm, and Japeth's arm trembled as if he felt something similar. Then Arthur noticed that Japeth had grown several inches, and his ragged shirt had restitched itself, even the string holding together his cuffs transforming into mother-of-pearl links.

"I will serve you too, Arthur, when I can," said Japeth, letting go of his hand. "Farewell for now, Master. Miss Suzy, if I may trouble you to explain, elucidate, or illuminate the workings of this wheel?"

He hurried over to the wheel and climbed in. Suzy showed him the lever that controlled its speed and the locked access hatch to the gearbox that could only be opened by Grim Tuesday or one of the Grotesques, to allow the wheel to use its stored clockwork power to go up the railway rather than down.

Japeth gently pushed the lever forward and the wheel moved off. The Denizen waved as he passed Arthur, then pushed the lever as far as it would go. The wheel accelerated away, and was soon lost in the rising shadows.

The rain had also just started again. Spotting drops, so far without the Nothing taint. The clouds were spreading out from the edges of the Pit, drawing closer to the fading sunburst.

Arthur stood still as Suzy sliced through his cape and shirt with a short, sharp knife — the knife she'd picked up in Monday's antechamber. Standing still while Suzy cut behind him reminded Arthur unpleasantly of being in the hospital, about to be injected in the upper arm.

After cutting the slits in his clothes, Suzy picked up one of the pieces of paper and quickly folded and tore it into two separate wings. The paper became fluffier and more feathery as she worked.

"Lie down," she instructed Arthur. He lay down but craned his head to see what she was doing.

Suzy put the wings on the ground and weighted them with a piece of ballast. She unrolled two pieces of twine and set them next to the wings. Then she picked up the stick of sealing wax and the matches.

"This'll sting a bit," she said as she struck a match against the ground. It flared with a loud *whoompah,* and a flame about three feet long shot up out of the match.

"Down," said Suzy. The flame receded. "Down some more. That's it."

Arthur couldn't see what she did next, but he felt it. A blob of hot sealing wax went straight onto his shoulder blade, then he felt the paper wing brushing his back and the string dangling past his neck. Suzy's thumb pressed hard into the wax.

"Don't move!" she warned. "Got to do the next one quickly or they'll grow unbalanced."

Arthur bit his lip to suppress a yelp as the wax dripped on the other side. It was worse when he expected it, but it was only a momentary pain.

"Done!" exclaimed Suzy with satisfaction. "They take about ten minutes to grow. I'll make mine, then you can stick them on for me."

"I don't know how!" Arthur protested.

"It's easy," replied Suzy as she quickly folded and tore the remaining paper into wings. "Just heat the wax, drop a bit on my shoulder, whack the wing and the string on, drop a bit more wax, then seal it with your thumb. There's already holes in my clothes from my regular wings."

"OK," said Arthur doubtfully. He took the wings and weighted them down with the same piece of ballast, and put the string next to them. Then he picked up the matches. They looked normal enough apart from the cover of the box.

"Hurry up," said Suzy, who was lying on the floor scratching her back through the holes in her clothes. "This stone is cold."

Arthur struck the match on the ground, flinching as it roared into life. The flame was even longer than the one Suzy had struck, and dancing around in an excited fashion that had nothing to do with any wind. It even seemed to have a tiny, grinning face.

"Down," said Arthur. "Down a lot."

The flame slowly ebbed, the face losing its grin and becoming sad. When it was only an inch or so high, Arthur picked up the sealing wax and quickly melted the end to drop a dollop on Suzy's back. Being nervous, he got it a bit wrong, so some wax fell on her coat and ran onto the skin. Arthur dripped a bit more on.

"What's the holdup?" asked Suzy. "It's not like it's a complicated spell or anything."

Arthur frowned and dripped a whole lot more wax, then he carefully pressed the wing and the string down, melted more wax on top, and pressed it down with his thumb. He expected that this would leave a thumbprint in the wax, but it didn't. Instead it made the wax glow in rainbow colors, followed by a perfect round seal, with a profile of his own head wearing a crown of laurel, and words around the outside in some weird alphabet that slowly changed into regular letters that read DOMINUS ARTHUR MAGISTER DOMUS INFERIOR and then changed again to LORD ARTHUR MASTER OF THE LOWER HOUSE.

"What are you waiting for?" asked Suzy in an exasperated tone. "Grim Tuesday to come and ask you to tea?"

"Sorry," said Arthur. He'd been briefly mesmerized by his own seal. Quickly he put on the second wing. It had already grown a bit on the ground, and was much more like feathers than paper. Clean, glowing white feathers, totally in contrast to the soot-stained stone and the gathering darkness.

Arthur felt his own wings begin to flap, sending a draft around his ankles. But they were still too small to lift him off the ground.

Suzy handed Arthur one of the jars of what looked like woolen frog finger-puppets, stuck the other in her apron pocket, then busied herself putting everything else back in the satchel. She hung it over her neck at the front so it didn't get in the way of her wings.

"There's six stickit fingers in the jar. Bung them on now, thumb and every second finger," she instructed, unscrewing her own jar. "They won't stick till you speak the spell, which is '*Stick by day and stick by night, stick for a minute each, left and right.*' Only one of your hands will stick at a time, so you can move about. Just remember which is sticky and which is about to unstick. I'll tell you how to take them off when we need to."

Arthur repeated the spell in his head to make sure he got it right, then put the six stickit fingers on his thumbs and alternate fingers. They were just like little woolen finger-puppets, only they wriggled and squeaked like little live mice as he put them on, which made it quite difficult.

He was concentrating very hard on that task, so he got an awful shock when Suzy suddenly picked up the copper rod he'd almost used as a weapon and swung it at something that came flying in like a pitched baseball. It was about the size of a baseball too, but black and fuzzy, almost like a lump of tar.

Suzy hit it. The end of the copper rod puffed into metallic mist as it struck, but whatever it was batted over the edge of the Pit and went straight down.

"A gobbet of Nothing," said Suzy with a frown. "Trying to find other gobbets to join to make a Nithling."

She looked up at the sunburst, which was very faint now. The clouds were practically solid again all around it, and she and Arthur were in twilight that was rapidly turning into darkest night. "I thought the sunburst would keep that sort of thing down for longer. You'd better grab some kind of club. Copper's better than steel, though neither's much use really against unformed Nothing. Need silver or something special like one of them blades made from frozen moonlight or burning with architectural fire, like Noon's. How're your wings? Can you reach your strings? Don't pull 'em yet."

Arthur craned his neck to look. His wings now stretched from his shoulder blades to his knees and were magnificently feathered and shining. They were beating slowly, as if they were warming up. The air they washed around him was cleaner, faintly orange-scented, and very refreshing. He felt for the strings, which were hanging down his chest on either side of his neck.

"I can reach them," he confirmed. He looked around and saw another piece of copper pipe, this one thicker and longer than the tube Suzy had appropriated. He started for it, was lifted off his feet, and overshot by several yards.

"Be ready," warned Suzy. "They'll flap proper-like in a minute."

Arthur bent down and half-crawled, half-pulled himself to the copper pipe. Just as his hand closed around it, his wings gave an almighty beat, lifting him ten feet off the railway.

Suzy was still on the ground, her wings warming up.

"You can lean to change direction!" she shouted. "Aim for the center of the Pit to start with. Harder to get shot at from the train or the road. If you get to the ceiling before me, you have to somersault just before you hit. That'll confuse the wings for a bit and they'll slow down. Use your stickit fingers to stick to the ceiling. It'll be easy!"

Arthur's wings increased the depth and the speed of their beat again, and he began to accelerate upwards. He looked down and saw a huge, only vaguely human figure that had long, wet dragonfly-like wings trailing down its back. As Arthur watched, it climbed up over the lip of the Pit and began to stalk towards Suzy.

She was looking up at Arthur, and obviously could neither hear nor see the Nithling.

"Suzy!" Arthur screamed. "Look out! A Nith —"

Chapter Ten

As the Nithling lunged at Suzy's back, the sunburst suddenly went out, plunging the Pit back into total darkness, save for the pathetic circle of light from the strom lantern clutched in Arthur's shaking hand.

Suzy didn't have a lantern — she'd only had the two fixed on the wheel taken by Japeth. Arthur strained his eyes, desperately trying to see what was happening, but to no avail. He couldn't hear anything either, over the beat of his wings and the rush of air.

"Suzy!"

There was no answer. Arthur's wings beat inexorably on, taking him higher and higher, faster and faster.

"Suzy!" he shouted again.

The only response came from above, a sudden swathe of rain. But Arthur's wings repelled or blew the drops away and surrounded him with an envelope of warm, dry air.

"Suzy!"

She must have escaped.

Arthur tried to recall that last split-second image before the sunburst died.

Suzy's wings had been fully extended, about to beat down, hadn't they? She would have taken off an instant before the Nithling struck her.

Right?

Arthur remembered what Suzy had told him about Nithlings. It seemed like only yesterday and he clearly recalled her words:

"A festering bite or scratch from a Nithling will dissolve you into Nothing. That's why everyone's afraid of them."

It *was* only yesterday, Arthur realized. They'd both survived Monday, but Tuesday was much worse. It had been bad enough to start with, but now —

Something flittered into the light of Arthur's lantern. Instinctively he hit at it with his copper tube, knocking it back into the rainy darkness. Only after he'd done it did he realize it was another one of those flying lumps of Nothing.

A gobbet. Seeking other gobbets to make a Nithling . . .

Arthur started to look everywhere feverishly, craning his head as far around as he could to either side.

What if a gobbet of Nothing hits me in the back of the head? Or in the wings?

Another gobbet hurtled past Arthur's foot. He kicked at it, and the point of his clog disappeared, sliced off as if by a guillotine. For a heart-stopping instant Arthur thought his toes might have gone as well, till he wriggled them.

For the first time Arthur experimented with changing direction. As Suzy had said, the wings only flew up, but he found he could quickly change the angle of his ascent. To avoid any gobbets that were targeting him — which they might be able to, he didn't know — Arthur leaned to the right, then the left, then backwards and forwards, till he started to spiral and had to try and remain still and straight to stop that.

Whatever he did, there were still gobbets flying around him. So far none had come from behind, or if they had, they were blown away by his wings. Soon Arthur was batting them away every few minutes with his rapidly diminishing piece of pipe. Every time he hit a gobbet, it dissolved several inches of copper and he had to be careful only to get them with the dissolved end.

Then one hit Arthur's lantern, boring a hole straight through it, extinguishing its flame, or whatever actually shed the light behind the glass. Arthur groaned, but the darkness only lasted a few seconds. A soft, mellow white light slowly grew all around him, and the gobbets of Nothing were rimmed with luminescence as soon as they got close.

The light was coming from Arthur's wings. That was comforting for a few seconds, till he realized that being lit up like a Christmas tree angel in the Pit was just an invitation to Nithlings, Overseers, and who knew what else.

Not that there was anything he could do, or any time to think about it. More and more gobbets were flying at him, most of them coming up from below, so he had to draw his knees and feet up and lean forward, which was quite difficult. Every time he leaned forward too far or let one knee fall lower than the other, he lost his balance and started to spin around.

After beating away at least a dozen more gobbets of Nothing, Arthur noticed that there were fewer of them, but the ones that were still attacking were larger. They were combining . . . becoming a Nithling.

Which worried him a lot, particularly when no more gobbets came hurtling up out of the darkness. Did that mean he was out of their reach, or that they had combined into something that was somewhere nearby, flying up with him?

Something touched his leg. Arthur flinched and cried out, till he realized it was just his useless lantern, brushing against his knee. He opened his hand and let it fall, the glass sending one last reflection back before it disappeared into darkness.

A second later, there was the sound of broken glass and an angry cry, partly muffled by rain and Arthur's beating wings.

"Ow!"

"Suzy!" Arthur called again. But as he called out, and relief rose in his heart, a nasty thought crept into his mind. Maybe there was some sort of Nithling that could imitate people? What if there was one that could take the shape of people it had dissolved or eaten? He had a vague half-memory of someone talking about that, or maybe he had read it in the Atlas. . . .

"Suzy?" he repeated, looking down. "Is that you?"

"'Course it's me!" came the retort. Arthur still couldn't see her, but she sounded closer. "Almost took my eye out, you idiot! There's enough rubbish in this hole without you chucking some more down."

That did sound like the sort of thing Suzy would say, Arthur thought. But what if the Nithling had absorbed her mind and memories, and had gotten all her vocabulary and word choices and everything?

He wished he could see her, but at the same time was afraid that he would see the distorted man-shape with the insectlike wings beating in a frenzy as it tried to catch up.

"What happened?" Arthur asked. He caught a glimpse of something below, but couldn't quite make out what it was. "The Nithling —"

"Missed me," called out Suzy. "Close-run thing. Bit off my right clog. I was kicking it in the teeth, so I s'pose that's fair."

Arthur relaxed. It had to be Suzy, narrowly escaped. *But if it's Suzy, why aren't her wings glowing like mine?*

"Better dim your wings!" Suzy called out, almost exactly as Arthur thought this. "The light's making Nothing come together into gobbets. Once there's enough of them around, they'll make a Nithling."

"How do I know you're really Suzy?" Arthur called in return, a slight edge of panic in his voice.

"What are you talking about?" came the exasperated reply. "Who else would I be? Shade your light!"

"Don't listen to her!" called another voice, one that also sounded like Suzy, but huskier. "Keep your light up, it's the only thing protecting you from the Nithlings!"

"Tarnation!" said the first Suzy voice. "The thing

that got my clog has patterned itself on me. Must have found a bit of toenail or skin."

"Don't listen, Arthur!" came the other Suzy voice. "I'm the real Suzy! Keep your light on, I'm catching up!"

Arthur stared down at the darkness. If only he could see the speakers, he was sure he'd be able to tell which one was the real Suzy. But there was nothing. . . .

"Arthur, tell your stupid wings to dim, and look out! That Nithling will get above you and swoop down at your face. It's blind, but it smells the power behind the light!"

Arthur blinked. That voice came from the left, and was accompanied by a faint sparkle of light, like a single distant star seen on a cloudy night.

"That's a lie! The light protects you!" screamed the second Suzy voice, from off to the right, and closer.

"Wings, please dim your light," said Arthur softly, and he raised the remnant of his copper tube and held it out like a sword before his face.

He was only just in time, as a nightmarish thing crashed into the tube, hurtling Arthur in a series of backwards somersaults, his wings thrashing to right themselves. The pipe was torn from Arthur's grasp as it stuck like a harpoon into the Nithling's breast. The creature plummeted past him and into the depths, shrieking.

Mid-somersault, Arthur caught a horrific vision of a figure the size and general shape of Suzy, but made from scales and patchwork crocodile hide. One of its fifteen-foot dragonfly wings beat so fast it blurred, while the other hung limp and useless with Arthur's pipe stuck into the chest muscles that powered it.

"How could you tellllll . . ."

Suzy's fingernail, thought Arthur. *That faint sparkle of light.*

Arthur's wings got him upright and level again, and resumed their steady, air-eating pace. They did not brighten, keeping the light at about the same level as that shed by a couple of birthday cake candles, so Arthur could hardly see his own hands.

"That was close," said Suzy.

"Very," said Arthur. "I know it's you, Suzy, but can you just brighten up your wings for a second so I can be sure? I'd hate to burn you into cinders with my power by mistake."

He said the second sentence louder than the first, in case it was another Nithling. It might get scared off.

"Oh, all right," said Suzy. Then she added in a louder voice, "Anything to avoid being incisorated."

Light bloomed a mere twenty feet below Arthur's feet, and he saw Suzy looking up at him. She winked, lifted her hands above her head, and pushed her palms together to make herself into an arrow shape. In response, her wings beat faster. She leaned to the left and rapidly drew up level with Arthur, a few feet to the side.

"Incisorated?" asked Arthur.

"Dunno," said Suzy with a shrug. "It sounds scarier, though, don't it? Incinerated is what they do with dead papers out on the Waste Waste, back home in the Lower House. That wouldn't scare me, not up here. Where's your incinerator?"

"I wish I was back home," said Arthur.

"So do I," replied Suzy briefly. "Wish I had one, let alone being there. Keep an eye out for more Nithlings. Too many gobbets flitting about below. They seem to be attracted to the wings. I'd wondered why no one ever used them here."

"What?" asked Arthur. "You knew no one ever used wings here?"

"Sure," said Suzy. "I just thought they were dumb plodders. Look, there's the train!"

She pointed. Arthur squinted into the dark and for a moment thought he saw a tiny spray of what might be sparks somewhere in the distance. Then he was plunged into a thick cloud, and even his wings couldn't keep all the moisture from him.

"An hour or so of cloud and then into the smoke next," said Suzy cheerfully. "Worse than Dame Primus's cigars. Old bat won't give me one, neither."

"Smoking will kill you with throat or lung or mouth cancer or heart disease," said Arthur, an asthmatic and the son of a doctor. "Not to mention years of bad breath, yellow teeth, brown fingernails, lungs full of tar so you cough like a cat throwing up hairballs, only the sputum is worse than hairballs."

"Well, you might be right about the yellow teeth and the fingernails, but smoking won't kill you in the House," said Suzy. "Unless you nick one of Dame Primus's cigars."

"Well, smoking will kill you back in my home," said Arthur. "Where I intend to be again as soon as possible. Where I should be . . . where I would be *now,* if it wasn't for the Morrow Days and the bits of the Will and everything."

"It could be worse," said Suzy.

"How?"

"You could have the Will stuck down your gob. It used to throb in my throat and make me feel like I'd got a bit of rice pudding stuck halfway down. Horrible, it was."

"And we're going to get another piece of it. If we can find it."

"It might be a better bit. Nicer. We'll find it. Has to be in the Grim's Treasure Tower, doesn't it?"

"Why?" asked Arthur gloomily.

"Stands to reason, doesn't it? Grim Tuesday's famous for stuffing 'is tower full of the best things ever made and the most valuable loot from the Secondary Realms. 'Course the Will will be in there somewhere."

"It can't be as easy as that," said Arthur.

"Well, we do have to get in there," said Suzy. "Through the wind vane and all. Might be a bit tricky, even with the stickit fingers. Then there'll be guards and so forth, I s'pose."

"Right," said Arthur heavily.

"And traps."

"Great."

"And there's an eel of a chance Grim Tuesday'll be there himself, though, if that is his train going down the Pit, he should be on that."

"Good."

"Probably. Though sometimes it's only one of the Grotesques takes the train — look out!"

Chapter Eleven

Arthur leaned desperately to the right as something plummeted past him. Once again he hardly had time to register what it was, beyond a jumbled snapshot of teeth, claws, and tiny, useless wings fluttering madly.

"What was that?!"

"Dunno," said Suzy. "Who knows how the gobbets decide what to make when they come together? Bad news for down below."

"What?"

"A Nithling'll probably survive the fall. It'll just be really cross. Look out!"

Arthur flipped his legs forward and threw himself back, tumbling end over end as something that looked like a cross between a boa constrictor and a weasel fell hissing past, its jaws almost close enough to close on Arthur's hand.

It fell still closer to Suzy, but she whacked it with her copper pipe. Arthur was surprised to hear the clear ringing tone of metal striking metal and to see that none of the pipe dissolved.

"Ouch!" exclaimed Suzy. "Jarred my hand!"

"Was . . . was that a Nithling?" Arthur asked as he regained his flying equilibrium. He kept looking nervously in all directions, though, ready to lean or tumble or do whatever it took to avoid whatever came flying up or falling down next.

"Who knows?" said Suzy. "Most shaped-up Nithlings are some sort of flesh, but whatever that was, it was made of metal. It bent my pipe."

"How long till we hit the ceiling?" asked Arthur.

Suzy frowned.

"Hard to say. We haven't even got to the smoky upper air yet. Maybe an hour or two."

Suzy had hardly finished speaking before they broke through the cloud and entered the layer of smog. Arthur had been out of it long enough that he could smell it clearly, many revolting odors combining to create something sharp and acidic in the choking smoke, with overtones of ozone, like from an electric appliance burning out.

Fortunately, the spell the Lieutenant Keeper had taught him was still going strong. Suzy, having been in the House long enough to be almost a Denizen, was unaffected, though she did wrinkle her nose.

The next hour passed uneventfully enough. There were still gobbets of Nothing flying around, and once a

Nithling fell just close enough to glimpse and cause Arthur a momentary panic.

Otherwise Arthur's wings continued their steady beat and they climbed up through the smoggy darkness. It was impossible to tell where they were, relative to the edges of the Pit or the ceiling of the Far Reaches.

After a while, Suzy pulled a fob watch out of her apron pocket, opened it, and peered at the face.

"I reckon we must be getting close," she said, closing the watch with a practiced one-handed snap. "Try and lie on your back. That'll slow the wings down so we don't crash into the ceiling too hard. Once we hit, use the spell to fully wake your stickit fingers and hold on to the ceiling. Then pull your string and lose the wings and we'll go hand over hand to the Treasure Tower."

"Which direction will it be in?" asked Arthur as he kicked and threw himself backwards. Unfortunately he just did a somersault, confusing him and not slowing his wings for more than a second.

"Mmm," replied Suzy evasively. She'd managed to lie on her back by folding her legs up and holding her feet against her face, which was a gymnastic maneuver Arthur couldn't hope to match. He drew his knees up instead and tried to keep them against his chest while he threw himself backwards with rather less vigor.

That sort of worked. Arthur's wings slowed as they tried to work out the best way to keep ascending.

"How will we know where to crawl across the ceiling?" asked Arthur again. "I mean, it could be miles away, in any direction, couldn't it? Without the light from our wings. In the dark and the smog, with no landmarks."

"We'll work it out," said Suzy.

"And we're just going to hang by three little woolen finger-puppets to the ceiling with a . . . a . . . a thousand-mile or whatever it is drop straight down beneath us?"

"Don't worry, Arthur," said Suzy. "Stickit fingers don't come off until you tell them to."

Arthur drew in an angry breath to answer, but before he could, he suddenly saw the ceiling. The breath left him as he frantically raised his arms and legs and braced for the impact.

He'd expected to hit solid stone, but what he hit was a deep layer of soot. He drove in at least a foot, and soot exploded all around him, smothering him in fine particles. There was so much soot his wings couldn't brush it away from him, and they flapped harder and harder to keep ascending.

Arthur scrabbled against the ceiling, finally getting his hands and legs braced against the solid stone beneath the soot, as his wings beat furiously in their efforts to push him through this barrier.

Suzy was nearby, soot cascading down all around her. Her and Arthur's impact had started an avalanche of soot. Hundreds, perhaps thousands of years of accumulated soot had been loosened. Arthur could see it raining down close by, and could hear it farther afield. It made a sound like ice cubes being cracked out of a tray.

"Ow!" Suzy exclaimed as her balance slipped and her wings drove her face-first into the ceiling. She got herself braced again, with her knees and elbows firmly against the ceiling, while her wings beat madly on her back.

"Stickit spell!" called Suzy. "Make sure you have your active hand stuck to the ceiling before you undo your wings. And remember, your sticky hand will change every minute!"

Arthur spat out a mouthful of soot and rubbed his mouth on his shoulder, a very difficult maneuver. But he only got more soot on his face. It was everywhere, billowing in clouds and sticking to every part of Arthur's body, except for his wings.

"This isn't going to work!" Arthur called out. He'd been too tired and too pleased to have any chance of escape from the Pit to think it through before. But with just one hand sticking to the ceiling, he'd be hanging from it and would have to swing his other hand, get it on the ceiling, and then wait till it stuck. He wouldn't be able to do that for very long before he misjudged the timing or got too exhausted and couldn't even raise his arms. Or worse . . .

"Our arms will get pulled out of their sockets!" he yelled.

"No they won't," scoffed Suzy. But then she frowned and said, "Actually, maybe *yours* will. Dame Primus didn't think of that!"

Arthur groaned. It took all his strength to stop his wings from smacking him into the ceiling again and again like a demented moth. Every time they beat, he was pushed into the ceiling and slid around a bit in the soot, bashing his knees and hands and, if he was un-lucky, his face or chest.

Slid around in the soot . . .

"What if we try to crawl with the wings keeping us pressed against the . . . oof . . . ceiling?" Arthur cried. "The soot makes it kind of slippery, so we can slide our hands and knees along."

He demonstrated, timing it so he slid on his hands and knees as his wings readied for the downstroke, bracing himself just as they flapped. He managed to get about four feet away from Suzy in that slide and was no more bruised than if he'd stayed still. And no more sooty. He was just about as caked in soot as it was possible to be. Only his teeth, the whites of his eyes, and his wings weren't totally black.

"It works!" he proclaimed.

"Very slowly," said Suzy dubiously. "I think I'll lose my wings and go hand over hand."

"No!" said Arthur. He had an image of Suzy forgetting to change hands quickly enough, or being distracted. There would be that moment where she would hang in the air, and then, with a despairing scream, fall into the endless darkness. . . .

"No," said Arthur again. "Try moving with the wings, like I did."

Suzy made an indistinct grumbling noise, but slid across the ceiling as her wings flexed up, barely bracing herself in time for the next wingbeat down.

"I s'pose it does work," she said. "But we'll be black and blue on the knees and elbows by the time we get there."

"I seem to be healing quickly," said Arthur, thinking about the Scoucher cut back in his own world. A slight current of fear ran through his mind as he wondered if he was being transformed into a Denizen. Then his wings flapped, he almost smacked his nose into the ceiling, and that brought his attention back to the task at hand. "Your bruises won't last long, will they?"

"No, but they still hurt while they're around," said Suzy. "Let's get going, then."

"But which direction?" asked Arthur. "Where is the Treasure Tower?"

"It's in the North-West corner of the Far Realms," said Suzy. "That's . . . uh, curse these wings . . . all I know."

"Which way is North — ouch, that *really* hurt — North-West?" asked Arthur. In the darkness, with smog and falling soot all around, there could be no hope of spying any landmarks.

"The opposite — *oof* — of South — ow — East."

Arthur didn't answer for a moment, as he waited for his wings to beat and begin to fold.

"You have no idea, do you?"

"I have one id —"

Whatever Suzy was going to say was lost as she slipped and her wings pushed her face-first into the sooty ceiling. She pushed herself off again immediately, spitting and cursing, resisted the next beat of her wings, then added, "One idea. Ask the Atlas!"

"Oh, yeah. That'll be . . . ah . . . really easy, won't it? Opening a book when I need both hands to brace —"

Arthur's knee slipped, and he was violently twisted and thrust against the ceiling, the wind knocked out of him.

"It may not have to open!" called out Suzy. "Just put one hand on it and ask. . . ."

Arthur nodded carefully. His mouth was so full of soot he couldn't speak. He was sure the Lieutenant Keeper's spell was the only thing preventing him from choking to death.

Slowly, he drew his elbows in towards his chest, so he could still brace against the ceiling and resist his wings but also touch the Atlas in his pocket with his index finger. Which didn't have a stickit on it.

"Atlas —" Arthur started to say, but he slipped again, his elbows splaying out as the right side of his face smashed into the ceiling. He had a black eye for sure now, Arthur thought as he struggled to get back into a good position. Not that anyone could tell under the cloaking soot. This time he managed to lock his elbows tighter and he waited till just after the downbeat of his wings.

"Atlas! Don't open! Show me which way is North-West."

Arthur felt the Atlas shiver under his hand, lost his concentration, and once more went face-first into the sooty ceiling. This time, when he pried himself off and braced again, his nose was bleeding and it felt like it might be broken, sending a savage pain lancing up between his eyes.

"Did it work?" called out Suzy.

Arthur didn't answer. He had his forehead balanced on the ceiling, every muscle straining to resist the next wingbeat, and all his attention on resisting the pain of a broken nose. Or maybe just a bruised one, as the throbbing began to fade. In the next second it stopped bleeding of its own accord — or had so much soot stuffed up it, no blood could get out.

"Did it work?" called out Suzy again.

Arthur steadied himself and looked back at his pocket.

"No," he said.

Then, "Or actually, yes, I think it has!"

A small compass made of four crossed golden arrows had materialized on his pocket and was slowly spinning around as if it were mounted on his shirt. Arthur stared down at it, grunted as his wings flapped, then pointed and slid at the same time.

"North-West is that way! Come on!"

Suzy followed, the two of them developing a rhythm where they slid when their wings folded up, and braced when their wings flapped. Though they could only slide four or five feet at a time, Arthur somehow found it easier to hold himself against the ceiling.

More importantly, he finally felt more optimistic. He might be pressed against the ceiling of the Far Reaches, but he was moving.

And he had escaped the Pit!

Chapter Twelve

They had been crawling across the ceiling for several hours when Arthur suddenly slid out of the smog and found himself buffeted by a strong breeze that ruffled the feathers of his wings and upset his sliding rhythm.

The breeze also took off the loose layer of soot on Arthur. He suddenly felt lighter and cleaner, even though there was still plenty of soot ingrained into his skin and clothes.

But it was neither the sudden disappearance of the smog nor the fresh breeze that made his mouth hang open and his jaw almost get broken on the ceiling when his wings flapped. Ahead of him, part of the ceiling the size of a football field shone as if there were hidden lights within it, sending down a shaft of clear golden light like late afternoon sunshine.

The light fell squarely on Grim Tuesday's Treasure Tower. It was a simple round stone tower without visible windows, about fifty stories high and maybe two hundred feet in diameter. It had a steeply pitched, tiled roof, surmounted, as Suzy had said, by a wind vane in the shape of a cockerel.

What Suzy hadn't mentioned was that the tower and the green lawns that surrounded it were entirely encased within a pyramid of sparkling glass, its apex just above the cockerel wind vane and fifty feet below the lit-up ceiling.

"That's new," said Suzy. "Guess old Grimbly didn't like his tower getting as scummy and sooted up as the rest of the Far Reaches. Dame Primus definitely didn't know about this."

"Or much else," said Arthur wearily. He was severely battered and bruised, and did not welcome another setback. He'd been looking forward to getting his wings off and standing up like a normal person. On the ground. Not to mention washing his hands and face. He knew a full-on bath or shower was an impossible dream.

"There doesn't seem to be any heat coming off the lit-up area," he added. "So we can get closer, I guess. But it's still a long way down. And how do we get through the glass?"

Suzy looked across at the tower and the pyramid. She had become much better than Arthur at letting her wings push her almost into the ceiling, resisting only to lessen the impact, rather than trying not to hit the ceiling at all.

"I guess we'll have to get as close as we can. . . . Drat these wings, the sooner they're paper again, the better. . . . Drop the wings, jump to the face of the pyramid, stick with our stickit fingers, then climb down and find another way in."

"But even at the closest, the pyramid will be forty or fifty feet below!"

"We can make that. You did almost as big a jump back in the Atrium, remember?"

"I had the . . . *arrggh* . . . rotten . . . Key then!"

Suzy thought for a while, white lines appearing on her forehead where the soot came off as the skin wrinkled up.

"How about you undo one wing, then jump," she suggested. "You'll corkscrew . . . but . . . one wing will still be lifting you up, so it won't be that bad."

Arthur looked down at the pyramid.

Jump sixty feet, corkscrewing around, maybe hit really hard, then have to climb down with hands that alternated between sticky and nonsticky?

"I should never have gone on that cross-country run," he muttered.

"What?"

"Nothing," said Arthur. He couldn't think of any other alternative, and he was tired of being a fly on the ceiling, particularly one that couldn't control its wings. And he was able to do a lot of things in the House that would be impossible or too dangerous back home. Hopefully this jump would be one of them.

"Let's get as close as we can," he told Suzy. "Then . . . then I suppose I'll have to jump."

It was more difficult sliding as soon as they left the sooty part of the ceiling, and Arthur developed even more bruises. He was a bit tentative about crossing the lit-up section, but it wasn't so bad. The light was quite soft and there was no noticeable heat. As long as he kept his eyes half-shut it was bearable. And on the plus side, the light made a bit more of the soot fall off.

At last they came to a point about twenty feet short of the point of the pyramid and fifty feet above it. Since he had to face the ceiling or be pulverized by his wings, Arthur could only glance down from side to side. But it looked as if this was as close as they could get. There was no way he was going to jump too close to the point of a glass pyramid, particularly with a single wing spinning him around.

"Ready?" asked Suzy. "Remember the stickit finger spell?"

"Yeah, I remember," said Arthur. "Just give me a second."

It was a long way down. Back in his own world he'd be sure to die from a fall that far. And what if the glass broke?

"What if the glass breaks?"

"The glass won't break," said a voice that wasn't Suzy's. Arthur almost tore his neck muscles whipping his head around to see who'd spoken and, for the thousandth time, got mashed into the ceiling by his wings.

Suzy shouted something, but Arthur missed it. He was partially stunned by the impact and still busy trying to crawl around so he could see who was talking.

He finally managed, only to see what looked like a black, soot-covered hairball the size of his head on the otherwise pristine, shining ceiling. But the winds were too strong for it to be a lump of soot. Besides, the blob had two deep-set silver eyes, eyes like bigger versions of the silver balls used in cake decorations. They flickered from side to side as Arthur met the thing's gaze.

It had a mouth as well, under the silver eyes. A mouth that also glinted silver, either from teeth or whatever lined the thing's throat.

"A Nithling!" exclaimed Suzy. She tried to draw her copper tube out of her belt while still bracing against her wings, but had to give up when she was mashed against the ceiling.

"I'm not a Nithling!" protested the blob. "I can help you!"

"I'll *help* you," muttered Suzy. She had braced herself on her elbows and was struggling to get something out from under the top of her apron. Probably her knife.

Arthur didn't know what she was going to do, but he was curious about this soot-encrusted hairy blob.

"Suzy, wait!"

He paused for a moment as his wings beat, then spoke to the thing.

"If you're not a Nithling, what are you?"

The sooty hairball spoke quickly, as if eager to convince Arthur of its story. As it spoke, it slowly unraveled, becoming less of a ball and more like a hairy, sooty slug. A very big hairy, sooty slug.

"More than nine thousand years ago I was one of Grim Tuesday's eyebrows, before I was wrenched from his forehead by an explosion of Nothing, down in the first, dark diggings of the Pit. I was lost there for centuries, next to Nothing. Slowly the emanations of Nothing transformed me and I became a thinking, living creature. Neither a Denizen made by the Architect, nor a Nithling born out of Nothing. The true Nithlings despise me and the Denizens fear me. Both attempt to slay me at any opportunity."

Suzy and Arthur looked at each other, then back at the hairy slug. It did resemble a vastly overgrown, animate eyebrow. A long, hairy crescent, caked in soot. It moved back a little under their combined stares, undulating sideways and making faint popping sounds.

"I am still attuned to Grim Tuesday," declared the thing. "I know some of his mind and secrets."

"It does look like a huge eyebrow," said Suzy hesitantly. "And strange things do happen near lots of Nothing."

"What are you doing up here?" asked Arthur. He wished he could consult the Atlas and check up on this . . . *eyebrow* . . . but it was too difficult in his present situation.

"I've been trying to get in the Treasure Tower," said the thing. "I need to be near the treasures. I want to feel the weight of the gold, bathe in the reflected light of the paintings, embrace the statues. Once I get in, I shall never leave. That's all I want — to get in the Treasure Tower!"

"If you can't get in yourself, how can you help us?" asked Arthur.

"I cannot get in by myself," said the blob, "but I can

help you, and then you can help me. For example, I have a diamond to cut the glass."

"Show it to us, then," Suzy demanded.

The blob undulated backwards and forwards, popping unpleasantly, and opened its mouth wider than Arthur would have thought possible. A black, sticky-looking tongue slowly poked out. Coiled up in the end of the tongue was a diamond as big as Arthur's thumbnail, sparkling in the light from the ceiling.

"Where did you get that?" asked Suzy.

"I madth ith," the blob started to say, then it withdrew its tongue and continued. "I made it from Nothing. I told you, I know much that the Grim knows. I also have some of his talents. But my tongue is not strong enough to hold the diamond and cut the glass. I need a hand."

"What's your name?" asked Arthur. When the blob didn't answer for a moment, he added, "What do you call yourself?"

"I suppose you could call me . . . Soot," said the thing. "Yes . . . Soot. I have breathed it, lived in it, and eaten it for so long that it is a fitting name."

"Eaten it?" asked Suzy. "Why eat soot?"

"Boredom," said Soot. "The Overseers fire their

steam-guns at me if I get too close. The Nithlings would eat me themselves. I have been unable to get into the Treasure Tower. What else has there been for me to do but brood upon the walls and ceiling of this realm and eat soot?"

"If we help you get into the Treasure Tower," said Arthur, "you'll have to swear to help us in every way you can against Grim Tuesday."

"Yes!" cried Soot. It practically bounced off the ceiling in excitement. Arthur wished it hadn't because he saw its belly, lined with lots of horrid-looking little suckers, like an octopus's tentacle. That was what made the popping sound when it moved.

"That story might be true, but I reckon that still makes it a Nithling," whispered Suzy, as she edged as close as she could to Arthur. "A clever one, so very dangerous. But we need that diamond."

"I'm sick of hanging upside down and getting smashed into . . . this stupid ceiling," Arthur whispered back. "Let's accept its help for now."

Suzy nodded reluctantly.

"We accept your offer," said Arthur to Soot.

"Fine! Fine!" burbled Soot. "It's a pleasure working with you. Whoever you are."

"I'm Arthur," said Arthur quickly, before Suzy could introduce him as Monday or the Master of the Lower House. "That's Suzy."

"And you'll be thieving just a few odds and ends from the Treasure Tower?" asked Soot. His voice sounded slightly anxious and he clearly took it for granted that Arthur and Suzy were thieves.

"We'll be reclaiming stolen goods!" snapped Suzy indignantly. "Goods as should have been returned to their rightful owner ten thousand —"

"Suzy!" interrupted Arthur. He didn't want Soot to know too much. If the thing did have some strange connection with Grim Tuesday, it was possible that Grim Tuesday might have a connection to it, as well.

"Reclamation," muttered Suzy. "Arthur only wants wot he's supposed to have already —"

"Suzy! Are you ready to do the stickit spell?"

"Oh, stickit fingers, is it?" asked Soot, peering with his silvery eyes at Arthur's hands. "Very nice workmanship. Not made by the Grim himself, but one of his better crafters."

"*Stick by day and stick by night, stick for a minute each, left and right,*" Suzy recited to her hands, keeping herself propped on her elbows and forearms. As she said the words of the spell, the little finger-puppet things on her fingers wriggled and squeaked and began to glow with a fuzzy green light.

Suzy braced against a wingbeat, then slapped both hands against the ceiling and pulled back. One hand stuck by the thumb and two fingers. Immediately Suzy used her other hand to grab both strings that hung around her neck. She pulled them. Wax seals cracked and her two wings instantly blew into a cloud of confetti that was whisked away by the breeze.

Suzy hung from the ceiling and turned to Arthur. She smiled, despite her two black eyes and a bruise on her chin, evidence of the damage done by being constantly beaten into the ceiling.

"That's a relief! I'll be dropping in about forty seconds, so you jump now, Mister Soot, and make sure you keep your distance on the pyramid."

Suzy punctuated her instruction by drawing the copper tube out of her belt.

Soot needed no encouragement. With a single flexing motion, accompanied by lots of tiny popping noises like exploding bubblewrap, it launched itself straight down. Caught a little by the breeze, it plopped onto the eastern face of the pyramid, about thirty feet below the apex.

"Good luck, Arthur," said Suzy. She quickly thrust the copper tube back through her belt to leave her hand free. "I reckon you should —"

The stickits on her right hand suddenly stopped squeaking and sticking.

Arthur watched Suzy fall. He almost couldn't bear to see her hit the pyramid, but she landed on her feet, then bounced and rolled down for a few seconds before she arrested her descent by slapping her sticky left hand on the glass.

She lay still for a few seconds, then rolled back and waved up at Arthur, shouting something he couldn't hear, the words carried away by the breeze and the beat of his wings.

Arthur looked back up, stopped himself yet again from being pushed into the ceiling, and took a deep breath. Then, propping himself so his hands didn't touch the ceiling, he spoke the words of the stickit finger spell. With the last word, he felt the ends of his fingers tingle, and the stickits on his left hand began to squeak.

Arthur used his right hand to pull the right string. He heard the wax crack, then confetti blew up past his ears. A second later, he began to fall, while his remaining wing beat harder and harder, trying to maintain its single-minded upwards thrust.

Arthur expected to corkscrew, but he didn't. Instead his single wing threw him head over heels, which rapidly became a series of wild somersaults.

An eye-blink later, Arthur hit the glass face of the pyramid.

Very, very hard.

Chapter Thirteen

Arthur screamed as he hit. There was an unbearable pain in his left leg, and he was sliding down the glass, faster and faster, while his single wing thrashed around his head so he couldn't see anything.

Then he managed to slap his sticky hand on the glass and came to a sudden stop. He pulled the string and almost choked on a sudden mouthful of confetti as it shot up all around him.

Arthur started to slide again as his hand became unstuck. He slapped his other hand down and stopped again. He could hear Suzy shouting something, and Soot too, but couldn't give them any attention. He had to see what was wrong with his leg. The pain was deep inside, but stabbing up into his body and down to his feet. He hardly dared to look.

But he made himself. Both his jeans and the pajama-like trousers the Lieutenant Keeper had given him were ripped. He could see some blood and what he had feared — something protruding that could only be bone.

He'd broken his tibia or fibula, the bones in the

lower leg. Maybe both of them, in a complex fracture. A bad one.

Arthur felt a terrible, sudden coldness sweep over him. He began to shiver. He tried to quell the shivers as he drew his leg up for a closer look. It made him feel sick to see his leg looking all lumpy and wrong, with that piece of bone thrust out through the skin.

Arthur gulped in a deep breath. He could feel his lungs tightening as panic set in.

I will not have an asthma attack, he told himself. *I can't have one. I'm in the House. Things are different here. Everything heals quickly. Even a broken bone will heal in time . . . but I haven't got time . . . can't stand the pain for long . . . I have to do something . . .*

Hesitantly, he laid his hand lightly over his shin, only just touching the lumpy broken part. Even so, it sent another stab of pain up his leg and into his head. He almost blacked out.

"By the power of . . . of the First Key . . . the power that remains in my hand," Arthur whispered. "Heal me. Fix the broken . . . bone."

His hand stopped shaking, though the rest of his body didn't. Then he felt it grow hot. As Arthur watched, the bone retreated back through the skin, which rejoined itself.

The pain remained for what seemed like several minutes but could only have been seconds, for it faded just as Arthur's right hand lost its stickiness and he had to slap his left hand onto the glass.

His leg still felt very strange, but Arthur was able to look around and refocus on what was going on. A moment later Suzy slid down next to him, stopping herself a little short with her sticky hand. Soot watched from a distance, silver eyes twinkling amid its black hair.

"What happened?" asked Suzy. "Are you sorely hurt?"

Arthur shook his head. The shakes were slowly subsiding but it took an effort to find his voice.

"I . . . I broke my leg. But I think I fixed it. . . ."

Suzy raised her eyebrows and grimaced when it made her black eyes hurt.

"Not bad. Don't s'pose you could fix up my bruises while you're at it?"

"Uh, I don't really know what I did," said Arthur. He lifted his leg and flexed it a few times. It felt stiff and clumsy, and Arthur experienced a stab of fear. The bone was healed all right, but his leg now looked and felt a bit crooked.

It hasn't set straight, he thought. *I'll be lame. No running ever. No baseball. No soccer.*

"Uh-oh," said Suzy, interrupting Arthur's thoughts. "Overseers."

Arthur looked down and started to slip. Quickly he changed hands again and temporarily forgot about his leg. Suzy was pointing to a band of Overseers that had emerged out of the smog down below and were running towards the base of the pyramid.

"Don't think their steam-guns'll reach us," said Suzy. "But they might have other weapons. We'd better start. It won't be quick with the stickit fingers."

"Yes! Yes!" called out Soot. It started undulating to the top of the pyramid. "We must get inside and join . . . see the treasures!"

Arthur nodded and pulled himself up as far as he could above his sticking hand and reached out to plant his other hand. Then he had to wait until it stuck, then repeat the process.

After ten minutes, they were still short of the top. Almost a thousand feet below and several hundred feet to the east, at the base of the pyramid, the group of Overseers was busy putting together something that looked suspiciously like a weapon. They had wheeled a steam engine in from somewhere out in the smoggy regions and were stoking it furiously, as other Overseers set up a long bronze barrel on a tripod mount and connected it to the engine by a hose of some silver-metal mesh.

"Steam-cannon," said Soot, looking down from its perch on the very apex of the pyramid. "Hurry, before they blast us off!"

"We are hurrying!" said Arthur as he pulled back on one hand to see if it was sticking yet. He kept looking down, not at the Overseers, but at his leg. As far as he could tell, it worked fine, but from a point several inches below his knee the leg was definitely not straight and it felt weird.

Suzy reached the top before Arthur. Soot immediately held out the diamond in his tongue

"Wait," said Suzy. "I'll have to time my stickits carefully."

She took out her pocket watch, left it hanging down the front of her apron, and waited till her stickit fingers swapped. Then she extracted a once-white handkerchief from her sleeve, used it to receive the gem, and gave it a good polish before she touched it.

"Keep an eye on my watch," she instructed Arthur as he arrived. "I'll cut till my stickit fingers are about to swap. Tell me when the second hand hits two."

Arthur looked at the watch dangling on its silver-gilt chain. It kept spinning around, so the face was difficult to see. The second hand was ticking around steadily, but as it reached twelve Arthur was distracted by his own stickits swapping over.

"Look out!" he called hastily as he stopped his sudden slide with a slap on the glass.

Suzy popped the diamond in her mouth and slapped her other hand down just in time. Then she resumed her work with the gem. The diamond didn't actually cut through the glass, but it scored it enough so a solid hit would snap off the pinnacle of the pyramid, allowing them to climb inside to the weather vane atop the tower.

"They're going to fire the steam-cannon," said Soot anxiously. "Hurry! Hurry!"

Arthur looked down. The bronze barrel was being elevated to target the top of the pyramid, Overseers frantically turning wheels and gears. Long wafts of steam were escaping from the end of the barrel, and the steam engine was blowing a steady stream of thick black smoke.

"Only a bit more to cut," Suzy said to Arthur. "You'd better hit it, rather than me. It will probably need the power of the First Key. Take the tube from my belt."

Arthur reached over and slid out the copper tube. Suzy finished the deeply scored line she'd drawn right around the pyramid, about four feet down from its point.

"Hit it!"

Arthur swung hard. The copper tube bounced off, jarring his hand. But there had been a definite cracking sound and his hands were hot. He swung again, and this time the cracking sound was so loud he had no doubt that the point of the pyramid had broken all along the diamond-cut line.

Together, Arthur and Suzy pushed at the top part of the pyramid. It resisted for a moment, then snapped off. The top three feet of the pyramid toppled over and fell down the other side, leaving a nice square access hole directly above the weather vane.

Arthur's stickits changed and he slipped back a few feet before he could slap his other hand down. Suzy quickly tested the edge of the inch-thick glass.

"It's not sharp," she said, and climbed up and inside the pyramid, her feet tapping the east-west crossbars of the weather vane to make sure they'd take her weight.

Suzy's right hand stuck to the glass as she lowered herself down. She pulled at it, then quickly said, "*Stickit fingers, my thanks to you, your work is done, till called anew.*"

"That's the spell, Arthur," she added, her voice suddenly fading as her head dipped below the lip of the hole. She waved at Arthur through the glass, and he faintly heard her say, "Come on!"

Before he could move, Soot swarmed past him, dived into the hole, and slid down the weather vane on the opposite side from Suzy. It continued to the roof of the tower and disappeared from Arthur's sight.

A second later, the first blast of long-range steam screamed up the side of the pyramid, clouding the glass as it came.

Arthur swung his legs into the hole and Suzy helped place his feet on the crossbars of the weather vane. He crouched down as low as he could, so he was almost entirely inside the pyramid. *Almost* — but his right hand was stuck outside, firmly glued by the stickit fingers.

Arthur opened his mouth to speak the unsticking spell, but he only got the first word out before the steam hit. Most of it hurtled above his head, but some spilled back down inside the pyramid. Arthur ducked down even more as it scalded his ears and the back of his neck. It hurt, but he'd only suffered the cooler edges of the blast.

Except for his right hand. That must have been right in the middle of the superheated stream of steam. But it didn't hurt. Arthur didn't look for a moment, imagining that he couldn't feel the pain because it was so intense, and all that was left were the bones. Then he discovered that his right hand was clenched against his chest and his left hand was stuck to the weather vane. The stickits must have swapped an instant before the steam hit, and Arthur had instinctively snatched his hand in just in time.

Arthur sighed a very deep sigh of relief and recited the spell. Immediately, the stickits on his left hand quieted down and stopped wriggling.

"This is hinged," said Suzy, who had climbed down to the roof and was examining the base of the weather vane. The whole thing was about six feet high and made of cast iron, so it would be very heavy. Arthur tapped the cold iron beak of the cockerel and wondered how they were supposed to lift it and get inside the tower, as Dame Primus had suggested. Even if it was hinged.

"There must be a catch somewhere," added Suzy. "A lock or lever . . . ah —"

She pressed a hidden button. There was a loud metallic *zing!* and Arthur was flung violently into the air. He smacked down onto the roof of the tower and rolled down the tiles to the gutter. His legs went over and he scrabbled desperately to get a grip, his fingers no longer sticky.

At the last second, he grasped the gutter, leaving his legs dangling over the side of the tower. Arthur tried to breathe a sigh of even temporary relief, but he couldn't get a breath.

Then there was a rattle on the tiles and Suzy's anxious face appeared, looking down at him and the ground, several hundred feet below.

"Sorry!" said Suzy. "It was spring-loaded. . . ."

"Help me up!" whispered Arthur. His breath was coming back. Once again he was grateful to be in the House. If he'd had the wind knocked out of him like that back home, he would've had an asthma attack for sure.

"Swing your feet back, I mean behind you," said Suzy. "The pyramid wall is only a few feet away. Push against it and I'll pull you over."

It took several minutes to get Arthur onto the roof. He lay on his back for a few minutes, panting, then wearily sat up.

Suzy was looking into the hatchway under the weather vane, which now hung at a right angle to the tower. Arthur slowly climbed up next to her, thankful that the pitch of the roof was not too steep.

"Bigger inside than out," muttered Suzy, still looking inside. "And that Soot thing has scarpered."

Arthur looked through the hatch. Even with Suzy's comment, he still expected to see something like a round tower room.

But the inside of the tower bore no relationship to the outside. It wasn't even round. It was rectangular and vast. It reminded Arthur of a nineteenth-century prison he'd visited on a school excursion. Large and gloomy, it had an open internal courtyard with many levels of cells built into the brick walls on each side, each traced by a cast-iron walkway.

The prison Arthur had visited had six levels, with a hundred cells or so on each side. The Grim's treasure prison had at least *fifty* levels, and the main courtyard was a mile long, maybe more. It was hard to tell, because the only light came from flickering oil lanterns — or imitations of lanterns — that were placed in wall brackets between every fourth cell. There had to be at least a thousand cells on every level, Arthur calculated, which meant there were more than fifty thousand rooms!

"It looks like a prison," said Arthur. "I mean, it looks almost exactly like one I visited back home. Only much, much bigger."

"That's what Grim Tuesday does," said Suzy. "Copies stuff. We'd better start looking for the Will."

"Start!" exclaimed Arthur. He looked down at the iron ladder that led to the top-level walkway, and the cells stretching to the left and right — a seemingly endless row of riveted cast-iron doors. "Where do we start?"

"Depends what you're looking for," said Soot, unexpectedly appearing out of the gloom at the top of the ladder. "Did I hear you mention . . . the Will?"

"Do you know where it is?" asked Arthur eagerly, before he remembered he didn't want their real business known to Soot.

Soot reared up and flexed, showing its nasty sucker underside again. Arthur leaned back from it, struck by the notion that it had gotten bigger somehow. It certainly looked about half again as big.

"The Will of the Architect?" asked Soot. "That part of it entrusted to Grim Tuesday?"

"Yes," said Arthur. Soot's voice had dropped in pitch as well. It sounded more menacing, less eager to please than it had before. As if Arthur and Suzy were less useful to it now that it had gotten into the Treasure Tower.

"I don't know where it is exactly," replied Soot. Its silver eyes weighed up Suzy, who had hefted her copper tube, and it backed down the ladder. "But I know where it must be. Follow me."

Soot slithered and popped down the ladder and onto

the top walkway. It didn't look back to see if they were following.

"It's got bigger," whispered Suzy. "Like a Nithling that's sucked the life out of someone."

Arthur nodded and bit his lip.

"We have to follow it," he said finally. "There are too many cells to check every one. Particularly since Grim Tuesday must know we're in here by now."

"What if it's leading us into a trap?"

"I still think we have to risk it."

"I s'pose so," said Suzy. "But keep your eye out for an architectural sword, or a light-ax, or something. If it gets any bigger, we'll need a better weapon than this copper pipe."

Arthur nodded and led the way down the ladder. His leg still felt weird and it felt weirder still when he finally stood up straight on the walkway. He took a few steps, stopped, then felt both his knees, his forehead wrinkled in puzzlement.

"What is it?"

"My leg . . . the one I broke," Arthur said hesitantly. "It's gotten shorter. It's an inch shorter than the other one!"

He bent down and felt his legs again. His clogs were long gone, fallen off into the Pit. He was standing in his socks, and there could be no doubt. He'd magically healed his broken bone, but he'd done it wrong. Not only was his leg a bit twisted, it was definitely shorter.

"It *is* shorter," confirmed Suzy in a conversational tone. "Come on, that Soot is going down those stairs to the next level."

"You don't get it!" cried Arthur. "My leg is shorter!"

He coughed as he said it, his breath catching. He could feel his lungs tightening, but it couldn't be asthma. Not here in the House. It was shock, or a panic attack, or something. It was bad enough having asthma and not being able to do everything. Now he was lame as well. Everything would be worse —

Arthur stopped himself.

I am not going to think about this now. I have to find Part Two of the Will, defeat Grim Tuesday, and get back in time to save the house and all our money and stop anything worse from happening. So one leg is a bit shorter? That's better than it being broken, isn't it?

"Come on!" repeated Suzy. She started off, and Arthur followed, lurching as he got used to his shorter leg.

They had to run to catch Soot, as the thing undulated down a set of iron steps to the next level, along it for a hundred yards or so, and then continued straight on down to the level below that.

Even in their socks, Arthur's and Suzy's footsteps rang on the metal walkway, the sound echoing through the vast open space in the middle.

"If there are guards here, they'll know where we are," said Arthur anxiously. His voice echoed out into the central courtyard, carrying even more than their footsteps.

"There are no guards," called Soot. It had stopped outside a cell door that looked the same as all the others. "Grim Tuesday allows no one but himself to enter the Treasure Tower. Not even the Grotesques are allowed in here. But at last I am where I should have always been — with all the lovely treasure!"

Arthur and Suzy grimaced and stepped back as thick, translucent saliva dribbled out of Soot's mouth and dripped down through the cast-iron mesh of the walkway.

"Is the Will inside that cell?" asked Arthur. It seemed a bit too straightforward for someone like Grim Tuesday to keep the Will here, even if no one but himself — or his former eyebrow — could know which of the five thousand rooms to look for.

"There should be a way to the Will inside," said Soot, its drool bubbling as it spoke. "But here I must leave you. Other, more easily digestible treasures await me!"

It leaped backwards and over the railing as Suzy rushed forward to hit it with the pipe. She and Arthur rushed to look over the side, only to see Soot several levels down, clinging to the side of the walkway there. With a loud popping, it slithered underneath the walkway and was gone from sight.

"Good riddance," said Arthur. "I suppose."

"If it's led us to the right door," said Suzy. She looked it over, then tried to slide back the inch-thick bolt. It didn't budge, even when she pulled with both hands and pushed with her feet against the rim of the door.

"Stuck, or magically locked," she said. "Not even a padlock to pick."

Arthur examined the bolt. It actually looked welded in place, with thick strands of metal between the bolt and the loops. As he touched it, Arthur's hand felt suddenly hot. Flakes of rust fell to the floor, the bolt rattled, and Arthur easily drew it back.

Suzy whistled in admiration.

"That's a good trick. Wish I could do the same thing to Dame Primus's biscuit pantry."

Arthur pushed the door open and stepped inside.

Chapter Fourteen

Arthur stepped into another room that was bigger inside than out. This was no tiny cell, but a room about the size of the big family room in Arthur's house — the house that they would lose if Arthur couldn't stop the Grotesques.

Apart from the overall size, this room had nothing in common with Arthur's family room. For a start, it looked more like a ship's cabin than a room. The brick walls of the prison were gone, replaced by wooden planking, sealed with tar that had dripped in numerous places. The ceiling and the floor were planked too, and everything creaked a little as Arthur walked farther in. The only light came from a lamp that swung on a chain from the ceiling, making the shadows shift and sway.

There was a neatly made-up bunk in one corner and some barrels and a chest in another, but most of the room was taken up by a long table of deeply polished wood. On the table were hundreds and hundreds of different bottles, all carefully laid flat, many of them mounted on wooden or ivory bases.

Every bottle had a ship in it. Many different kinds of ships, in many different sorts of bottles. Glass of all colors, thick and thin, sealed with corks, or wax, or lead, or sprung metal stoppers. Ships with one mast, two masts, three masts, or no masts and lots of oars. Big ships that might have crews of hundreds of sailors and little ships just for one.

Arthur walked closer. The lamp swung, and the shadows shifted. Arthur saw a red glow suddenly flare in the corner at the end of the table and stopped as he saw it came from a pipe in the mouth of a man who was sitting there. An oldish man, white-haired and white-whiskered, his face looking like it hadn't seen a shave for a week but wasn't yet up to a beard.

He was wearing a heavy blue coat, the sleeves showing dark bands where four gold braided bands might once have been. Instead of the ubiquitous clogs of the Far Reaches, he had on rubber boots, with the tops folded over above the knee.

His eyes were deep-set, bright blue, and very piercing. He met Arthur's stare, carefully placed his pipe on a stand, still smoking, then put down the quill pen he held, snapped shut the top of the inkwell, set down the huge bronze-bound book he was writing in, and spiked a piece of paper that looked like an old-fashioned telegram on a long metal spike that held hundreds of similar papers.

Then he stood up, all six feet six inches of him and came into the light.

"It's the Piper!" shrieked Suzy, and she fell to her knees, either in worship, a faint, or some sort of faked fall to distract the man. Arthur didn't know. But he was slightly relieved this man wasn't Grim Tuesday, which is what he'd thought.

The relief only lasted a second as the man reached into the shadows and pulled out a nine-foot-long harpoon that glittered and shone all the way from its incredibly sharp-looking point to the eyehole on the end where a rope would normally be attached.

"Nay, lass, I'm not the Piper," growled the man, his voice deep and carrying. "That would be my youngest brother you're thinking of. Now tell me your names before I must do as Grim Tuesday bids me, and send you to perdition."

"Ah, is perdition some part of the House?" asked Arthur.

The man chuckled.

"In this case, perdition means 'total destruction,'" he explained. "But I'm a kindly man and hold no grudge against you Denizens. My friend here will snip your skein of destiny, sharp as you like, and that will be the end of it."

He slapped his harpoon as he spoke, and it shone still brighter.

"Now, give me your names. I've a lubber's employment now, keeping the register straight for Grim Tuesday, and I mislike pawing over a cold stone corpse to find a name to strike off the roll. Speak!"

"Off the roll?" asked Arthur. "Do you mean the register of indentured workers?"

"Aye, I do, and I must return to it, so kindly give me your names. Or must I prick it out of thee at the point of my companion?"

"I'm not an indentured worker," said Arthur, though he quailed a little as the man lifted his harpoon and made as if to strike. "I'm the Master of the Lower House and I've come to get Part Two of the Will."

The man's eyes narrowed, but he put the harpoon aside and strode over to Arthur. Standing above him, he gripped the boy's chin and pushed his head back till their eyes met. At the same time, he blocked an attempted blow from Suzy's copper pipe, grabbed her by the collar, and lifted her up without looking.

"Master of the Lower House, are ye?"

"Yes . . . yes, I am!" stammered Arthur. Suzy's lips were turning blue and her eyes were rolling back in her head. "Leave her alone!"

He reached out and tried to drag Suzy down. At first he couldn't move the man's arm at all, then once again his hand felt hot and, with a sudden lurch, Suzy was dropped.

"Well, well," said the man. "So you are, after all."

He held out his hand. When Arthur hesitantly took it, they shook vigorously.

"You can call me . . . let's see . . . Captain Tom Shelvocke," the man said. "A mariner, temporarily becalmed by that slavemaster Grim Tuesday. And who's this young lady, Master?"

"Call me Arthur," said Arthur as he helped Suzy up. She gave Tom a nasty look and massaged her throat. "This is Suzy Turquoise Blue, Monday's Tierce."

"Sorry about the neck-wrangle," said Tom, offering his hand to Suzy. "Though by rights, you'd be stuck through and through by my friend, as is my orders from Grim Tuesday. 'Any indentured workers that step through that door are to be slain,' he said. But if one of the other Days orders me to leave her alone, well then,

Tom has to wait and think about it and maybe not do anything at all."

Suzy reluctantly shook Tom's hand, then stepped back, out of his reach.

"Who are you?" asked Arthur. "I mean, are you a Denizen . . . or something . . . someone . . . er . . . else?"

"I'm a treasure," said Tom. "Collected by Grim Tuesday from a place called Earth. You've heard of it?"

"Yes," replied Arthur. "I'm from Earth. I mean, that's where I live, only I have to be the Master, but not yet. . . . It's a long story . . . but why would you be a treasure?"

"Because I'm neither mortal nor Denizen nor Nithling," said Tom. "Like my brother, the Piper, who Miss Blue has obviously met. I'm one of the sons of the Architect and the Old One, in a manner of speaking. The Old One sired the three of us on mortal women, and the Architect brought us up in the House, with all the changes that brings. When She chained up Dad, we slipped back to the Secondary Realms. I went to Earth and signed up for a few seafaring journeys, here and there and back again. First I knew of Mother disappearing was when Grim Tuesday took me from the deck of my ship and stuck me in here. Took all the power of the

Second Key to do it, and that wouldn't have been enough if I was ready with my friend at hand. Or in all truth, if I'd drunk a little less rum at dinner, which I wouldn't normally have done, you understand, if it wasn't for that blamed bird I shot by accident . . . but there you have it. I'm bound here by the power of the Key, can venture no farther than the worldlets in my bottles, and must serve Grim Tuesday as an inky-fingered secretary."

"Nothing wrong with inky fingers," muttered Suzy.

"What's that?" asked Tom sharply.

"What's your 'friend' made out of?" asked Suzy quickly and more respectfully than Arthur had seen her speak to anyone.

"She's made from the luminous trail of a narwhal's wake under the aurora borealis in an arctic sea," said Tom. "Mother made her for me, as a birthday present when I was a century old and set fair for a seafaring life."

"Good," said Suzy. "There's a Nithling outside who should meet your friend."

"A Nithling? Inside the Tower?"

"It used to be Grim Tuesday's eyebrow," Arthur explained. "Or so it says."

Tom laughed again, a deep, booming laugh, and rubbed his hands together.

"Looks like Tuesday's glass is set for storms. Now, am I right in thinking you're looking for something in particular in this Treasure Tower, Arthur? Anything I might be able to help ye with?"

Arthur had been thinking about that, and about what Tom had said. A few things had caught his attention.

"What are these 'worldlets' in the bottles?" he asked.

"Ah, the bottles are something I taught Grim Tuesday myself," Tom said. "You see, if you've got the art and the craft and the power, and a bottle made special, you can copy a little piece of the Secondary Realms and stick it in that bottle. It'll stay there, right and tight, place and time and all, unless someone pulls the stopper. And if you've got the secret of it, you can visit whatever place you've got in your bottle."

"So they're all copies of real ships in real places?" Now that Arthur looked closely at the bottles, he could see that the ships were moving, the sea splashing, the sun — sometimes more than one sun — shifting in the sky.

"All but one bottle," answered Tom. "There's one

that holds a real place, not a copy. One where time flows like it should, not round and round for a few copied hours."

"What do you mean?" asked Arthur. "What's in that one bottle?"

Tom smiled. "I'm as pleased as punch you asked that question, for it's the one I've been wanting to tell you. That single bottle holds a sun, and several worlds, and a sunship, the finest ever built. Sail into the sun, she can, right to its blazing core — with the crew none the hotter for it."

"Why would you sail to the center of that sun?" asked Arthur.

"Why, you'd sail there to see what Grim Tuesday might have put there ten thousand years ago."

"The Will?"

Tom smiled and shrugged.

"Can you take us there?"

"I could take one of the Seven Days into any of these bottles at their command, for Grim Tuesday never said nay about that."

"Well, I, Arthur, Master of the Lower House, command you to take me and Suzy to the center of the sun where Grim Tuesday went ten thousand years ago."

"It will be my pleasure to go a-sunfaring with the

two of you," replied Tom. "We'll just need some bright-coats, star-hoods, and Immaterial Boots."

The mariner went over to a chest behind the barrels and reached way down inside it, far further than it was deep. He quickly produced several long overcoats that shimmered in different colors, like mother-of-pearl. He threw these to Arthur, who nearly collapsed under the weight of what felt like a hundred pounds of wool. Then he threw across several pairs of boots identical to the ones he was wearing himself, that just looked like ordinary rubber seaboots. Finally he gestured to the corner of the table.

"And we'll need the saltshaker off the luncheon corner of my board, Miss Blue, if you don't mind. Likely Old Tuesday will have left some Fetchers aboard."

Arthur separated out the pile of coats into half a dozen garments. One looked to be his size, so he happily discarded his apron and tried it on. The coat fit perfectly. Despite its weight, it was very cool and very soft, and Arthur immediately liked it.

"Star-hood in the collar," said Tom. He put on a brightcoat himself and took the huge silver saltshaker from Suzy and put it in his pocket. Then he folded up his collar and unfurled a hood that was made from what Arthur thought must be loosely woven starlight. It sparkled and shimmered, barely visible, save for the faint outline where it touched Tom's hands.

"Drag it right over, you won't come to harm," Tom instructed. He pulled the hood completely over his face and down to the top button of his coat, where it fastened with a single press of his thumb.

"Immaterial Boots on and you'll be equipped for any trouble of a starry nature," said Tom. "Just remember to pull your hands into your sleeves if it gets a little hot. Not that you need any of this gear aboard the *Helios,* as I call her, but it's best to be prepared — we might have some trouble docking."

"What do we dock with? What's at the center of that star?" Arthur asked as he struggled to get the Immaterial Boots on. As soon as his feet were snug, they rippled and changed shape to look like his normal runners. Suzy's became shiny patent leather half-boots.

"A place Grim Tuesday made," Tom replied. "That's all I can say. It may be a little hot disembarking there, and hotter still when it's time to sail away. Are you ready?"

"I'm ready," said Suzy.

"I just want to look at the register," said Arthur. He walked over to look at the bronze-bound book. It was about two feet thick, with very thin paper like onionskin. The open page was printed up with headings and lines, and had some clear copperplate writing filling in each section, obviously copied from the yellow forms that were on the spike.

There was NUMBER, OCCUPATION, FORMER NAME, ORIGIN, MISDEMEANORS, PUNISHMENTS, and the same headings Arthur had seen on Japeth's indenture card, EARNINGS and OWING.

The figures under EARNINGS and OWING changed as Arthur watched, written in clear numerals unlike the copperplate hand that had to be Tom's.

"One of Grim Tuesday's conceits," said Tom darkly. "The register can write everything itself, but he enjoys setting me to enter the new arrivals. That register took over for more than two thousand clerks. Freed them up to go down the Pit."

"I have to destroy it," said Arthur. "So the indentured workers can be freed."

"Many's the time I've tried to rip it apart or wrench it from the table," said Tom. He was bent over the bottles, carefully reaching across to get one that shone with a clear yellow light. "Grim Tuesday makes strong stuff, particularly when it's got slavery at the heart of it."

Arthur tried to rip out the open page. But he couldn't get a grip. His fingers slid off. Then he tried to pick up the book, but it didn't budge at all. It felt like a solid lump of metal bolted to a concrete block.

"I promised Japeth I'd free him and the other workers," said Arthur. He put both his hands on the open pages of the register and took the deepest breath he could manage.

"I, Arthur, Lord Monday, Master of the Lower House, call upon the power of the First Key to destroy this register! Turn every page to dust and . . . and break its binding into fragments!"

Arthur's hands got hot and smoke billowed out from under his palms. But the book didn't turn to dust or explode into fragments. When Arthur stepped back, it looked just the same.

"Made with the Second Key," said Suzy. " 'Spect you need that to destroy it."

Arthur didn't reply. He stared down at the register, watching the OWING figure increase for some poor Denizen who had the former name *Sargarol* and was now just a thirteen-digit number and *Driller Fifth Class*.

As he stared, a yellow form fluttered out of the air and landed next to the book. Arthur picked it up, expecting to see the record of a newly indentured worker.

But this was a telegram, just five lines of uneven capital letters from some really old typewriter that said:

CAPTAIN STOP THIEVES IN TOWER
STOP SLAY ALL INTRUDERS STOP
NO EXCEPTIONS STOP REPORT ANY
INCIDENT IMMEDIATELY STOP GRIM
TUESDAY END

Chapter Fifteen

Arthur glanced across at Tom. The old mariner was rearranging the bottles, intent on his task. Without looking directly at the telegram, Arthur slowly dropped his hand over it and then slid it across the table towards his waist. He coughed as he crumpled the paper to disguise the noise, and thrust the balled-up telegram deep into the pocket of his brightcoat.

"How do we get inside?" Suzy asked as she bent over to look inside the bottle Tom had carefully placed in front of her. "Is that the sunship?"

"The *Helios*. A fine vessel, one of the finest in my fleet. Though she sails with the solar winds of space rather than on the seas I love, I rate her as my third most favorite ship, after the sloop *Polly Parbuckle* and my Ophiran quinquereme."

"Looks like a metal turtle," said Suzy. She looked at Tom and quickly added, "No insult meant, your honor."

"None taken, young miss," Tom replied. "She does look like a metal turtle, and that's a fine shape for sun-faring. Now, I'll ask you to place your left hand upon the bottle and look deep at my *Helios* while I ready the spell to take us in. Mind you — stare at the ship and not at one of the planets or the sun itself. Are you ready, Arthur?"

Arthur hesitated. Having experienced the awfulness of the Pit firsthand, he really wanted to destroy the register and free the indentured workers before he headed into the sunship.

"What if you helped me take the register?" he asked Tom, struck by a sudden idea. "You're the son of the Old One. I've got some of the power of the First Key. Maybe together we'd be strong enough to remove it?"

"Remove it together? Perchance we could," said Tom. "But what then?"

"Could we drop it into the sun we're going to visit?" asked Arthur. "Out of the sunship?"

"Aye, we could. But that might not destroy it. It depends upon the protections Grim Tuesday wove into its making."

"Oh . . . and I guess if we drop it in the sun it would just keep on working and we couldn't even get it back to try and destroy it some other way."

Tom shook his head. "If it was not destroyed, it would find its way back here. That is the nature of such artifacts."

"Maybe we could drop it into the Pit and it would be destroyed by Nothing," Arthur offered. He reached up and felt the outline of the Atlas in his pocket. "I'll ask the Atlas."

"The Atlas? *The Compleat Atlas of the House*?" asked Tom, with obvious surprise. "You have it?"

"Yes," answered Arthur. "Why?"

"It disappeared at the same time as Mother, ten thousand years ago," replied Tom. "It is one of her greatest works, after the House itself and the Secondary Realms."

Arthur took out the little green notebook and looked at it. It was certainly useful sometimes, but he hadn't really thought of it as anything much more than a faintly annoying and difficult-to-use database. Though it had helped him to escape the Scoucher . . . and had shown him the direction to the Treasure Tower . . .

"I guess it is kind of amazing," he said without conviction. Then, in case the book had feelings and might be offended, he continued, "I mean *really* amazing. And helpful. I'll ask it if the register of indentured workers can be destroyed by dropping it into the sun."

Arthur held the Atlas out and focused upon it, concentrating all his willpower upon the question. The book shivered under his hands, but didn't open or grow to its full size. Arthur tried again, mentally repeating his question. But the Atlas did not respond.

"It's not working," Arthur admitted. He tried to open it like a normal book, but just as when he'd first tried it in the hospital, it felt like all the pages were solidly glued together.

"You need to be Mother, or have a Key to use the Atlas," said Tom. "Many's the time I tried myself, an Atlas being in my line of work."

"I opened it before," Arthur insisted. "After I gave the First Key to the Will . . . Dame Primus. She said it would answer some of my questions even without the Key."

"That would be because the First Key's power lingered in you." Tom's piercing blue eyes fixed on Arthur. "There is some scant residue of that power left. But very little, a mere sip in the bottom of the glass. You must have used it without stint. Even a mortal vessel will hold a great deal of the Key's power."

"I guess I . . . I healed my leg . . . not very well," said Arthur, wincing as he looked down at his twisted, foreshortened leg. "And I opened your door, and I tried to remove the register. Before that I pushed one of the Grotesques . . . and I used the power to get to the Front Door. I didn't know I could use it up."

He had very mixed feelings about losing the power he had gained from the First Key. If he'd been back home and all was well, he would have been pleased to return to normal. Right now, in the House, with danger on every side, it would be comforting to have just a little magic.

"You might be the better for it," said Tom. He looked away from Arthur, towards his bottles, and spoke as much to them as to the two children. "The power of the Architect, in her person, or from her Keys, is perilous to mortals."

"Do you think I have enough power left for us to take the register?" asked Arthur.

Tom shrugged and started to say something. But his words were lost in a deep booming thud that echoed through the room and made the floor and walls vibrate with a dull buzz, and the bottles hum a high-pitched note.

"The pyramid," said Tom. "Grim Tuesday has lifted the western side to gain entry. He will come straight here. Let us try the register!"

Arthur didn't hesitate. He grabbed one side of the bronze-bound book with both hands as Tom grabbed the other side.

"One, two, three . . . heave!" Arthur called out.

The register groaned like a man in pain, then shrieked like a cat whose tail is trodden on, and came away from the table with a sound like a car screeching to an emergency stop.

The book was so heavy that Arthur's end dropped almost to the floor, even though Tom was taking most of the weight. Together he and Arthur staggered over to the sunship bottle.

"Arthur, touch the bottle with your nose and stare at the sunship!" Tom gasped as he leaned forward and planted his beaklike nose on the glass. "Miss Blue, your hand will do."

It was extremely difficult for Arthur to get his nose against the glass, but fortunately the bottle was quite big.

"I can't see past your head!" exclaimed Suzy. Arthur slid his nose back a bit and Suzy leaned over his shoulder.

"Look at the ship!" Tom commanded again. Then he roared out something that sounded like a poem, in a language that was nothing like any Arthur had ever heard. It was all roars and deep, husky noises, and it made him shiver all over.

His eyes slid away from the ship, drawn to a planet with many feathery rings, like Saturn but much brighter.

Desperately Arthur forced his dizzy eyes back to the sunship. It *did* look like a huge metal turtle, as Suzy had said. A metal turtle eighty feet long made of beaten gold, with hundred-foot-long front flippers of glowing red-tinged light. Its head had two big eyes that were obviously windows, made of a deep blue material the color of an old-fashioned glass fishing float.

Arthur stared at those windows. They seemed to get closer and closer, until he could see blurry figures moving behind them. When he was closer still, he could see the figures were Tom and Suzy and — even more strangely — Arthur himself.

Tom roared a final, deafening word and all of a sudden Arthur was looking out through the blue glass windows at a distant, feathery-ringed planet. Tom and Suzy were by his side, and the register was on the deck between them. A deck of golden metal planks, fixed with silver nails.

"Welcome aboard the *Helios*," Tom said, but his blue gaze looked past the two children, and he drew the silver saltshaker from his pocket.

Arthur looked around too. They were on the bridge of the *Helios*, an oval-shaped chamber about twenty feet in diameter. There was a wheel, lashed in position with a bright white rope. There were several strange-looking gauges around the wheel and a map box of mirrored metal that showed the planets and the sun in three dimensions, like shining fish in a deep, clear aquarium. There were the two huge blue glass windows at the front, and a gangway at the back going down, through an open hatch.

"Here," said Tom, handing the saltshaker to Arthur. "Go below and clear away any Fetchers or such-like that may be lurking. I'll get us under way."

"What about the register? And Grim Tuesday? Can he get us out of the bottle?"

"The register can stay where it is, but we'll need to watch it for any tricks. As for Grim Tuesday, we should return a scant minute after our embarkation. Time flows slowly here."

Tom began to unlash the wheel. Arthur hefted the saltshaker and looked at Suzy.

"Lead on," she said. "I want to see the rest of the ship."

Arthur climbed down the gangway, grimacing as his left leg lurched down the steps. Like the rest of the *Helios,* the gangway and the passage below were made of golden metal that shone with a soft light, so there was no need for lanterns. Or maybe, Arthur thought, it was a very bright light, lessened by his protective gear. He felt the faint presence of the star-hood over his face, but he didn't dare take it off to test his theory.

There were two decks below the bridge. Arthur and Suzy searched every cabin, space, and store methodically, but found no Fetchers. They did find a bronze bottle, sealed with a lead stopper, but as far as Arthur could see it was secure. If it held Nothing, none had leaked out.

They found many other things of interest, since the *Helios* was well stocked with equipment and food, for venturing on planets as well as deep in space or inside a sun. Many things baffled both of them, but others, like the cutlasses they discovered in the armory, they admired and immediately acquired. When they climbed back up to the bridge, both had broad-bladed but short cutlasses thrust through their belts, the edges of the blades shimmering with curdled moonlight. Suzy had also acquired a diamond-set gold earring, one much more resplendent than the indentured tag in Arthur's ear, and a bright red bandanna she'd tied around her head, over the top of the star-hood.

The view through the blue portholes had changed considerably. The two long flippers of the *Helios* were extended even farther out the front, so they now looked more like matching spinnakers of insubstantial red light.

There was no sign of the many-ringed planet; instead, the stars were moving with considerable speed past the portholes, and the sun had grown much larger, filling half the view.

"We didn't find any Nithlings," Arthur reported.

"Call me 'sir' or 'Captain' aboard ship," said Tom, but not unkindly.

"Yes, sir."

"And 'aye, aye' or 'aye' rather than 'yes,'" Tom continued. "I'll make sailors of the pair of ye before we're through."

"Is everything working properly, uh, Captain?" asked Arthur, with a glance at the rapidly enlarging sun.

"Indeed it is. We're set fair for the star's fiery heart, and the *Helios* dances light as she ever did."

"And we definitely won't burn up?" Suzy asked. "Captain, I mean, sir."

"Not unless we stay too long," replied Tom. "But a quick visitation should prove no problem for the *Helios* or for ourselves. Now I should bend my attention to the ship, for we must beat against the solar wind, and I need to trim the sails."

Arthur and Suzy watched for more than an hour as Tom turned the wheel this way and that. He occasionally pulled or pushed upon one of the levers that were mounted against the wall ahead of the wheel or tapped the glass of an oscillating gauge to steady it. The sun grew larger and larger, until it filled all the portholes. There was nothing else to see but blazing white light.

Arthur was very grateful for the shining metal of the sunship hull and the blue portholes. He knew that without them his whole body would have been burnt to ash many millions of miles out from the sun. He was grateful for his star-hood too, for saving him from instant blindness.

Tom spun the wheel a half-turn in anticipation of a shift of the solar winds and pointed to a circular ring on the floor near his foot.

"Arthur, you see that ring?"

"Yes . . . I mean, aye, aye, Captain."

"Take hold of it. When I say 'heave,' pull it up and out as far as you can. Then when I say 'let go,' release it."

"Aye, aye, sir!"

Arthur hurried over, knelt down, and gripped the ring. He looked up at Tom, who was staring intently through the portholes and moving the wheel in quarter turns, continually to the right.

"Heave!"

Arthur wrenched back on the ring. It came clear of the floor, and a brilliantly sparkling chain that seemed to be made of crystals or perhaps even diamonds came rattling out behind it. Arthur staggered backwards, pulling on the ring. Yards and yards of the glittering chain emerged, spreading all over the deck.

"Mind you don't get caught up!" Tom shouted.

Arthur had already realized that, but it was easier said than done. There was chain spreading everywhere, at least a hundred yards of it, and Arthur had to go down the gangway to avoid it, while still pulling on the ring. Suzy retreated to one corner, eyeing the chain with suspicion.

"Hold there, Arthur!" Tom called out. He suddenly stepped away from the wheel, looped the chain around the register on the floor, sprang back to the wheel, and shouted, "Let go!"

Arthur let go. The ring shot away from his hand, and the chain rebounded back to wherever it had come from. The loop around the register tightened. For a few seconds, the chain stopped, and the register stayed stuck to the deck. Then as Arthur leaped back up the gangway, he saw the register screech across the floor, deep scratches in the floor testifying to how hard it was fighting the pull.

"It won't go through there!" Arthur shouted, pointing at the saucer-sized chain-hole. But when the large bronze-bound book reached the hole, it *did* go through, though not without a final, earsplitting scream that sent Arthur tumbling down the gangway again, his hands pressed against his ears.

A moment later the ship ran into something. There was a thud and a groan from the hull. The deck rocked from side to side.

Arthur dragged himself up to the bridge, shaking his head from side to side, his ears ringing.

"It had to be a surprise," Tom was saying to Suzy. "The register would have defended itself better if it knew I was going to wrap it in the anchor chain. I trust you were not too disturbed?"

Suzy looked up at him, tapped her ears, and shook her head.

"Good!" declared Tom, not realizing that Suzy was shaking her head to try to clear her ears. "We've docked, in a manner of speaking. We'll swing on the chain a little and should be able to see —"

The white light in the porthole changed. Arthur stared as he saw lush green trees drift into view. Trees hung with vines and dense green leaves, interspersed with bright white flowers.

"It looks like a jungle!" he cried out, surprised.

"It is, of sorts," replied Tom. "A tropical island, preserved in a bubble of Immaterial Glass, here in the heart of the sun."

"How do we get across?" Suzy asked, much too loudly. Her hearing hadn't fully come back.

"We're beached on her sandy shore, broadside on through the Immaterial Wall," said Tom. "So we can wade in. But we need to wait a moment, to make sure the anchor has taken bite. It wouldn't do to drift back into the sun's embrace before we're back aboard."

"What are we going to wade through?" Arthur asked.

"A patch of sea, caught with the island," Tom replied. "The Immaterial Glass that encloses this place knows to let the *Helios* impinge. Any other vessel would just bounce off."

He bent down and gave the anchor ring a few heaves. A few yards of chain came out, but then snagged. Tom gave a few more steady heaves, then let the ring go.

"She's fast," he declared, "unless a storm comes up. But now — let's go ashore!"

Chapter Sixteen

Arthur half-shut his eyes and pulled his hands up into the sleeves of his brightcoat as Tom opened the portside hatch. But as Tom had promised, the hatch opened onto clear blue water, with a sandy beach only yards away, with the jungle verge beyond. A small surf of one- to two-foot waves swept around the sunship's hull and crashed onto the beach.

Even though he'd seen it through the porthole, this was *not* what Arthur had expected. He'd thought there'd be some indication they were in the heart of a sun. Brighter light for example, or a ring of fire in the distance.

There was normal sunshine overhead and the air was warm and humid. Arthur poked his head out the hatch and saw ocean stretching out to the horizon, broken a mile or so out by a long line of what must be coral reefs.

All in all, it looked good enough to become a post-card from an unspoiled tropical holiday destination.

"Where do the waves come from?" Arthur asked Tom as they jumped down. The sea was warm, but the waves were bigger than they looked from the ship, and as the beach shelved away steeply, the water was deeper. Arthur had to jump up to keep his head out of a passing wave in order to hear Tom's reply.

"It is unlike the other bottles, in that this place is both here and there, in a manner of speaking," said Tom. He grabbed Arthur and Suzy by their coat collars and lifted them up as an even larger wave swept past. "But the only way for us to get to it is here. If we went to where it is on the old Earth, we wouldn't see it and would turn away — or, in unlucky circumstances, we would wreck and drown some way off. You should be able to wade now."

"Thanks," muttered Arthur as Tom dropped them in the wash and strode up the beach. The boy picked himself up clumsily, his lame leg stuck in the wet sand for a moment.

"Hey, I'm dry!" exclaimed Suzy after one step up the beach. She'd been sodden and dripping a moment before.

"So am I!" said Arthur, patting his coat. There was some steam rising off it, but otherwise the coat and everything else he was wearing had dried the instant he left the sea.

"This is a great coat," said Suzy. "I hope I can keep it. And these shoes keep the sand out *and* they'll be great for kicking Nithlings. Immaterial Boots are proof against everything you know, even Nothing. For a while, anyway."

"You're cheerful," Arthur observed wryly. But he felt much better himself. The clean air and the sunshine were very heartening, and with Tom's help he felt sure they would soon find the Will. Once they had Part Two, then it could sort out Grim Tuesday and all would be well.

This moment of optimism was slightly spoiled as he stumbled in the sand, his shortened leg betraying him once more. He kept trying to walk like he always had, but he couldn't. He had to learn to take different steps and think ahead to where he'd put his left foot.

Tom had already gone into the jungle, following a rivulet of fresh water. The trees and undergrowth thinned out a bit on either side of this narrow stream, making it the next best thing to a path.

"Too green for me, and too damp," remarked Suzy with distaste as they splashed up the stream. She looked up at the canopy of leaves and vines and shuddered. "Could be anything hiding in the shrubbery. Give me a nice street any day."

"What about your old place with the dinosaurs?" asked Arthur. "That had trees."

"Only a few, and it was inside the House. . . . Where did Tom go?"

Arthur and Suzy stopped and looked around. Tom had been only a little way ahead. Now they could neither see him nor hear him splashing. There was only the gentle burble of the stream and the soft noises of the wind rustling the upper levels of the jungle canopy.

"Tom?" called out Arthur. "Captain?"

Paranoid thoughts began to creep into his brain.

Maybe Tom had somehow seen the telegram from Grim Tuesday after all? Or maybe he'd always planned to get us here. He's brought us here to trap us. He'll leave us here, on this jungle island in the middle of the sun. We'll never escape —

"Up here!" Tom called out.

"Where?" Arthur shouted back. He could hear Tom, but couldn't see him. There was only the jungle all around, and Suzy next to him, slowly scanning the trees.

"Here!" called out Tom again, and this time Arthur saw a hand thrust down through the thick mass of leaves, waving. "You can climb up on the other side."

Arthur and Suzy left the stream, pushed their way between some vast bushes with pale yellow flowers and odd elongated seedpods, and came to the trunk of a large, spreading tree. The trunk was wrapped in vines that grew in all directions, making a natural ladder up into the jungle canopy. Arthur and Suzy climbed easily, maneuvered through the leafy canopy, and emerged out into the sunshine.

Tom was waiting for them, perched on a thick spreading branch next to something that could only be described as a nest. A circular platform of branches and vines wove together in a haphazard fashion to make a cross between a balcony and a treetop bed.

In the middle of it, apparently asleep, was a small bear. It was a sleek black in color, apart from a lighter muzzle and a bright yellow crescent-shaped blaze across its chest. It also had a tail, which Arthur wasn't sure was normal for bears. If it was a bear. It wasn't that big, about half Arthur's size, though it was plumper around the middle.

"That's it," said Tom. "Part Two of the Will. And, if I recall from one of my journeys to the Spice Islands, in the shape of a sun bear."

Arthur climbed across to look at the sun bear more closely. It didn't stir, but the slow rise and fall of its chest suggested it was merely asleep. Arthur leaned closer still and looked at its fur. Sure enough, when he was only an inch or two away, he could see thousands of tiny letters swirling about, rather than actual fur or flesh.

"What's wrong with it?" he asked, as the sun bear didn't awaken or show any sign of being aware of its visitors. "Is it asleep? Or hibernating?"

"Sun bears —" Tom began to say, but he got no further, as the sharp crack of an explosion sounded from the beach. Arthur, Tom, and Suzy snapped around to look and saw a huge geyser of steam spout into the air — from where the *Helios* was beached.

"Uh-oh," said Suzy. Her hand fell to her cutlass hilt. "Is that Grim Tuesday arriving?"

"No," Tom replied. "Apart from the Improbable Stair, there is no way to reach this island but the *Helios*, and Tuesday wouldn't dare the Stair. It is more likely we have woken a guardian or watcher. I will deal with it."

All of a sudden, Tom's harpoon appeared in his left hand, glittering with its strange mix of light and darkness.

"But what about the Will?" Arthur asked. He prodded the bear with his finger, keeping a wary eye on its long, sharp-looking claws. A faint golden glow spread over Arthur's finger, but the bear didn't move. "What do we do with it?"

Tom had begun to climb down, but he stopped and looked back up, his forehead furrowed in thought. He kept glancing back towards the beach, where the steam continued to spout a hundred feet into the air.

"What did you plan to do with it?" the seafarer asked.

"I don't know," replied Arthur in exasperation. "I thought it'd be like the first part of the Will. You know, it would tell me what to do. Not just lie there."

"Bring it, then. We should not linger here," said Tom. Then he was gone.

"You reckon we can lift it?" Suzy asked Arthur. "Pretty solid-looking bear. Even if it is made of words."

"I don't know," Arthur snapped, showing his irritation. "Why can't it just wake up and be useful?"

Making sure he had a good foothold on the branch, he bent down and tried to lift the sun bear under one arm. But he could barely raise its front legs an inch off the nest. It was extremely heavy, heavier than any bear of real flesh and blood.

Suzy tried to lift it too, but could only get its rear legs up, while its round midsection stayed firmly planted on the woven leaves. Even lifting together, they could only bend it into a U-shape. It still didn't wake up.

"It's too heavy!" Arthur conceded.

"The Captain could carry it," said Suzy. "That steam's stopped . . . oh . . . smoke."

She pointed. The steam geyser had gone, but in its

place there was a dense column of smoke. Then they heard a strange crackling noise, and a soundless vibration passed through Arthur and Suzy, making them shiver. It was followed by an inhuman, very high-pitched scream — and a triumphant shout from Tom.

"Reckon that was the Captain's 'friend,'" whispered Suzy as she felt her teeth with one dirty hand. Arthur's teeth felt odd too, kind of fuzzy. But the sensation passed quickly.

"As long as it gets used on the right side, I don't mind," said Arthur. He cupped his hands over his mouth and shouted, "Captain! Captain! We need you to carry the Will!"

"Aye, I hear you!" came a returning shout. "I'm coming back!"

Tom followed his shout several minutes later, emerging through the canopy, once again without his harpoon. "We must speed on. That was a Sunsprite. There are others trying to drag the *Helios* off. They have some means of getting in through the Immaterial Glass."

"I thought you said there was no way in except the Stair and your sunship," Suzy said as Tom picked up the sun bear and slung it over one shoulder as easily as if it were a pillow.

"So I thought, lass, so I thought," Tom muttered. "I wonder . . . but this is no time for wonderings. Quickly, to the ship!"

"What's a Sunsprite?" Arthur asked Suzy as they hastily climbed back down into the cool shade of the jungle. Tom easily outdistanced them into the greenery, even with the sun bear on his shoulder.

"Dunno exactly," replied Suzy. "There's a mort of different Sprites, and I never learned 'em. Basically they're Nithlings that got out of the House and into the Secondary Realms."

"Miss Blue is correct, to a degree," Tom called out. He was ten or twenty yards ahead and hidden, so his comment came as a minor shock to Arthur and Suzy. "All Sprites were once Nithlings, but they take on the nature of the place they inhabit out in the Secondary Realms. Sunsprites are essentially self-willed entities composed of stellar plasma. But even they should not be here, at the hot heart of a star. They usually swarm around the fringes of a sun."

"He's got good hearing," whispered Suzy.

"Swarm?" asked Arthur. He didn't like hearing that word.

"Typically the original escaped Nithling divides into several hundred Sprites. If they come upon us, do not let them embrace you. Even a brightcoat and star-hood will not endure long against their kiss."

"Uh, let's just get back on board without meeting any," Arthur suggested. He picked up his pace, splashing Suzy with his strange, stumbling gait.

"Too late for that," said Tom as another geyser of steam erupted out of the sea, just as all three of them burst out of the jungle and onto the sand.

The Sunsprite wasn't visible, but the column of steam slowly moved towards the beach, the water fizzing and boiling all around it

"Can't the sea quench it?" asked Arthur.

"Eventually, if there was some means of keeping it in the water," Tom told him. He held out his left hand and his harpoon appeared there out of nowhere. He immediately handed the weapon to Arthur, who accepted it with surprise.

"My friend does not willingly fly from another's hand, but she will help the Master of the Lower House. Aim high, for the upper torso of the Sprite — and keep your distance. My friend is best thrown as far as you can."

"But . . . but what are you going to do?"

"I must ready the *Helios* for our departure, before the other Sprites drag it back into the sun. You will need to distract this Sunsprite, then finish it. Miss Blue, your cutlass will cut several times before the blade melts. Use your weapons well."

He rushed into the surf just as a man-sized cloud of writhing steam emerged from the sea. A moment later the steam wafted away and Arthur caught a glimpse of a dark charcoal-colored creature, just before it exploded into flame. Even through his star-hood, Arthur felt the heat of it on his face.

Without even thinking about it, he threw Tom's harpoon at it, aiming for its upper chest. Once again there was the strange crackling noise, like wrapping paper being mangled, magnified a hundred times. The harpoon flew so fast Arthur only saw a luminous aftertrail.

"Ow!" exclaimed Suzy, and Arthur groaned as the harpoon hit. Both of them clutched their mouths, as they were hit by a sudden toothache that radiated through into their cheekbones and eye sockets.

It was much worse for the Sunsprite. It screamed and ropes of flame shot from its hands up into the sky, then came back down and wrapped around the harpoon that stuck through its chest. When it seemed as if it might pull the harpoon free, Suzy dropped her hand from her mouth and drew her cutlass. But the flaming ropes dimmed and the Sunsprite's fire went out completely as it crumbled into ash and chunks of charcoal.

The harpoon disappeared. Arthur flinched as it reappeared in his hand with a solid *whack!*

Suzy looked at the harpoon, ran her tongue across her still-aching teeth, and shook her head. "That's nasty, that is. I wouldn't want to be any closer next time you use it."

"I hope there won't be a next time," Arthur replied as he hurried into the sea. He held the harpoon away from his body as far as he could, as if it might turn and strike at him. "Let's get aboard before another Sunsprite comes through, and —"

A wave slapped him in the face before he could continue. The star-hood stopped him from swallowing anything, but he had to stop where he was in order to regain his balance.

At that moment, steam exploded just in front of him. He stumbled back into Suzy, and both of them fell over in the soft sand, the wash spilling over their legs as another steam-wreathed Sunsprite reared up out of the sea.

It was too close to throw, and he was blinded by steam, so Arthur simply thrust Tom's harpoon up and out, while Suzy scrambled away on all fours as fast as she could.

Arthur felt the harpoon shudder in his hands at the same time an intense heat blasted across his face. He pulled his hands into his sleeves as far as he could, and leaned back into the wash, setting the shaft of the harpoon into the sand.

A moment later, he had to let go of the weapon, as a biting ache struck every bone in his body and spread through his teeth and across his face. He screamed and beat at his mouth with his sleeved hands, desperate to stop the pain. The intense heat of the Sunsprite was nothing compared to the deep, vibrating ache beneath his skin, throbbing in agonizing time with his increasing pulse.

Rushing to escape the harpoon's awful influence, Arthur squirmed away through the sea and sand. He didn't care whether he'd gotten the Sunsprite, whether it was following to kiss him and burn him to death. All he wanted to do was get away from the Captain's terrible weapon —

Something slapped into his right hand, and Arthur screamed again. The harpoon had come back. He couldn't get away from it!

That meant the harpoon thought it would soon be used again.

Chapter Seventeen

Even though the harpoon was back in Arthur's hand, the pain suddenly ebbed away, disappearing as quickly as it had come, leaving only a lingering discomfort in his teeth and a horrific memory.

Arthur found he was lying facedown in wet sand, and hastily rolled over. There was no sign of the Sunsprite or any other geysers of steam. Wearily, he sat up, then staggered to his feet and looked around properly. Suzy was lying still on the sand about six feet away, just above the tide line.

"Suzy!" Arthur called, panic in his voice. What if the side effects of using the harpoon had killed her?

Suzy lifted her head, probed her face with her fingers as if to make sure it was still there, then shakily stood up.

"Are you all right?" Arthur asked urgently, taking a step towards her. She backed away and held up her hands.

"Keep your distance with that sticker, Arthur. I'll just follow on behind."

"Arthur! Miss Blue! Quickly, we need to cast off!"

Tom's shout galvanized both children into action. Arthur flung himself into the waves, turning sideways to get through them more easily, though he had to kick as well, as a bigger wave lifted him off his feet. Suzy, despite her words, plunged in and soon caught up to him.

As they approached the portside hatch and the rope ladder hanging from it, the water all along the golden bulk of the sunship's hull began to fizz and bubble. Tom leaned out of the hatchway and shouted again.

"Faster! The Sunsprites have done something to the Immaterial Glass, our anchor's dragged, and our starboard sail is filling!"

Arthur redoubled his efforts, but stumbled just before he got to the ladder. He fell completely underwater. Hot water. He pushed off the sand and felt a hand under his arm, and when he burst back out, Suzy was right behind him, helping him up.

She practically threw him onto the ladder. Arthur dropped the harpoon as he grabbed the bottom rung, but it didn't fall. It just disappeared.

"Don't come back to me," muttered Arthur under his breath as he clambered up. At the top, he turned and reached back to help Suzy. The water was really boiling now all along the sunship, and Arthur could see a red glow spreading through the clear blue-green sea.

Suzy leaped aboard with alacrity, hardly needing Arthur's help.

"Shut the hatch and dog it!" roared Tom from somewhere inside.

Arthur pulled and Suzy pushed on the hatch. It was very heavy, made of the same golden metal as the hull, and at least a foot thick. It moved very slowly along a top and bottom rail. As it closed, Arthur saw dozens of gouts of steam explode up through the waves outside. The columns of steam were motionless for a second, then all turned towards the still open hatch.

"Sunsprites!" shouted Arthur. "Lots of them!"

He gave up pulling the hatch and ran around to help Suzy push.

"Heave!" he yelled. "One, two, three — heave!"

A ropy arm of fire thrust itself inside just as the hatch rolled shut. Cut off, it rolled and twisted around Arthur's and Suzy's feet, till Suzy stamped on it. Its fire went out and it collapsed into black dust.

Arthur picked up the long metal bar and slid it in place, locking the hatch. He'd barely gotten it in place when there was a sudden beating on the hull, a sound like many hammers striking metal.

"I hope they can't get in," said Suzy. "I lost my cutlass in the sea."

"So did I," gasped Arthur, feeling his side. He couldn't remember when he'd last had it. "Let's get some more. I'm not using that harpoon again."

"All hands to the bridge!" Tom bellowed.

Arthur and Suzy hurried along the passage and then up to the bridge. Tom was steering the wheel with one hand and reaching out to pull levers with the other. Through one blue porthole, Arthur and Suzy saw the island, now hidden in steam and smoke. The other porthole showed only bright light and indistinct figures that had to be Sunsprites. The metal hammering noise was just as loud here, making it hard to hear and even harder to concentrate.

"They're trying to tow us somewhere," said Tom. "But we've got the solar wind with us. Grab those two levers and pull back as hard as you can."

Arthur and Suzy hurried over to the levers, jumping across the dormant Will. It was lying on the floor behind Tom, still asleep or unconscious.

The levers were much harder to pull down than Arthur expected. In the end, he and Suzy had to hang on to each one to drag them down into position.

"Sunsprites are trying to spoil our rigging, but the *Helios* is a tough ship," shouted Tom. "Tuesday might be a penny-pinching slaver, but he can make a good vessel."

"Grim Tuesday made the *Helios*?" shouted Arthur.

"Aye, he did," roared Tom, even his mighty voice almost lost in the constant hammering ring. "Copied, of course, from some inventor out in the Secondary Realms. Not from Earth, for a change. Probably ⓒⓒⓒⓒⓒⓒⓒⓒ or *ÆΩ∂∞f‡*."

"Where?" asked Arthur. "Who?"

He couldn't even begin to understand the noises Tom had just made, which he presumed were names of other worlds. Or maybe just countries. Or maybe they were the inventors' names.

Tom didn't answer. He was intent on a gauge that was slowly filling with a red dye. As it got to two-thirds full, he spun the wheel and held it fast, straining against some unseen pressure. The gauge almost immediately became totally suffused with the red dye and stayed full.

"A good wind and both sails taut," shouted Tom. "They're trying to hold us back, but they'll fall away. Aye, there they go!"

Arthur couldn't see anything in the portholes, or at least he couldn't be sure what he was seeing. But the hammering lessened, and the indistinct shapes in the brightness were no longer all over the place but bunched up in the bottom corners of the portholes. From there, they slowly disappeared.

After five minutes, there was no more hammering. Tom relaxed a little at the wheel, though he didn't lash it or let go.

"We'll be returned to our mooring afore too long with this wind," he said cheerfully. "Then back into the House in a trice."

"And we'll get back only a minute or so after we left?" asked Arthur. He was thinking about the telegram in his pocket and what Grim Tuesday would do. And the even bigger question: What was he going to do with a sleeping Will?

"As long as it takes to speak both spells, the embarkation and disembarkation," replied Tom. He frowned and added, "I trust you'll do something with that Will. I've no more mind to follow Grim Tuesday than I ever did, but if he commands me in person with the power of the Second Key, I must obey without question or slipperiness. I don't want my friend to shorten your future."

Arthur and Suzy shook their heads in an instant mutual reaction.

"Why is nothing ever easy?" asked Arthur. "I just want the Will to wake up and tell Tuesday to hand over the Key to me. Then I can sort everything out, get back home, and forget about this blasted House and everything in it!"

"It could be worse," said Suzy philosophically. "We could be soaking wet."

Arthur let a slight chuckle escape as he walked around the sun bear.

"And I could be having an asthma attack. And all our teeth might fall out because of . . ."

He glanced at Tom and decided not to say anything about the harpoon. Maybe it had feelings and would be offended. Or Tom might be.

Arthur stopped circling the sun bear and took a series of breaths, each one a little deeper than the last. Now he was outside the House, he couldn't quite fill his lungs, the familiar catch still lurking there, but it could hardly be called asthma. It was just a minor annoyance. Nothing compared to his short, twisted leg.

Forget about the leg, he told himself. *Get on with it.*

"Okay, I have to wake the Will up. How do you wake up a sleeping bear? Or a hibernating one? Does anyone know?"

Suzy shook her head. Tom adjusted the wheel, then almost absently said, "I know sun bears don't hibernate."

"They don't?"

Tom shook his head, and, out of the corner of his eye, Arthur saw the Will's eye flicker too. Just a rapid, momentary lift of an eyelid so it could get a snapshot of the room and the situation.

"It's not even asleep," cried Arthur, crouching down next to the bear. He tapped it on the snout and said, "Wake up, Part Two of the Will."

Nothing happened.

"Tell it who you are," suggested Suzy. "I mean, the Master and everything."

"I'm Arthur Penhaligon. Master of the Lower House. Rightful Heir to . . . uh . . . the Keys to the Kingdom, the Lower House, the Middle House, the Upper House . . . um . . . the Far Reaches —"

"The Great Maze, the Incomparable Gardens, and the Border Sea," recited Suzy, helping Arthur out.

"Says who?"

For a second Arthur didn't know who'd spoken, till he saw the corner of the sun bear's mouth lift up. It had a high-pitched, squeaky drawl, and it could speak with barely a movement of its snout or lips.

"Says Paragraphs Three to Seven of the Will, who chose me in the first place," said Arthur angrily. "I didn't want the job, but I've got it, so you can get up and help me out."

The Will opened one eye fully and slowly looked Arthur up and down. "How do I know you're telling the truth? You could be anyone. Where's the First Key if you're Master of the Lower House?"

"I made Dame Primus — that is, the first part of the Will — my Steward," Arthur answered, trying to muster authority into his voice. "She's got the Key. I need you to make Grim Tuesday hand over the Second Key to me, so you'd better stay awake and start thinking about doing it."

"Not as easy as that," said the Will. Its high-pitched voice was quite annoying. "I need to see it in writing that you're the Rightful Heir. Proper official notice from Dame Primus. Part One chooses the heir, fair enough, but the least she can do is the proper notification. I can't do a thing without it. Wouldn't be prudent. Don't bother me again unless you've got the notice."

It shut its eyes. Arthur reached forward and tapped it smartly on the nose, then retreated even more smartly as one claw snapped out and raked the air where his hand had been an instant before.

"I said, don't bother me," squeaked the Will. "I'm meditating."

"Even more irritating than the first bit," remarked Suzy. "Though I s'pose it's a benefit not having it in your throat."

"We'll have to get it — and ourselves — away from

Grim Tuesday, out of the pyramid, and up to the Lower House," said Arthur. "Somehow or other. Did Dame Primus tell you what to do once we got the Will?"

"Nope," said Suzy. "Maybe I should've asked, from experience, like. With her last plan coming unstuck and everything."

"This one's come unstuck too," said Arthur. He scratched his head. "We've got an hour or so sailing back, haven't we, Captain?"

"Half that, or maybe a third," replied Tom. "The solar wind is with us now."

"So we come back out a few minutes after we left," said Arthur, as he paced lopsidedly around the bridge. "Surely it'll take Grim Tuesday ten minutes to get up to your room, Captain?"

"Depends. There are weirdways inside the Treasure Tower. If he climbs the stairs at his usual pace, it'll be ten minutes or more."

"Weirdways? In the prison . . . I mean the Tower? Where?"

"Ah, a slip of the tongue there," Tom said with a twinkle in his eye. "I've been expressly ordered not to mention the weirdways. Can't tell anyone where they are either, though I suppose I might nod my head or give a wink, if someone was to ask where they're not or such-like roundabout questions."

"Grim Tuesday wouldn't put a weirdway right into the chamber with the bottles," said Arthur slowly, watching Tom's face. "But he might put one close . . . like the cell next door. . . ."

Tom slowly winked.

"Even if someone did put a weirdway in a cell next door, they'd be sure to disguise it," continued Arthur. "Like maybe behind something on the wall. Or behind a trapdoor in the floor. Or the ceiling. Or disguised as something else —"

Tom nodded slowly at the last sentence.

"How would you disguise the entry to a weirdway, Suzy?" asked Arthur. "How are they normally disguised?"

"Could be anything," snorted Suzy. She glanced at Tom and said, "A cup of water is quite common. Or a teapot. Or a candlestick. Sometimes a book. Or a painting. A hook on the wall. I remember an old geezer had one you got in through a coin stuck to the floor. Then there's flowers. A loose brick. Mirrors is popular. Water closet, though that's disgustin' and not proper. A chest or drawer. Maybe a box of some kind. Wardrobes. Cigarette case. A pianoforte or harpsichordicle. Clocks —"

She stopped. Tom had winked at "clocks."

"So a clock in one of the neighboring cells is the entry to a weirdway. I wonder where it comes out? I guess it must still be inside the pyramid, since Grim Tuesday is so paranoid about keeping people out."

"I wonder if he left the door open?" mused Suzy.

"You said he lifted the west side of the pyramid to get in," said Arthur to Tom. "Can you talk about that?"

"The entire west face of the pyramid is hinged as a door," said Grim Tuesday. "It's no secret, for no one else is strong enough to lift it. Even I could not open that door. Not alone."

"And all my power's gone," said Arthur.

"Maybe he left it open," suggested Suzy. "He was in a hurry."

Arthur shook his head. "Leave open the door to all his treasures? I doubt it."

"Just being optimistic," said Suzy. "You should try it. It doesn't hurt. Least, it doesn't hurt me. Maybe it would give you a pain in the midsection."

Arthur ignored the comment. His mind was racing over the possibilities, trying to work out what to do.

"We'll have to get Grim Tuesday to open the pyramid for us," he said. "Or maybe Soot. It must have gotten even bigger and stronger from eating the Grim's treasures —"

"Ah, the Nithling," interrupted Tom. "I fear that it will not be able to serve you. I am sure that Grim Tuesday will call upon me to slay it immediately. I am surprised he did not send a telegram to that effect. It is his preferred means of communication, fitting for one so mean with words."

"Oh, yeah, right," said Arthur. He slipped his hand into his pocket and felt the telegram there. He'd hoped it had become a sodden, unreadable mess, but the brightcoat had kept it dry, or had dried it out perfectly. "Sure. I guess you chasing around after Soot will distract Grim Tuesday anyway. That's better than nothing. . . ."

Arthur's voice trailed off as a thought slowly rose to the front of his mind.

"Telegrams," he said.

"What?" asked Suzy.

"Telegrams!"

"What about telegrams?"

Arthur clutched Tom's sleeve. "If you can receive telegrams in your room, does that mean you can send them?"

"Aye, if I've the coins to pay. Grim Tuesday allows nothing on account."

"Have you got any coins?" asked Arthur feverishly. "I mean can you lend me some?"

"Only the coins in my ears, for paying Davy Jones in case of drowning," said Tom, pushing back his graying hair to show two large gold coins hanging from his earlobes. "Superstition, I know, but I've grown accustomed. . . . Anyways, once we're ashore you can have the loan of one of them. I need to be keeping one, against unfortunate circumstance."

"Would it be enough?" asked Arthur, eyeing the coin. It looked pretty thick and heavy. The laurel-crowned head stamped into it looked pretty smug and self-satisfied too about being on such a valuable coin. "To send a telegram and pay for a reply?"

"Aye, it should. Who would you send it to?"

"Dame Primus. Then she can send one back confirming that I'm the heir. I show that to this . . . to the sun bear. It sorts out Grim Tuesday. Everything'll be okay!"

Chapter Eighteen

"Telegram's not good enough," said the sun bear without opening its eyes. "When I say proper notification, I mean *proper*. Stamped and sealed."

"You're a proper pain, aren't you?" commented Suzy. But the Will didn't respond.

"I'll send the telegram anyway," said Arthur, with as much conviction as he could muster. His brilliant idea didn't seem so brilliant now. "Maybe Dame Primus can help us escape from the Tower and the pyramid. Or send the proper notification some other way . . . or something. I guess we'll just have to try to get out ourselves in the meantime. And make sure Grim Tuesday doesn't find us."

"Good idea," said Suzy. "Only we can't carry the bear. Not without the Captain."

"I thought I was the one who needed optimism," Arthur reminded her. He prodded the sun bear's rear with the toe of his Immaterial Boot. "It can walk. How about that, Will? You should come with us just in case I do turn out to be the Rightful Heir, which everybody tells me I am."

"I'm not going anywhere till I have adequately assessed the situation," said the sun bear, still without opening its eyes. "It would not be prudent to move until I have considered all possibilities, or must comply with appropriate authority."

"You're not staying on board the *Helios*," announced Tom. He turned from the wheel and stooped down to look at the sun bear. "Part Two of the Will, do you know who I am?"

"No," said the sun bear, squeezing its eyes even more shut. "Nor do I care to play twenty questions to discover your dubious identity."

Tom held out his hand. There was a rush of cold air, and his strangely dark and bright harpoon appeared in his hand. He tilted it down, till the point touched the deck a few inches from the sun bear's nose.

Arthur and Suzy retreated to the companionway and took a few steps down, almost falling over each other in their haste.

The sun bear reluctantly opened one eye.

"Do you know me now?" growled Tom.

The sun bear opened its other eye, lifted its snout with obvious effort, and sniffed the air several times.

"The Old One's second son," it squeaked.

"The Architect's adopted son."

"Yes, yes," admitted the sun bear. "That is true enough."

"And I say Arthur *is* the Master of the Lower House and so must have been chosen as the Rightful Heir."

The sun bear rolled its eyes and gave an annoyed snort.

"Character witnesses are all very well, but I stand by my position. I will not act on behalf of anyone until I am in receipt of the correct notification from Dame Primus."

Tom scraped the point of the harpoon across the deck towards the sun bear's snout. It made a nerve-jangling, harmonic sound that filled the bridge and made Arthur and Suzy take several steps down the ladder.

But the sun bear did not retreat. It merely pulled back its head.

"Nor am I moved by threats!" it added.

"This is not a threat, you furry backslider," Tom roared. "But if you won't at least go along with Arthur, then I'll see if Mother's gift can spill some of Mother's words out of your gizzard."

The sun bear looked distastefully at Arthur and wrinkled its nose.

"I suppose that I have to go somewhere, since my

pleasant retreat has been destroyed. Perhaps, ipso facto, pursuant to the circumstances, I may accompany this potential heir-designate until further information is forthcoming one way or another."

"Pleasant retreat!" said Arthur. "That was a prison — you . . . you were supposed to break out of it and do your duty. Let the Will be done, my foot!"

"I trusted that I would be released at the correct and proper moment to fulfill my obligations," said the Will stiffly. "Certainly not rousted out by such an unorthodox . . . ahem . . . party, with such peculiar —"

"That's enough!" ordered Tom. His harpoon vanished, he spun the wheel and pushed back several levers. The red dye in the central gauge ebbed away. "We're almost at the mooring point. You will need to gather around me for the transfer back to the House."

The Will frowned, but stood up with visible effort and waddled the few steps to Tom's feet.

"Fat little rat," whispered Suzy. "Nothing like Part One."

"I guess they could all be different," whispered Arthur back. "Not that I want to find out."

"Stand close," said Tom. He reached into his pocket and drew out a silver carving fork. He frowned, returned it, and pulled out a very large silver soup spoon, rubbing it carefully against his sleeve. Then he held it up so it caught the blue light from the portholes.

"Focus on your own reflection in the spoon," he instructed. "Don't look at anything else. Don't get distracted. Don't look away. Everybody looking?"

Arthur and Suzy nodded.

The Will sighed and reared up on its hind legs, its stubby tail helping it to balance.

"Hold it a little lower, if you please? Yes, I am looking."

Arthur stared fixedly at the curved back of the spoon. His reflection was curved and fuzzy, mixed in with Suzy's and the reflection of the bear. Arthur tried to concentrate on maintaining his stare, but his mind was wandering ahead, trying to think about other options. But he couldn't think of anything other than sending the telegram to Dame Primus and trying to stay one step . . . or preferably many more steps . . . ahead of Grim Tuesday.

Tom began to bellow his spell (or poem or chant or whatever it was). Having an extremely loud, incomprehensible shout going on and on above his head was very distracting but Arthur forced himself to keep staring at the shiny spoon and his own curved face.

It got easier to look after the first minute. The other

reflections drifted away, and Arthur lost all sense that there was anything or anyone else around him. There was only his shimmering reflection. He was alone in the universe, looking at himself, and that was all there was —

Tom finished the spell and wrapped his weather-beaten hand around the spoon.

Arthur blinked.

They were back in Tom's room in the Treasure Tower. Arthur could hear distant bellowing and shouting. No words were distinguishable, it was all angry roaring, until a few distinct words came through, one voice cutting through the other. Arthur recognized the quieter voice as Soot's.

The louder one's shout was, "Captain! To me!"

Tom cursed.

"I must obey!" he explained. "Good fortune, Arthur. Here!"

He tore the gold coin from his right ear and flipped it to Arthur as he strode to the door, his "friend" materializing in his hand on his second step.

Arthur caught the coin, sticky with Tom's blood, and looked over to the table.

"Thanks! But how do I send a —"

He was too late. Tom had gone, the door swinging shut behind him.

Suzy hurried over to the desk, while the Will climbed awkwardly into Tom's chair and recommenced looking haughty and disapproving.

"There'll be a telegraph blank here somewhere," Suzy explained, quickly sorting through the papers. "You just write in the squares. Here!"

She took a quill and an ink bottle from deep inside her shirt, unscrewed the bottle, licked the point of the quill, and handed it to Arthur.

"You write it," he said. He tried to hand the quill back. He'd never used anything but a ballpoint or felt tip.

Suzy shook her head. "I'm still taking penmanship. Dame Primus says my letters are a disgrace. Particularly the esses. And the haitches."

Arthur looked at the telegram blank. It was a simple printed form, headed THE ELEVATED AND WORSHIPFUL TELEGRAPHIC, TELEPHONIC, AND MESSAGE SERVICE OF THE HOUSE. Under that, there was TO and a line of seven word boxes, MESSAGE and five lines of seven boxes, and FROM with its line of seven boxes, plus a red-inked circle in the corner about the size of the blood-dappled gold coin Arthur held. There was also a very small box with the words REPLY PAID under the circle.

Dipping the quill in the turquoise-blue ink, Arthur somewhat blobbily wrote *Dame Primus*. He had to re-ink for the -*mus,* ignoring Suzy's unspoken but evident scorn at his clumsiness with the quill.

He thought for a few seconds, then with several re-fills, numerous splotches, and some scratching, wrote:

IN TREASURE TOWER GOT WILL IT WON'T RECOGNIZE ME SAYS NEEDS OFFICIAL FORM SEND FORM OR HELP HELP!

He hesitated at the FROM boxes, then simply put *Arthur* and ticked the box next to REPLY PAID.

As soon as he'd ticked the box, the red-lined circle began to glow with a silver light, and the handwritten annotation 12R appeared.

"Lob the coin down," Suzy instructed.

Arthur placed the gold coin on the circle. The whole form immediately vanished. In its place were four silver coins of varying sizes and designs.

"Lucky you got the change," said Suzy, sweeping the coins off the table and into her pocket. "They embezzle it half the time."

"We'd better find that weirdway next door," said Arthur, suddenly conscious that he couldn't hear any shouting outside.

"Which side?" asked Suzy.

"Forgot to ask," Arthur shouted as he made his way to the door. "Come on! You too, Will."

"If you must call me anything, you may address me as Most Excellent Testamentary Clause," said the sun bear.

"Claws?" said Suzy, as she tilted the chair to speed the bear on its way. "Orright, Claws, hop to it."

"No, no, no," protested the sun bear. "Most Excellent . . ."

"Claws it is," said Suzy loudly. "After you, Claws."

"I said . . . oh . . . just don't speak to me," huffed the Will as it waddled after Arthur.

Out on the walkway, Arthur was already trying the door on the left. It opened easily enough, but the cell beyond was completely empty and quite dark, illuminated only by the spill of light from the walkway lanterns. Arthur dashed in, quickly scanned the room, and dashed out again.

"The other one!" he said. He tried to keep his voice down, but it still echoed.

The echo was answered by a shout from below. A harsh, powerful voice that was not Tom's. It echoed up from a point not as far below as Arthur would have hoped. Perhaps only three or four levels down.

"Captain! Did you hear that?"

"What?" came the reply from Tom, while Arthur and Suzy crept along to the next door, gently slid back the bolt, and pushed open the door. There was a light inside this cell, and Arthur immediately felt more hopeful. They would find the weirdway quickly and get away, at least for the time being.

"That was no Nithling! It must not have eaten the other intruders!" the voice continued.

"Let us deal with the Nithling, Lord Tuesday," said Tom. "It is strong, and grows stronger. We must find it first."

"Come here, Nithling!" roared the voice, which Arthur now knew must belong to Grim Tuesday. "I do not have time to waste searching for miscreants!"

He growled out something else, then more clearly shouted, "By the power of the Second Key, all intruders stand before me!"

Arthur felt unseen hands tug at him, dragging him back towards the nearest steps down. Suzy also took several steps back, a look of surprise on her face. Only the Will appeared unaffected. It stood to Arthur's left, watching him struggle as his Immaterial Boots slid backwards across the woven iron floor.

Arthur grimaced and threw himself forward. But he

just fell face-first onto the cold iron and began to slide back, as if dragged by invisible captors. He tried hooking his fingers through the mesh of the walkway floor, but had to let go before they were broken or torn off.

Flailing wildly for some other handhold, Arthur touched the Will's tail. As soon as he did, the dragging force disappeared. Arthur immediately gripped the tail hard.

"How dare you!" squealed the Will, its high-pitched voice echoing out into the central void.

Arthur didn't reply. He reached out and grabbed Suzy's hand as she was dragged past. She stopped too and started to crawl back.

"Unhand my tail!" squealed the Will. It turned on Arthur and tried to scratch him, but he kept his grip and jumped behind it.

"I'm not letting go until we go through the weirdway in that cell," gasped Arthur as he jumped again, Suzy jumping with him. She managed to get a grip directly on the Will's tail as well.

"This is outrageous behavior. I protest!"

"Who is that?" bellowed Grim Tuesday. His shout was followed by heavy footsteps ringing on the iron steps.

"Hurry up!" snapped Arthur to the Will. "You don't want to meet Grim Tuesday either, do you?"

The bear turned again and sped into the cell far faster than Arthur had seen it move before. The two children barely hung on, both running hunched over and scraping the door frame.

Arthur kicked the door shut with his foot, jarring his bad leg. He could hear Grim Tuesday's shouts reverberating outside as he hastily looked around the room. It was mostly empty, but there was an armchair sitting opposite two exquisite clocks on the wall: an ornate cuckoo clock made of finely sculpted gold, and a very simple, small ivory dial set in a walnut frame.

"Let go, let go, let go!" whined the Will. "I insist that you let go."

Arthur looked at Suzy, then tentatively loosened his grip. When they weren't struck by invisible forces, they both let go completely and stepped well back to get clear of the Will's claws and to look at the two clocks.

"If you've rumpled my fur, I shall send you the cleaning bill," said the Will as it curled around to inspect its tail.

Arthur ignored it. Instead he stretched up and touched the door of the cuckoo clock. It was solid gold, with an emerald-set door handle. Arthur opened it and was not surprised to find the door expanding as he pulled it, stretching down and across till there was no sign of the clock. Instead there was a normal-sized doorway in the wall, leading to a dark corridor whose walls, floor, and ceiling rippled as if they were made of stretched cloth rather than the solid stone they otherwise appeared to be.

"Come on!" Arthur held the door open for Suzy. Strangely, it still felt as if he was reaching up to hold a tiny clock door. "Claws, come on!"

"How many times must I repeat myself, you may address me as —" the Will started to say. It made no move towards the weirdway.

Before he could finish, Arthur suddenly slapped his hand to his mouth and groaned, as the now-familiar ache struck. Tom had used his harpoon, a fact confirmed by a shriek of agony from Soot and another inarticulate bellow from Grim Tuesday. It sounded like they were all very close.

"Go through!" screamed Arthur in frustration as the Will turned around to inspect its tail again.

Then Grim Tuesday shouted again, from right outside the door.

"Finish the Nithling, Captain! I'll fix the other thieves!"

Chapter Nineteen

Grim Tuesday's shout finally galvanized the Will into action. The sun bear shot into the weirdway and Arthur dived after it. He had a momentary glimpse of the cell door opening and the shadow of Grim Tuesday falling on the armchair. Then the cuckoo clock reassembled itself, closing the weirdway.

Arthur shivered. He did not want to meet Grim Tuesday without the Will's help. He needed to be taught the spells or incantations he would need to wrest the Second Key from the unfaithful Trustee.

The Will had already caught up to Suzy. Arthur ran after them both, steadying himself with his hands as he wobbled from side to side. This weirdway was even more fluid underfoot than the one he'd used in the Lower House to get to Mister Monday.

It was a lot shorter too. Arthur came to the end and ran straight out without even realizing that the darkness was the exit, not another turn. He stumbled against Suzy and the sun bear, then fell over a waist-high palm tree.

"Tuesday's in the cell," gasped Arthur as he pulled himself up on the palm, shredding most of its fronds. He could still see the weirdway exit, a strange inky doorway standing between two twelve-foot palm trees. "How do we shut the weirdway?" he asked.

"Blood ought to do it," said Suzy. She got out her knife and then, before Arthur could do anything, suddenly gripped his hand tight and stuck the point of the blade into his thumb. "A Day's blood, that is. Yours. Sorry about that. Bung some in."

Arthur flicked a few drops of blood at the dark doorway. Instead of going through, they splattered as if on glass. The weirdway gave a strange, cooing sigh that made Arthur step back as it closed in on itself, leaving only air between the palm trees.

Arthur looked around. The air was clean and bright, and they were surrounded by healthy-looking palms and carefully tended shrubs with pale pink trefoil flowers. For a moment he thought they were out of the Far Reaches altogether. Then he saw the wall of the Treasure Tower and the sparkle of the pyramid glass.

"Yep," said Suzy, noting his look. "We're in the garden around the Tower. Still inside the pyramid."

"We'd better find somewhere to hide," said Arthur. "What's that?"

He pointed up at the pyramid wall. It was hard to see through the shining glass, but somewhere in the distance Arthur could just make out big red-bursting flares that had to be very bright to make it through the smog. They were exploding near the ceiling of the Far Reaches and then drifting back down.

"Rockets," said Suzy. "Ooh, that was a good one!"

"Why . . . who would be firing rockets?" Arthur asked. He tilted his head to catch a distant, muffled noise. "I can hear bells too. Electric bells, like the elevator bells. Lots of them, all going off at once. Like the fire alarm at school . . ."

He looked at Suzy and said, "Those rockets are distress signals. The bells are alarms."

"Grim Tuesday's problem," said Suzy, with a shrug. She started to push through a line of thick bushes to see if there was a good place to lurk.

"It must be Nothing," said Arthur. "That's what everyone's afraid of."

"I'm not afraid of Nothing," said the Will. "Or anything else. Nothing cannot divert me from my duty."

"You should be afraid," Arthur warned. He was sick of this part of the Will. It was all bluster and wind. "Dame Primus was afraid of Nothing. I'm afraid of Nothing, like anyone with any sense. What if it all breaks out and destroys the foundations of the House and the whole . . . everything . . . the complete universe?"

"The Architect's work is far too superior for that to happen," said the Will smugly. "You need not worry on that score."

"You've been locked up for ten thousand years," Arthur pointed out angrily. "Grim Tuesday has dug a huge great Pit into the foundations here in the Far Reaches, right into Nothing. The Atlas says it is a great danger to the House — and I bet it knows more than you."

"The Atlas?" asked the Will, sitting up and losing its supercilious look. "You have *The Compleat Atlas of the House*?"

"Yes, I do." Arthur took it out and flashed it in front of the Will's nose like a police badge, then thrust it back in his pocket. "Because whether I like it or not, I am the heir to this whole mess!"

"Ah, perhaps I have been a little too rigorous in applying the principles laid down at my creation," the sun bear said with a couple of delicate coughs. "If I might make a closer examination of —"

"Arthur! Take a look at this!"

Arthur pushed through the bushes. Suzy was standing

on a long stone bench, looking out over a well-manicured hedge towards the eastern side of the glass pyramid.

"Get down!" Arthur called nervously. "He'll see us."

"Come and have a look!" answered Suzy.

Arthur glanced around, then jumped up, knowing from past experience that Suzy wouldn't get down until he took a look at whatever it was she wanted him to see.

"I think Grim Tuesday has got a whole lot of new problems," said Suzy, pointing to the border between the windswept clean air and the ceiling-high wall of smog.

Arthur stared. Through the swirling edge of the smog, he saw the fringe of a great crowd. Hundreds and hundreds, maybe even thousands, of Denizens were marching north, towards the station and the elevators. They were waving their leather aprons as they marched, throwing them in the air and trampling upon them.

Closer to the pyramid, a few dozen Overseers were running in all directions. A few ran towards the glass wall. Arthur could see they were shouting, probably to Grim Tuesday, for help, though he could only hear the ringing bells and the deeper, rough noise of the crowd.

"The register of indentured workers," he said. "It *was* destroyed by the sun!"

"Sure was." Suzy took out the indenture ticket from around her neck and looked at it. All the columns had reset to zero. Suzy took it off, bit it with her teeth to start a tear, then ripped it to pieces.

"I can make another register," said a harsh voice behind them. "The other Days will sell me more workers. It is merely an annoyance."

Arthur spun around. Even though the boy was standing on a bench, Grim Tuesday was taller. A hard-faced man with no eyebrows, his arms were corded with muscle, and his leather jerkin was torn near the heart with the telltale marks of a Nothing burn upon his chest. He wore gloves of flexible silver metal, bound with golden bands.

"I . . . I am the Rightful Heir," said Arthur, though his mouth was suddenly dry. "I claim the Second Key and Mastery of the Far Reaches."

Grim Tuesday's eyes narrowed. "You are the boy Penhaligon."

"Yes. I am Arthur Penhaligon. Give me the Second Key and . . . and I will be merciful."

"I do not recognize your claim," said Grim Tuesday with finality. He raised his right hand and made a chopping motion. Though he didn't come any closer, Arthur felt a savage blow strike his chest. He was knocked backwards over the bench, and crashed down to the grass behind.

Arthur lay there, stunned and wheezing.

I have to get up. I have to get up and get away. I have to —

Before he could get up, Grim Tuesday stood above him. This time he raised his left hand and made a claw.

Arthur covered his eyes with his arm and cried out.

I hope it's quick. I hope Dad and Mom will be okay and they keep the house and everything. I hope Michaeli gets to university. The plague had better not come back. Suzy should run right now, she might make it. If Nothing bursts out, everyone will die anyway. The Will should do what it's supposed to do. I tried my best. I tried to do the right thing and sometimes evil does win anyway no matter what you do. . . .

"Before I extract your heart and gild it for my . . . depleted store of treasures," Grim Tuesday said, "I want you to give me the Atlas. Take it from your pocket and hand it to me."

Arthur moved his arm and opened his eyes. His mind was racing furiously again, but his thoughts were more concentrated.

"No," he said.

The Atlas must be like the Key. Grim Tuesday can't take it, even from my dead body. It has to be given freely.

"Give it to me," Grim Tuesday ordered, without inflection. He might not have even heard Arthur. He clawed the air with his hand, and Arthur felt his heart stabbed all around by a thousand needles.

"No, I won't." Arthur raised his voice and half-shouted and half-sobbed out, "Will! I call upon you as the Bearer of the Atlas and the Rightful Heir to do your . . . do your job. Just do . . . do what you're supposed to do. . . ." he finished in a whisper.

"Give me the Atlas!" roared Grim Tuesday. "Why am I thwarted at every turn?!"

"Cos you're a rotten bastard," said Suzy as she popped out from the hedge and swung a large paving stone at the back of his head. But she would have done better not to speak. Grim Tuesday spun like a top, a blur of motion, and smashed the stone to powder with his fist. Suzy was also caught by the blow, flying through the air to smack into a palm tree. She struck with enough force to snap its trunk, and fell down with it.

"Now, Penhaligon, the Atlas!"

"No," whispered Arthur. "You give me the Key."

"You shall know pain," threatened the Grim. "Unspeakable pain, until you give me the Atlas."

"Ahem!"

Grim Tuesday looked surprised by the interruption.

He glanced around at normal head height, but it wasn't until the second "ahem!" that he saw the Will near his feet. His eyes narrowed and he clenched his fists.

"What?!" Grim Tuesday raged. "You, *here*! I shall soon fix that!"

"I think not," said the Will, and for once Arthur was glad to hear its stuffy, self-satisfied tone. "You tricked me once, but not again. And I have taken the precaution of enlisting assistance."

The bushes parted and Tom strode out, his harpoon in his hand. He nodded curtly at Grim Tuesday and reached down to help Arthur up.

"You are bound to me, Captain," snarled Grim Tuesday, raising both his hands. "By the power of the Second Key —"

"Which I now officially place in dispute," announced the Will. "I revoke your status of Trustee, pending further inquiry."

Grim Tuesday shook his head. "You cannot. I will not allow it! I do not allow anyone to take things away from me! What is mine is mine forever."

"Your sooty old eyebrow proved that one wrong when it ate up a bunch of stuff," said Suzy, staggering over. Her nose was bleeding but otherwise she seemed to be all right. Grim Tuesday took a step towards her and raised his hand, but did not persist when Tom made a slight motion with his harpoon.

"Your wishes are immaterial, Lord Tuesday," declared the Will. "I have spoken. While I am not ready to pronounce on the matter of a Rightful Heir, it is clear that you cannot continue to wield the power of the Second Key."

"You must allow it," said Grim Tuesday with cold satisfaction. He pointed at the bursting rockets up in the smoggy regions. "Those are distress signals from the depths of my Pit. The bells confirm it, as will the screams of my former workers. Nothing is breaking out. Only I can stem it, and I must have the power of the Key to do so. But I know when to cut my losses. You may all leave my domain. I shall not prevent you."

"The outbreak of Nothing is not my concern," continued the Will. "I shall establish an inquiry into the Rightful Heir, and once I have examined all the relevant documents and heard from material witnesses, whoever is granted the Second Key, whether it is returned to your trust or not, shall deal with the Nothing. We must not be too hasty. Prudence is a virtue, as I always say."

This speech was somewhat lost as everyone else was

staring up at the distress rockets and the gobbets of Nothing that were already beginning to fall down upon the pyramid, despite the cleansing winds.

"There's no time for an inquiry," said Tom. "Declare Arthur the heir. He must go down and repel the Nothing. Grim Tuesday's day is done."

The sun bear sighed and seemed about to launch into another speech when a particularly large gobbet plummeted onto the glass a few hundred feet above. It ran down the side and joined several other gobbets, which writhed and coiled together until they became a Nithling. A large Nithling, with a sort of human head and torso upon a cricket's body, all of it covered in stiff, rod-like red hair. It fiddled its back legs together, then set about punching holes in the glass with the spikes on its elbows.

"One here, a thousand down below," said Grim Tuesday. "And raw Nothing everywhere, eating away at the foundations of this House. Confirm me in my power, Most Excellent Testament, and I shall secure those foundations as I have always done."

"You dug into them for your own greedy purposes, using Denizens as slaves!" Arthur pointed out with indignation. He took a deep breath, the deepest he'd ever managed, and looked down at the Will. "I don't want to be the Heir," he continued. "I don't want the Second Key. I really don't want to go and deal with the Nothing. But I have to, because I was in the wrong place at the wrong time. When Dame Primus picked me, I had to do the right thing — and I have to try to keep on doing it. You don't want to confirm me as the Heir, but I think you have to do the right thing too, so I can at least attempt to put things right."

"I don't want to make a mistake," said the Will softly. "Better not to make a decision than to make a mistake."

"The whole House is going to fall down if you don't make a decision!" Arthur argued. "Everything the Architect made will return to Nothing. You have to choose me . . . or Grim Tuesday, and Grim Tuesday has already gone against the Architect's Will."

The Nithling above stopped making holes and started punching the side of the pyramid. The glass didn't shatter, but cracks began to appear.

The Will stood up on its hind legs. The sun blaze upon its chest grew brighter and brighter, and its fur became less furlike and more full of words. It grew larger, the words spreading out, weaving a larger body. It changed shape, continuing to grow, though it still remained a bear.

"I will be strong," it said. The blaze on its chest turned black and the words that made it up darkened and became furlike once more. It now stood almost as tall as Grim Tuesday, and was twice his bulk. No longer a sun bear, but an imperial grizzly of forbidding aspect. "I will stand by my decision with tooth and claw. I am the Second Part of the Will of the Architect, and I say the Second Key must be —"

Just then, a huge square of glass exploded, and the half-insect Nithling leaped down with a chittering scream.

Chapter Twenty

Huge shards of glass came falling down, shining in the artificial sunlight from the panels in the ceiling high above. The Nithling fell between the shards, screaming its strange insectoid scream.

For an instant, everyone stood still, staring up. Then Arthur dived under the stone bench just as Suzy dived from the opposite direction. The Will grabbed a palm tree and uprooted it, holding it over its head like an umbrella.

Grim Tuesday stood his ground, raised his hands, and shouted . . . but nothing happened. His mouth gaped in surprise, for he had forgotten that the Will had revoked his power over the Second Key.

Tom spun his harpoon above his head and shouted a word in the strange rasping language he used for his magic. Arthur and Suzy clapped their hands over their ears, but it was no good. The pain struck them, eating into their jawbones as the harpoon shone with its arctic glow. The light caught the falling glass, and suddenly it wasn't glass anymore, but a great wave of freezing seawater.

The wave crashed down, sweeping Arthur and Suzy out from under the bench. It carried them about ten yards away, depositing them all tossed together against a stand of trees.

Both Grim Tuesday and Tom had managed to stand against the wave. Now they faced the Nithling, which jumped at Tuesday, gripping his jerkin with its spiky insectoid legs as it raised its elbows to spike into his head.

Tom raised his harpoon, but could not strike without spearing Grim Tuesday as well. But his intervention was not needed. Even without the power of the Second Key, Grim Tuesday was a mighty Denizen. He gripped the Nithling's arms and with a sound like a lobster being cracked open, he split the thing completely in half. He threw the remains into an ornamental pool, where the thing's Nothing-rich blood bubbled away.

Grim Tuesday snorted, bent down, and wiped his gauntlets clean on the grass. Arthur and Suzy straightened themselves out, and the Will thrust its tree umbrella back into the ground.

"As I was saying," it boomed, "the Second Key will go to the winner of an appropriate contest, the two contestants being Arthur Penhaligon and Grim Tuesday."

"What?!" exclaimed Arthur. He looked up at the mass of gobbets floating around above the pyramid and the distant flare of the distress rockets coming out of the Pit. "We haven't got time —"

"I am ready for any competition," declared Grim Tuesday, clapping his gloves together. They sounded like crashing cymbals and didn't do anything for Arthur's confidence. "What is it to be? Mortal combat?"

"Naturally not," said the Will. "In keeping with the powers of the Second Key, it shall be a contest of making. In light of the urgency of the Nothing situation, it shall be an expedited competition. Each of you shall be allowed three minutes with the Second Key to create a work of art. The creator of the greater work will win the competition and be declared either the Trustee or the Rightful Heir to the Second Key and shall assume the Mastery of the Far Reaches."

"But I've never even used the Second Key!" protested Arthur.

"Wot a swizzle!" said Suzy. "I've played fairer games of Uncle Jack."

"I have made my decision!" roared the Will. Arthur opened his mouth to protest again, but didn't. As a huge grizzly, the Will was considerably harder to take lightly. "All that remains is to appoint a judge. Naturally it must be someone of appropriate rank —"

He was interrupted by another fall of Nithlings.

Three things that looked like a cross between a lizard and a monkey came sliding down the pyramid and fell through the gaping hole.

Tom's harpoon leaped into the air with its crackling noise and impaled all three Nithlings, transforming them into harmless puffs of dark vapor. Arthur and Suzy clenched their teeth, but the effect of the harpoon wasn't so severe when it struck at a distance.

"The appropriate rank and power," continued the Will crossly. "One of the other Days would be suitable if it were not for the fact —"

"They're a bunch of traitors," whispered Suzy.

"Hurry up!" Arthur and Grim Tuesday implored together. They glared at each other as they spoke. Arthur did not drop his eyes, though it took all his willpower to meet Grim Tuesday's angry stare.

"Quiet!" bellowed the Will. "To cut straight to the heart of the matter, the contest will be judged by the Mariner. Who wants to go first?"

"I will go first," declared Grim Tuesday. "But only if you will restore my right to the Key's powers."

"For three minutes," the Will conceded. "No more. Captain, stand ready for any trickery."

Arthur was not even mildly surprised to see the grizzly bear pull a large pocket watch out of its nonexistent waistcoat. The Will fiddled with one of the several knobs on the watch, then raised one hairy paw and waved at Grim Tuesday.

"Begin!"

Grim Tuesday smiled and raised his hands. Arthur and Suzy flinched, but Tom did not seem perturbed.

The Trustee muttered something under his breath. Arthur tried to hear what he said, in case it was some secret to using the Key. Which, he now guessed, must be one of the strange silvered metal gloves that Tuesday wore. Or maybe both gloves, in the same way that the First Key had been a minute hand and a clock hand, which united together as a sword.

A gobbet of Nothing came hurtling down through the hole in the pyramid, summoned down by Grim Tuesday. He caught it easily and held it in both hands, in front of his face. He directed his gaze upon it, and the Nothing lost its darkness and began to shine. Grim Tuesday started to shuffle his hands around the shining ball, still muttering.

It shone brighter and brighter as the Grim moved his hands in short, sharp gestures. He kept talking under his breath, but Arthur couldn't hear him. Even with his starhood still on, he couldn't look directly at whatever Tuesday was doing to the gobbet.

The Will's watch chimed, three falling notes.

"Time!" called the grizzly.

Grim Tuesday grasped the dazzling object he'd made and lowered it to the park bench. The light slowly faded to reveal a fourteen-inch-high tree made of precious metals. Its trunk and branches were platinum shot with gold, and its thousand leaves were beaten gold, veined with silver. The leaves caught the breeze coming down through the hole in the pyramid and made a sound like a windswept xylophone.

It was the most beautiful object Arthur had ever seen. But only a fleeting smile of satisfaction passed over Grim Tuesday's face.

"Arthur can do better than that standing on 'is head," said Suzy, but her heart wasn't in it.

"Give Arthur the Second Key," instructed the Will.

Grim Tuesday scowled and slowly stripped off the silver gauntlets. When they were off, he held them for several seconds before reluctantly handing them to Arthur.

As Arthur took the gauntlets, two yellow envelopes materialized in the air above them. Grim Tuesday snatched them out of the air. He grunted as he read the address on the first one and threw it at Arthur's feet. The second one he ripped open and read quickly. Then he turned to the Will.

"Yan warns that the whole eastern buttress of the lower Pit is leaking Nothing," Grim Tuesday reported. "It will fail within the hour if I am not there to repair it! End this ridiculous contest now and return the Key to me!"

Arthur put the surprisingly light gauntlets under his arm and picked up the other telegram, which was addressed to him as Master of the Lower House. He opened it and read:

ARTHUR SHOW WILL ATLAS HELP
COMING HOLD ON BE BRAVE DAME
PRIMUS

"The competition has begun and it must finish," the Will was saying as Arthur read the telegram. "Arthur, you must begin immediately."

Arthur handed the telegram to Suzy and put on the gauntlets. While they appeared to be made out of flexible silver metal bound with gold, they didn't feel cold or metallic. In fact, they were soft and warm and felt very comfortable. Arthur found himself standing straighter once they were on, and he felt more confident.

I bet the Second Key works just like the First Key or the Atlas, he thought. *I just have to think what I want them to do and say it aloud. That's why Grim Tuesday was muttering —*

"Begin!"

"Get me a gobbet of Nothing!" called out Arthur as he raised his hands and looked up to the broken pane of the pyramid.

"A small gobbet!" he hastily added as he saw several huge gobbets head towards him.

They swerved aside, and a football-sized gobbet of Nothing came sailing down through the hole. Arthur raised his hands to catch it, fighting down his apprehension and all thoughts of what might happen if he fumbled and it landed on his unprotected face.

He didn't fumble the catch. Once he had the gobbet firmly in his grasp, he went to work. He'd already thought of what he would make, ironically inspired by the sound of Grim Tuesday's precious-metal tree.

Arthur knew he had no hope of matching Grim Tuesday's artistry with a sculpture or a painting or anything like that. But what he intended to do might not work either. It all depended on what criteria Tom was judging the results on.

"My xylophone," he muttered to himself, as he pictured it in his head. "The one Dad and Mom gave me for my sixth birthday, that Dad borrowed all the time. With wooden bars on a metal frame, and two mallets."

He tried to stretch and shape the gobbet with his gauntlets as he focused his mind on remembering the xylophone. It was hard to tell if it was working, but the gobbet was shining, though not as much as it had for Grim Tuesday. Or perhaps it was, Arthur saw, as he took a swift look at everyone else shielding their eyes.

But I can only spend a minute getting this xylophone, Arthur thought desperately. *How do I know when it's ready?*

His fingers twitched without Arthur meaning them to. *Was that a sign from the Key?*

Arthur's fingers twitched again. Taking the second twitch as a definite sign, Arthur gently put the glowing former gobbet onto the ground and stepped back. The glow faded, and there on the grass was Arthur's xylophone, with its two mallets.

"Is that it?" asked Suzy.

In answer, Arthur clumsily knelt down and picked up the mallets. He took a deep breath, something he wasn't able to do the last time he played, and immediately started the tune that he'd spent two years composing, from when he was eight to almost ten. It was his thank-you song, composed for Bob and Emily, to express his gratitude for them adopting him. It started off sad and slow and quiet, and got happy and loud.

He didn't think it was the greatest song in the world, but he'd composed it himself, and it did express something of what he felt when he learned he was adopted, how he'd come to terms with it, and how grateful he was to be in a family that loved him and accepted him and treated him no differently than any of his other siblings.

He finished just as the Will called, "Time!"

The last fading note of the xylophone merged with the watch's third chime.

There was silence for a moment, then Grim Tuesday gave a scornful laugh and held out his hand for the gauntlets. But the Will stepped between him and Arthur.

"We must await the adjudication," it said sniffily. "Captain?"

Tom looked down at Grim Tuesday's gold-and-platinum tree and scratched his chin.

"That's a beautiful piece of work," he said. "There's not many that could work a masterpiece out of Nothing. A real work of genius."

Arthur's head sank. He'd gambled on what he'd heard about Grim Tuesday's nature and what Tom might think was important, and he'd lost. Even if Grim Tuesday did let them go as he'd promised, and if he went down and stopped the Nothing breaking out, Arthur's family would still lose everything. Maybe the whole world would slide into an economic depression, and all because Arthur couldn't do —

"A real work of genius," Tom repeated. "Only not *your* genius, Lord Tuesday."

"I made it!" roared Grim Tuesday. "I wrought it from Nothing!"

"But it is a copy," insisted Tom. "I have seen it before, though you have replaced silver with platinum. It was in the workshop of del Moro in Rome, upon the old Earth, when I was master of a Genoese trader, buying candlesticks and silver-gilt basins on my own account. I saw it again, in a much later time, in the collection of Froment-Meurice. I suppose the original is now in your Treasure Tower."

Tom turned to Arthur and continued. "Arthur's tune, on the other hand, I have not heard, and I have heard many songs. It made me think of returning home from a long, lonely voyage to a glad welcome, but also gave me the joy of boarding a new vessel, the deck fresh-scrubbed and the tide about to turn. I declare Arthur the winner of the competition!"

"No!" screamed Grim Tuesday. "No!"

He threw himself at Arthur and his pallid, wiry fingers gripped Arthur's hands, lifting the boy bodily off the ground. But when the Grim tried to pull off the gloves, they wouldn't budge. Arthur's arms were almost wrenched out of their sockets and he was flung all over the place as Grim Tuesday raged and pulled, till he was restrained by Tom and the Will.

Even those two powerful individuals had trouble holding Grim Tuesday back, till Arthur held out his palms and yelled, "Stop!"

The gloves wriggled against his skin, and Arthur felt the zap of an electric charge cross the air. He didn't see anything, but Grim Tuesday suddenly stopped struggling and became still. As still as a statue.

"You must claim the Second Key properly, milord," said the Will rather humbly. "Repeat after me: I, Arthur, anointed Heir to the Kingdom, claim this Key and with it the Mastery of the Far Reaches. I claim it by blood and bone and contest, out of truth, in testament, and against all trouble."

Arthur quietly repeated the claim. His left side twinged as he spoke, reminding him of when he'd claimed Monday's key. He also felt the gloves move on his hands, wriggling about till they fitted most comfortably.

"Well done, Arthur! Like a walk in the park!" declared Suzy. The fact that she could hardly stand up and her nose and chin were caked in blood somewhat lessened the effect of this statement. She clapped Arthur on the back, making him lose his balance and once more reminding him of his misshapen leg.

"You shall not have long to enjoy your triumph," whispered Grim Tuesday. "When the eastern buttress fails, Nothing will burst forth and destroy us all!"

Chapter Twenty-one

Arthur closed his eyes for a second and tried to summon up all his remaining strength. Grim Tuesday was defeated. He had the Second Key. But he felt no thrill of victory, because he still hadn't won. He couldn't rest, or go home, or do anything he really wanted. He had to take on yet another huge problem that he was quite unsuited for and totally unprepared to deal with.

"I'll fix the buttress," he said. "Will you tell me how to do it?"

Grim Tuesday snarled and spat at Arthur's feet.

"I have lost the Key, my domain, and all my treasures," he growled. "But I shall have the satisfaction of returning to the void with them around me, and my enemies in confusion!"

"That means *no*," said Suzy helpfully.

"I suppose I'll just have to work it out." Arthur looked out through the glass wall to the smog-shrouded Pit. "Only, how do I get down there quickly enough?"

"You can't," sneered Grim Tuesday. "The buttress

can hold for less than an hour, yet even my train takes days to reach the face of the Pit!"

"But you were going to get there," said Arthur. "You said you would fix the buttress. So there has to be a way."

"You can't fly," said Suzy as she looked up towards the ceiling. "Not with all those gobbets floating around."

"Tom? Do you know a way to the bottom of the Pit?"

"Nay, save for the Improbable Stair," replied Tom. "But it would be very dangerous, so close to so much Nothing. The Stair skirts Nothing closely everywhere, but never so close as here. I doubt that Grim Tuesday would risk the Stair himself."

"You can compel Grim Tuesday to answer your questions with the Key," said the Will. "It will harm him, but that is of little account. You must not allow Nothing to break out. I suggest you move swiftly, milord Arthur."

"If you'd helped me in the first place, then we'd have more time," Arthur pointed out bitterly.

Something caught his eye over in the smog. A flicker of light, then another. It was not the red flare of the distress rockets, but steady beams of light coming down from the ceiling.

"Elevators!" Suzy exclaimed, following his look.

"Dame Primus, I guess," said Arthur. "Late and useless as usual."

He turned back to Grim Tuesday. The Denizen seemed shorter than he had been and less fierce. Diminished in all respects.

Arthur reluctantly raised his hands, then dropped them as a thought struck him.

"Elevators! There must be an elevator to the bottom of the Pit! Where is it?"

Grim Tuesday didn't answer.

"I don't want to do anything nasty to you," said Arthur. "But I will use the Key on you if I have to. Is there an elevator to the Pit?"

"Do your worst," said Grim Tuesday. "I care not."

Arthur shook his head, then raised his right hand and pointed his index finger at Grim Tuesday.

"By the power of the Second Key, I command you to answer my questions truthfully."

Once again Arthur felt the static electric shock. This time he saw sparkling ultra-fine tendrils of light extend from his finger to Grim Tuesday's head, winding into his ears and nose.

Grim Tuesday grimaced and shook himself like a dog coming out of water, but did not speak.

"Is there an elevator from here to the bottom of the Pit?"

"Yes," growled the Grim through clenched teeth. "Emergency elevator. Small. Only for me."

"Where is it?"

Grim Tuesday clenched his teeth still tighter, but his right arm rose up and one finger uncurled. A bronze button appeared out of nowhere. The Grim tried not to press it, but his hand lunged forward. As the button depressed, an electric bell rang and a second later a narrow elevator, no larger than a phone box, erupted out of the ground.

Only Grim Tuesday was ready for it. He toppled forward, but the elevator door was not quite open. Rebounding from it, the Denizen was seized again by Tom and the Will. He did not struggle.

Arthur looked at the elevator. As well as being very narrow, it looked a lot worse for wear. There were many tiny holes like acid burns all over the plush leather interior, and the wooden paneling in the ceiling was blackened and burned.

"Let's go!" said Suzy. She stepped shakily inside, still partially stunned by her encounter with the palm tree. Once in, she took up more than half the space. The elevator was clearly made to just fit the lean body of Grim Tuesday.

"No," said Arthur. "I think I have to go alone."

"We'll fit," said Suzy. "I'll breathe in."

Arthur shook his head and pulled her sleeve. His gauntlet tingled against his skin and a surprised Suzy found herself unable to resist. Before she could jump back in, Arthur jumped in himself and slid the door closed.

"Wait, Arthur! You might need my —"

Her voice was cut off as Arthur pressed the button with the down arrow clearly marked upon it. The elevator lurched, knocking Arthur off his feet. He bounced off both walls, then managed to wedge himself into the corner.

"All the way down *again*?" asked a disembodied voice. "You know this elevator's only good for a few trips down *there*."

"All the way to the bottom," instructed Arthur. The elevator increased its downwards velocity, and Arthur felt himself rising up towards the ceiling, as if he were in free fall. While he was wedging himself even more firmly into the corner, he added, "What do you mean *again*? When was this elevator last used?"

"Half an hour ago," said the voice. "Fair gave me a turn. Haven't had to run this elevator for more than twenty years. Beautifully mothballed it was, everything sealed up, waxed, and greased. Look at it now!"

"Who was the passenger?" asked Arthur. Who could possibly have gone to the bottom of the Pit half an hour ago?

"Dunno," said the voice. "He had the proper authority, though. From on high."

"You didn't ask *me* for any authority."

"You got the Second Key, haven't you, sir? Hold on, we're almost there."

The elevator slowed dramatically. Arthur slid down the wall and onto the floor, his stomach attempting to run out through his Immaterial Boots. Then after a series of frightening bangs and lurches, the elevator came to a stop and the door slid open.

"Bottom of the Pit, thank you!" said the voice. Arthur stepped out into darkness. The door slid shut, and the elevator vanished.

For a frightening second it seemed like Arthur was trapped in total darkness. But as his eyes adjusted, he saw lanterns some small distance away. Then his gauntlets began to glow with a cool green light that slowly spread up his arms and all over his brightcoat and boots.

.

One of the lanterns bobbed nearer. Arthur hurried to meet it. As he got closer, he saw that the bearer was very short and broad. One of Grim Tuesday's Grotesques.

"You're only just in time, sir!" called the Grotesque hoarsely. "It's fair oozing Nothing —"

The Grotesque stopped as he realized that Arthur was not Grim Tuesday. A peculiar expression crossed his face — one of relief, sorrow, and a twist of anger.

"You're not the Master!"

"I am the Master of the Far Reaches now," said Arthur, holding up one clenched fist.

"The Grim . . . that would explain the indentured workers . . . I thought it had to do with all the Nothing. . . ." muttered the Grotesque. He appeared confused and kept shaking his head. Then he looked at Arthur and said plaintively, "I am Yan. Will you remake us as we were? As three, instead of seven?"

"I guess . . . I'll try," said Arthur. "Only first, you need to take me to this buttress that's about to break."

Yan shook his head again. "The buttress? We need not go anywhere. We are at its foot."

Arthur looked around, but could see only darkness beyond the circle of light from his own strange glow and Yan's lantern. But he could hear something off to his right. A kind of creaking, like the night wind in the trees at home.

"Cast a sunburst up about a thousand feet," said Yan hurriedly. "That is the first step, sir. You will remember to make us three?"

"Yes," said Arthur. "Uh, how . . . oh, never mind . . ."

He cupped his hands and concentrated on the gauntlets.

Sunburst, he thought. *A sunburst to fly up to a thousand feet and explode like the one I saw before. Hot and glorious, a miniature sun to shed light on everything down here and send the Nothing back into its holes —*

Something jetted out of his grasp, heading skyward at incredible speed. Arthur stared up after it, a shooting star that reached its thousand-foot-tall ceiling in a few seconds. He was still looking when it exploded into light. His star-hood saved him from the worst of it, but he still had to blink and cover his eyes with his arm.

He was just about to lift that arm and take a look around when Yan suddenly cried out. Arthur heard him fall and his lantern smash upon the stone.

Arthur instinctively jumped back. He saw Yan go sprawling, and he saw a tall, immaculately clad top-hatted

Denizen step forward and stab the Grotesque through the heart with a sword-cane that had a shining silver blade.

"He might have helped you repair the buttress," said the Denizen, his voice smooth and cultured, his handsome face unmoved by what he had just done. "And we can't have that, can we?"

"You killed him!"

The Denizen gave a small shrug.

"Perhaps. He is one-seventh of a higher being. He might recover. It is all rather academic, with Nothing about to overwhelm the entirety of creation."

He pointed with his sword-cane. Arthur flicked his head to look, but only for an instant, keeping his attention on that silver blade. In that moment, he saw that they were standing only yards from the foot of a vast wall that stretched as far as he could see to the left and right and up towards the sunburst. It was made of deep red bricks set in yellow mortar, but there were many dark cracks and lines of leaking Nothing among the bricks.

"I should give up if I were you, Arthur," said the Denizen. His voice was quite hypnotic and Arthur found himself listening intently. He wanted the voice to go on and on. "This is all beyond you. Much easier to give in to fate. Let the buttress fail, let Nothing wash away the House, the Secondary Realms —"

He lunged at Arthur's throat on the last word, but the Key was ready for him even though the Key's wielder was not. The gauntlets caught the blade, twisted and broke it. Then Arthur found himself plunging the broken end of the blade deep into the Denizen's red silk waistcoat.

"Ah, proof against the voice," sighed the Denizen as he backed away. He looked down at the golden blood that was trickling down his waistcoat. "A hit! One is enough to end the bout, by any rules. Now others shall take their turn!"

With that, he slapped a button that appeared in the air. The elevator sprang into visibility, its door open. The Denizen staggered into it. The doors closed and a beam of light shot up towards the far distant ceiling, well beyond sight.

Arthur stared at the fading beam, totally confused. The Denizen was obviously not one of Grim Tuesday's servants. Nor was he a Nithling. Or was he? Why did he want Nothing to destroy the House?

Where were the Nithlings, for that matter? Grim Tuesday had said, "One up here, a thousand down below."

Arthur turned back to look up at the buttress and

saw where the Nithlings were. They were hundreds of feet up the face of the buttress, clawing out bricks with their hands and claws and tentacles and talons. Thousands of them, swarming over the face of what Arthur now realized was effectively a dam wall.

A huge dam made of special bricks, holding back the great void of Nothing itself.

A leaking dam, getting weaker by the second.

A dam wall Arthur had to fix.

Bricks are no good, Arthur thought. *The Nithlings can pull out bricks. Reinforced concrete, that's what we need. Magical reinforced concrete.*

He raised his gauntleted hands and began to concentrate, muttering to himself.

"Bricks into reinforced concrete. Special reinforced concrete. Immaterial Concrete, like my boots but a thousand times stronger, a thousand times tougher."

He felt the gloves vibrate with the power of the Key, but when he looked up at the dam, there was no change. The streaks of thick, dark Nothing were spreading as the Nithlings splintered the mortar and crumbled the bricks.

Someone croaked something behind Arthur. He whirled around, ready for another attack. But it was only Yan, raising himself up on one elbow.

"Touch the bricks," Yan whispered. "Touch the bricks to transform them!"

Arthur nodded and ran towards the buttress. A brick sailed past his ear, and then another one struck his misshapen leg. He screamed and fell, holding his hands over his head.

"Key, protect me!"

The green glow in Arthur's brightcoat spun itself into a sphere all around him. More and more bricks came raining down, but when they hit the green barrier, they splintered into dust. Coughing and partially blinded, Arthur staggered forward and got both his palms onto the wall.

He looked up for a second, to see Nithlings of all shapes and sizes coming down towards him. Some of them flew, some simply jumped, some scuttled, and some ran as if the wall were horizontal rather than vertical. But none could get to him for at least thirty seconds, Arthur judged.

He leaned into the wall, resting all his weight on his palms, and once again thought of the dams he had seen, either in person or in pictures.

The biggest, strongest dam anywhere. Reinforced concrete. Reinforced Immaterial Concrete. Dozens of yards thick, on top of the existing brickwork. Impene-

trable. Impervious to Nothing. Too smooth for fingers, claws, talons, or tentacles, or teeth. A real dam wall. A mighty buttress! Built with the power of the Second Key!

Arthur felt that power flow from the gauntlets into his body and then out again. He was both a pool and a conduit. The power welled up inside him, then when he was full of it, it spilled over, back through his hands. He could feel the new dam wall building, the Immaterial Concrete spreading from his hands, expanding out like spilled ink upon a page.

"It's working!" he cried, just as a bullheaded Nithling landed heavily near him and rushed to the attack, its sharp horns aimed directly at his unprotected back.

Chapter Twenty-two

The Nithling fared no better than the bricks, for the Key had continued to divert some small part of its power to fulfill Arthur's spoken command. The boy felt a spray of something against the back of his neck, but it was not enough to distract him from his task.

Other Nithlings landed and charged, only to meet the same fate. None could prevail against the power of the Second Key. Many realized it and, instead of attacking, they fled, hoping to find some way into other parts of the House or the Secondary Realms. Others climbed higher up the buttress as the new wall rose. They tried desperately to pull out just one more brick, to erode one more line of mortar. Many were caught, as reinforcing metal wove its way around and through them, and were drowned by the rising columns of Immaterial Concrete.

Only one Nithling neither attacked, tried to pry a few bricks away, nor fled. A strange Nithling that watched Arthur from a place of concealment behind a many-holed boiler that had rolled down to its final resting place, here at the lowest part of the Pit.

The lurker did not look like any normal Nithling. If seen from the left side, it looked just like a boy. In fact it looked just like Arthur in his school uniform. But from the right side, it was a skeleton, bare bones of red ochre bereft of skin. Front-on, it was a hideous split-faced thing, half smiling boy and half grinning skull.

When it was clear that the buttress was going to be rebuilt and there was no chance of Nothing breaking through in the immediate future, the Skinless Boy laid himself down completely in the boiler and folded one fleshy hand and one bony one across his chest. He was in no hurry. The messenger who had come to watch his unusual birth had presented several interesting possibilities and opportunities, depending on what happened with the buttress. Arthur's success had not been considered likely by the messenger, but he had prepared for it and told the Skinless Boy what to do.

Arthur, unaware of his strange watcher, felt his fingers twitch. He looked up and saw his sunburst fading, but the concrete wall that he had made sparkled with starlight, and that was enough to see that it was complete. There was no sign of any leaking Nothing. No Nithlings. Only Yan, no longer propped up on one elbow, but sprawled in a heap.

The Grotesque was still breathing, but only just. He opened one eye as Arthur slowly walked over to him.

"No need to remake us now," he whispered. "Who'd have thought the Grim wrought so badly? One sword-thrust to slay all seven . . . We did not want to be what we became, Arthur. Remember that."

His eye clouded over and his head fell back. As it touched the ground, Arthur saw the Grotesque's face flicker and change, showing him the three handsome Denizens who had gone into the making of Grim Tuesday's seven students. Then it was just Yan's face again, cold and dead.

Arthur looked away. Now he was truly alone, in the very depths of the Pit. The sunburst was just a faint spark above, the shadows creeping up the dam wall.

He felt completely done in, too tired to do anything, even clean away the brick dust and the peculiar slime that coated his back and hair. His arms were sore too, as if he'd been carrying a heavy weight for a long time.

Arthur let his weariness carry him to the ground. He sat down, then lay on his back and looked up into the gathering darkness.

Light descended from above. A bell rang, and an elevator door opened.

"Going up," said the disembodied voice. "Least, I hope we are. Last trip down here for this elevator. All aboard who's coming aboard."

Arthur groaned and staggered to his feet.

He hobbled over to the lift and got in.

"This could be a bit tricky, sir," said the disembodied voice. "Taken some damage, this elevator. Not to mention that last passenger, with his emergency rise."

"Emergency rise?" asked Arthur with a yawn. "What's that?"

"Well, strictly speaking, this elevator only goes up to the top floor of the Far Reaches. But that last passenger went right through to the Atrium of the Lower House. He had the paperwork, of course, but it does terrible wear and tear to an elevator."

"Who was he?" asked Arthur sharply.

"Dunno. Someone important," said the voice. "Him as went down before you."

The elevator lurched and shuddered as Arthur thought about a suitable reply to that. Instead he wedged himself in the corner as the lift gathered speed.

"This could be a bit slow, sir," said the voice. "Would you care for some music? I can play the clarinet a bit. Something soft, you understand, nothing too strident . . ."

The elevator did take a long time to get back up. Several hours at least, though Arthur lost track, as he fell asleep listening to odd, disconnected, half-familiar tunes played not very well on a clarinet of highly variable volume.

He was rudely awakened by the lift's bell, and a stop that was more like an impact with a solid object above them than a controlled halt.

Arthur picked himself off the floor and staggered out of the elevator. He emerged blinking in the artificial sunlight to discover that the glass pyramid had entirely disappeared. The Treasure Tower had been partially whitewashed, and the palm tree gardens turned into a large expanse of lawn. Forty large white bell tents — almost the size of circus big tops — were set up in a circle around the Tower, and there were long lines of former indentured workers waiting outside them, each line stretching off into the smog. As far as Arthur could tell from the tables outside the tents and the groups of teacup-toting Denizens that were milling around between the lines, the tents were there to serve afternoon tea.

There was a reception committee waiting for Arthur, assembled in a semicircle around the elevator. Dame Primus was at the front, but there was also Monday's

Noon and at least a hundred armed Commissionaire Sergeants, Metal Commissionaires, Midnight Visitors, and others.

Suzy was sitting on the park bench, eating a particularly large chocolate éclair. She was once more dressed in her usual shambolic collection of clothes with her favorite squashed top hat. Arthur noticed she'd kept her Immaterial Boots, and the rolled-up bundle at her side must be her brightcoat.

Suzy waved. Arthur waved back.

Dame Primus seemed to think this was a more formal greeting to her. She saluted Arthur with the First Key, which was in its sword form. She was even taller than Arthur remembered, and imposingly dressed in some sort of uniform, all electric blue and gold lace, and a ridiculously tall fur hat like the British guardsmen wore outside Buckingham Palace. Her wings were not visible, but there was a kind of hint of them, a shining in the air above her tightly bound-back platinum hair.

"Welcome, Arthur," she boomed, her voice deep and penetrating but not quite as gravelly as it sometimes got. "Well done. Very well done."

"I'm tired," Arthur burst out. "I want to go home. I

want to have a long rest. I don't want to be bothered again for at least six years like you promised!"

"That is understood, Arthur. However —" Dame Primus began. Something about her voice made Arthur look at her more closely and interrupt.

"You're both of them now! I mean you're both parts of the Will!"

"Yes," said Dame Primus. "We are one, as was always the intention of the Architect. It was the unfaithful Trustees who broke me apart."

"Speaking of breaking things, I need you to fix my leg," said Arthur. "I can't go home like this."

"A hot towel, sir?" asked Sneezer, appearing at Arthur's elbow and making him jump. "You seem a little, *ahem*, disarrayed. Perhaps if I take your coat? And perhaps a cup of coffee? Or a ginger beer? And I'll just nip that earring out."

Arthur didn't even notice the earring's removal. He took the towel and wiped his face. For some reason he couldn't feel it, then he remembered the star-hood. He rolled that back, and Sneezer slipped off his brightcoat in one expert motion. When Arthur finally got it to his face, the hot towel was almost too hot, but it refreshed and woke him up a little. It also magically removed the soot, brick-dust, and slime from all parts of his body, even though he only wiped his face. He looked around and noticed that both Grim Tuesday and Tom were nowhere in sight.

"Where is Grim Tuesday? And Tom?"

"The Mariner has once again chosen to avoid responsibility in this House," sniffed Dame Primus. "He has left, probably to illegally enter the Secondary Realms. Naturally I have promulgated arrest orders for him should he return."

"But Tom helped me," Arthur protested. "You can't arrest him. And what about Grim Tuesday?"

"The Denizen formerly known as Grim Tuesday has been put to work," said Dame Primus. She pointed at the Treasure Tower. Arthur looked and saw a tall, bony figure in white overalls struggling with a huge tin of paint. An enormous paint roller, easily twenty feet wide, was propped up against the wall.

"There are many tasks awaiting our Lowest Assistant," said Dame Primus. "The top level of the Far Reaches will be rehabilitated first, then the Pit must be filled in — which his former Overseers will be employed to do — and the spring reestablished. Not to mention the original treasures he has stolen that must be returned to their proper places in the House or the Secondary

Realms. There is a great deal of work to be done, Arthur. Work that would benefit greatly from the presence of the true Master of both the Lower House and the Far Reaches. So I am very pleased to return the First Key —"

"No!" shouted Arthur. He pushed Sneezer's silver tray and proffered coffee cup aside and walked away. "Didn't you listen to anything I said? I want to fix my leg and go home, and then I don't want to be bothered again! Haven't I done enough?"

"You must control your temper," said Dame Primus. "It is not fitting for the Rightful Heir to have a temper tantrum in front of —"

"I am *not* having a temper tantrum," Arthur said as coldly as he could manage. "I am letting you know that I want my leg fixed and then I am going home."

"That would be extremely unwise," replied the Will. "You can only return if you give up the Second Key, and if you do that, you will be unprotected. The danger is even greater than before. It is clear that the other Days are exploiting loopholes in their Agreement and actively working against you. Superior Saturday's Dusk is believed to have been here, for example —"

"I think I met him," said Arthur. "He killed Yan, and all the Grotesques died. With a single thrust. But I wounded him and he ran away. For some reason he wanted to —"

"You see," interrupted the Will. "I even think that they might flout the Original Law and strike against you in the Secondary Realms."

"Well, you should try and stop them here," said Arthur. "I have to go home. I want my regular life back!"

"That is not possible," sighed the Will. "However, if you insist on returning, then it shall be so. But you must appoint a Steward for the Second Key, as before."

"Okay, I appoint you," said Arthur. He stripped off the gauntlets that were the Second Key and handed them to Dame Primus.

"This is most unorthodox," said Dame Primus. "But I suppose . . . repeat after me . . . 'I, Arthur, Lord of the Far Reaches, Master of the Lower House, Wielder of the Second and First Keys to the Kingdom . . .'"

Arthur gabbled the words. He had the curious sensation that if he could get away quickly enough then everything would be all right, that he wouldn't be caught up in anything else.

"I grant my faithful servant, the combined First and Second Parts of the Great Will of the Architect, all my powers, possessions, and appurtenances, to exercise on my behalf as Steward, until such time as I shall require them rendered unto me once more. There, finished!"

Dame Primus took the gauntlets and carefully put them on. They shed a ruby light as her fingers went in, and rose petals fell from her palms.

"A nice gesture," said Dame Primus approvingly.

"Can you fix my leg now?" asked Arthur anxiously. He pushed it forward so that its foreshortened length and twist were obvious.

Dame Primus bent down to examine it. She frowned and held out her hand. A pair of pince-nez appeared, which she fixed to the bridge of her nose before looking again.

"How did this happen?"

"I broke my leg falling on the pyramid," said Arthur. "Then I fixed it with the power of the First Key, the power that was left in my hands."

"Ah," said Dame Primus. "Then there is a problem."

"A problem?" whispered Arthur. "Can't you fix it?"

"I can use the First Key to reverse what you did. But then your leg will be broken, and as it will effectively have been broken by the Key, it cannot be mended by any magic that would not transform you completely."

"Transform me?"

"Into a Denizen. You would no longer be mortal, which I gather you still wish to be. The Architect knows why!"

Arthur thought about how much his leg had hurt when he'd hit the pyramid. He thought about his life. His regular life. He wanted it, every boring bit that he'd ever complained about. New school and all.

"If that's what it takes," he said slowly. "But I still want to go back. Only . . . if I can go straight back home, that would be good. I don't want to be lying around with a broken leg in the street."

"I am sure that can be arranged," said Dame Primus. "There is now no reason not to use the Front Door. In fact, I shall make a point of using it, and at the same time post warnings with the Lieutenant Keeper that you are to be left alone."

"The Lieutenant Keeper . . ." Arthur said, suddenly struck by a thought. "Does he come under the Lower House? I mean, he said something about there being no Captain Keeper for ten thousand years. Was that because of Monday not signing something? Why don't we . . . *you* just promote him?"

"The Captain and Lieutenant Keeper are appointed by all the Days," said Dame Primus. "The current Captain Keeper is merely missing, so cannot be replaced until his fate is determined, if it ever is."

"Oh," said Arthur. "I owe the Lieutenant Keeper a favor, so I thought maybe . . . also, there are a couple of Denizens who helped me here. If you can, give them good jobs. A new indentured called Japeth, who used to be a Thesaurus."

"A Thesaurus is always useful," said Dame Primus. She nodded to Monday's Noon, who bowed to Arthur and made a careful note in a little linen-bound notebook.

"And a Supply Clerk called Mathias."

Arthur glanced over to the bench where Suzy was now attacking some sort of cream-filled pastry.

"And Suzy, of course. I could never have done any of it without her. Maybe you could give her a holiday or something like that?"

"Suzy is always taking holidays," replied Dame Primus. "Whether she should be having them or not. But some reward can doubtless be discovered through negotiation."

"And Tom," added Arthur. "The Captain. Please don't have him arrested."

"Very difficult character to arrest," muttered Noon.

"Shouldn't like to try it myself. Amazed Grim Tuesday managed to capture him."

Dame Primus gave Noon a quelling glance.

"Since you ask, Arthur, we shall not bother the Mariner unless he bothers us or comes to our attention in such a way that we cannot ignore his transgressions."

"I think that's everyone," said Arthur. "Let's get on with it. How do we get to the Front Door?"

"Transfer Plate," said Dame Primus. "To Doorstop Hill in the Lower House. Now, where have they gotten to? Sneezer!"

Arthur started again as Sneezer stepped out from behind him.

How had he gotten there without me noticing again?

"I have two Transfer Plates, ma'am," said Sneezer, placing two quite ordinary-looking yellow-and-white china plates on the grass. "The Combe pattern. Miss Blue has the third plate for her cakes."

Suzy was already hurrying over, stuffing a cake in her mouth while she wiped the crumbs off the plate she was carrying. She put it down next to the others.

"Where are we going?" she asked cheerfully, with her mouth full.

Dame Primus grimaced and looked away.

"Doorstop Hill," she said. "Arthur is going home.

You simply step on the plate, Arthur. Not too briskly. With Grim Tuesday deposed, all lines of communication — and credit, I am pleased to say — are open once more between here and the other regions of the House. Noon, you are in charge here until I return."

With that, she stepped on the plate in front of her and vanished.

Arthur was about to step onto his plate when Suzy fell against him and gripped his elbow.

"Oops!" she said loudly, but at the same time she slipped something in his hand and whispered in his ear, spraying his neck with crumbs.

"Captain told me to give you this. Don't let the old madam see it."

She pushed herself upright and stepped on her plate. Arthur was tempted to open his hand and see what he'd been given, but Noon was watching, so he stepped on his plate too.

And took another step onto the grassy slope of Doorstop Hill.

The Lieutenant Keeper was waiting by the Front Door. A huge door of dark wood that stood between white stone gateposts on top of the green hill that overlooked the Lower Atrium. Arthur glanced up at the glowing ceiling and the many beams of light that shot back and forth between the ceiling and the town below. He knew better than to look at the Door directly. You could see too much in the Door and easily go mad.

"I greet you, Arthur Penhaligon," said the Lieutenant Keeper as he saluted. Arthur waved back and, on the return motion, slipped whatever Suzy had given him into his shirt pocket next to the Atlas. It was small and flat, so it fit easily.

"Are you ready, Arthur?" asked Dame Primus. "The Lieutenant Keeper will carry you through when I am done."

"Almost ready," said Arthur. He stripped off the pajama-like shirt and trousers, but put his Immaterial Boots back on. They looked like sneakers anyway. Now that the moment had arrived, he couldn't help put it off just a little. And it wasn't just because his leg was going to be broken. He turned to Suzy and held out his hand.

"Thanks," he said awkwardly. He wanted to say more, but didn't know how.

"See you," said Suzy. "Next time you come back, we'll get some proper wings. No more of those rotten ascension ones."

"Definitely not," said Arthur. He turned to face Dame Primus, nodded quickly, and shut his eyes.

He didn't see what she did, but there was an explosion of pain in his leg. He cried out and fell. The Lieutenant Keeper caught him with a swooping motion that carried them both into the Door.

Every step the Lieutenant Keeper took was agony for Arthur. The pain in his leg was terrible, and every jolt sent it out of his leg and up his side all the way to his head.

"Steady," said the Lieutenant Keeper. "Not much farther."

Arthur hardly heard him. He wasn't sure if his eyes were open or not. All he could see were exploding blossoms of bright colors. All he could think about was his leg.

"You are brave, sir," said the Lieutenant Keeper. "A slight jolt, and —"

Arthur blacked out. When he came to, he was lying on the landing at the bottom of the steps from his room. Doors were banging. There was shouting. He realized that he was screaming.

"Shut up!" called Michaeli. He heard slow footsteps on the stairs, then very fast footsteps and a shout in a very different tone. "Dad! Eric!"

Arthur forced himself to stop screaming. It was surprisingly easy. Too easy, in fact, until Arthur's pain-drenched mind realized it was because he wasn't getting any air.

I'm having an asthma attack! The stupid Will has reversed everything *the First Key did to me! I've got a broken leg and I'm having an asthma attack!*

"Help," Arthur croaked with what little air he had left. "Asthma . . ."

It was all too much. As Michaeli turned to dash back up the stairs to get his inhaler and Bob rushed up from his studio, Arthur blacked out again.

Chapter Twenty-three

Arthur woke up in the hospital. There was a drip in his arm and an oxygen mask on his face. He felt extremely sick and there was a constant dull ache in his leg. It also felt very odd, which was explained when Arthur raised his head and saw that it was wrapped up in some sort of plastic and carefully placed out of the covers.

"Arthur?"

He looked across and saw his parents. Bob was asleep in a chair, almost snoring, his head rising an inch with every heavy breath. Emily was getting out of the other chair, putting down her folder of luminescent e-paper.

"Mom . . ."

"You're going to be absolutely fine," Emily said. She came over and straightened his blankets and smoothed his hair back. "Not a bad asthma attack. But you have broken your leg. I don't how you did it. Jack — the surgeon who set it — said it looked like a parachute-jumping injury. But it will be okay too."

"Our house . . . the real estate agents . . ."

"Don't worry," soothed Arthur's mom. "Everything's messed up, with the Sleepy Plague and all. Someone just got things confused in the city records and thought the property tax wasn't paid. We'll sort it out. You just go back to sleep."

"I don't feel sleepy," said Arthur.

"How is the pain?" asked Emily. "Shall I fetch your nurse?"

"No, no . . . it's not so bad," Arthur answered truthfully. He looked around again, taking in the normality of the white walls, the stainless steel fittings, the panel with its numerous buttons and gauges and connections for oxygen and everything else.

Then he saw the clock, only he couldn't quite see its face.

"What time is it?"

"Just after five in the morning," said Emily. "You've been out since noon yesterday. The operation finished at seven last night, so you've done very well to sleep till now. That's a good sign."

She was hiding her concern with her "doctor" manner, Arthur saw. He felt her hand shaking as she smoothed his hair again.

"Five in the morning on Wednesday," said Arthur.

"Yes," Emily replied with a smile. "Michaeli and

Eric were here, but I sent them home. And your friend Leaf dropped in."

"Leaf?" asked Arthur quickly. "Is she okay?"

"How did you know she was hurt?" Emily sounded surprised. "She came in around the same time we did. We met her in the emergency room. Nasty cut, but straightforward. It's hard to believe that people would try to rob a house during a quarantine emergency. But I guess I shouldn't be surprised."

"Is Leaf still here, in the hospital?"

"Yes, she is. Since her parents and brother are here for Q-observation, she's gone in with them. And some sort of aunt with a peculiar name."

"Mango," said Arthur. He leaned back into his pillow, stretched his hands underneath, and immediately felt some things that shouldn't have been there. The Atlas, a square of cardboard, and the small round-shaped object that Suzy had given him from Tom.

"I might go to sleep now," he said to Emily, with a yawn. "You should go home."

"I might as well wait for the snore monster to wake up," said Emily. "But I've got some papers to look at. You just rest up."

Arthur watched her go back to her chair and pick up

her papers, their pale green glow lighting her face. When she started tapping on them with her smart stylus, he rolled over and touched whatever was under his pillow. But he didn't pull the items out.

Instead he withdrew his hand. He knew without looking that whatever was under the pillow would take him farther away from the normal life he so wanted to lead. It was already five hours into Wednesday and Arthur was sure the Morrow Days wouldn't leave him alone. That had been a foolish hope, one he was not going to cling to anymore. If he could survive the Pit and take on Grim Tuesday, then he could face any further challenge. He might not succeed, but it wouldn't be for lack of trying.

Arthur reached back under the pillow and pulled all three things out. The Atlas was first. It seemed to be its usual self so Arthur put it back. Next came a small disc. Arthur surreptitiously checked it out in the light from the call button. It was bone — probably whalebone, he thought. One side was carved with lots of tiny stars, and the other had a ship on it. A Viking longship, with the sail up and oars out between a row of shields. The disc had a hole at the top, so it could be worn on a leather strap. Arthur looked at it for a long time, then put it back.

The last thing was, as Arthur had felt, a square of stiff cardboard. White cardboard, with gilt edges and several lines of elegant copperplate writing.

It said:

LADY WEDNESDAY

TRUSTEE OF THE ARCHITECT AND DUCHESS OF THE BORDER SEA

HAS GREAT PLEASURE IN INVITING

ARTHUR PENHALIGON

TO A PARTICULAR LUNCHEON

OF SEVENTEEN REMOVES

TRANSPORT HAS BEEN ARRANGED

RSVP NOT REQUIRED

About the Author

Garth Nix was born on a Saturday in Melbourne, Australia, and got married on a Saturday, to his publisher wife, Anna. So Saturday is a good day. Garth used to write every Sunday afternoon because he had a number of day jobs over the years that nearly always started on a Monday, usually far too early. These jobs have included being a bookseller, an editor, a PR consultant, and a literary agent. Tuesday has always been a lucky day for Garth, when he receives good news, like the telegram (a long time ago, in the days of telegrams) that told him he had sold his first short story, or just recently when he heard his novel *Abhorsen* had hit *The New York Times* bestseller list.

Wednesday can be a letdown after Tuesday, but it was important when Garth served as a part-time soldier in the Australian Army Reserve, because that was a training night. Thursday is now particularly memorable because Garth and Anna's son, Thomas, was born on a Thursday afternoon. Friday is a very popular day for most people, but since Garth has become a full-time writer it has no longer marked the end of the workweek. On any day, Garth may generally be found near Coogee Beach in Sydney, where he and his family live.

NEXT

Drowned Wednesday